BITCH
I
PLAY
FOR KEEPS 2
FINESSED BY:
NIKKI NICOLE

Acknowledgments

Hi, how are you? I'm Nikki Nicole the Pen Goddess. Each time I complete a book I love to write acknowledgements. I love to give a reflection on how I felt about the book. I've been writing for almost three years now and this is my 2nd book. When I first started writing I only had one story I wanted to tell and that was Bitch I Play for Keeps. I'm so excited to revamp this book to see what you guys think. I appreciate each one of you for taking this journey with me. I'm forever grateful for you believing in me and giving me your continuous support.

Book 2 the realest shit I ever wrote and the only story I ever wanted to tell! If I never write another book again; I don't care because this is the only one, I EVER wanted to write because this message wasn't being conveyed and it's still not 3 years later!

I speak for the strong queens, I rep and put on for you. I speak for the ones that ain't laying down crying over nann nigga! I speak for the queens that ain't scared to buss a man in they shit!

I speak for the ones that ain't scared to buss a bitch in they shit! I speak for the ones that got a few replacements and free agents on call! This one is for you! BITCH I PLAY FOR KEEPS

I want to thank my supporters that I haven't met or had a conversation with. I appreciate y'all too. Please email me or contact me on social media. I want to acknowledge you and give you a S/O also.

I dedicate this book to my Queens in the Trap **Nikki Nicole's Readers Trap**. I swear y'all are the best. Y'all go so hard in the paint for me it's insane. Every day we lit. I appreciate y'all more than y'all will ever know. The Trap is going the fuck up on a Sunday. I can't wait for y'all to read it.

It's time for my S/O **Samantha, Tatina, Asha, Shanden (PinkDiva), Padrica, Liza, Aingsley, Trecie, Quack, Shemekia, Toni, Amisha, Tamika, Troy, Pat, Crystal C, Missy, Angela, Latoya, Helene, Tiffany, Lamaka, Reneshia, Misty, Toy, Toi, Shelby, Chanta, Jessica, Snowie, Jessica, Marla Jo, Shay, Anthony, Keyana, Veronica, Shonda J, Sommer, Cathy, Karen, Bria, Kelis, Lisa, Tina, Talisha, Naquisha, Iris, Nicole,**

Koi, Drea, Rickena, Saderia, Chanae, Shanise, Nacresha, Jalisa, Tamika H, Kendra, Meechie, Avis, Lynette, Pamela, Antoinette, Crystal W, Ivee, Kenyada, Dineshia, Chenee, Jovonda, Jennifer J, Cha, Andrea, Shannon J, Latasha F, Denise, Andrea P, Shelby, Kimberly, Yutanzia, Seanise, Demetria, Jennifer, Shatavia, LaTonya, Dimitra, Kellissa, Jawanda, Renea, Tomeika, Viola, Barbie, Erica, Shanequa, Dallas, Verona, Catherine, Dominique, Natasha K, Carmela, Paris B, Amy,

If I named everybody, I will be here all day. Put your name here_____ if I missed you. The list goes on. S/O to every member in my reading group, I love y'all to the moon and back. These ladies right here are a hot mess. I love them to death. They go so hard about these books it doesn't make any sense. Sometimes, I feel like I should run and hide.

If you're looking for us meet us in **Nikki Nicole's Readers Trap** on Facebook, we are live and indirect all day.

S/O to My Pen Bae's **Ash ley, Chyna L, Chiquita, T. Miles,** I love them to the moon and back head over to Amazon and grab a book by them also.

Check my out my new favorite Author **Nique Luarks** baby girl can write her ass off. You heard it from me. I love her work! Look her up and go read her catalog!

To my new readers I have six complete series, and three completed standalones available. Here's my catalog if you don't have it.

Crimson & Carius 1-2

Cuffed by a Trap God 1-3

I Just Wanna Cuff You (Standalone)

You Don't Miss A Good Thing, Until It's Gone (Standalone)

Journee & Juelz 1-3

Giselle & Dro (Standalone)

Our Love Is the Hoodest 1-2

Join my readers group **Nikki Nicole's Readers Trap** on **Facebook**

Follow me on Facebook Nikki Taylor

Follow me on Twitter @WatchNikkiwrite

Like my Facebook Page AuthoressNikkiNicole

Instagram @WatchNikkiwrite

GoodReads @authoressnikkinicole

Visit me on the web authoressnikkinicole.com

email me authoressnikkinicole@gmail.com

Join my email contact list for exclusive sneak peaks.
http://eepurl.com/czCbKL

https://music.apple.com/us/album/victory-lap/1316706552

Table of Contents

TORN
IN BETWEEN
THE
TWO...

Chapter-1

Barbie

"Oh my gosh. What the fuck just happened? I know it didn't go down like this? We just had everything under fuckin' control. Where did those niggas come from and what the fuck did they want with my sister? Give me my phone, Ketta. Let me call Lucky and let him know some niggas just ambushed us and kidnapped Kaniya," I argued. I started crying and yelling to no one in particular. My emotions were getting the best of me. My feelings were a wreck, I was tipsy, but I sobered up quickly. If anything happens to her, I would never be able to forgive myself.

A lot of people were just out here standing around and looking. See, that's the fuckin' problem with black folks. They're always acting like they didn't see anything. That's the shit typical black motherfuckas do. The fucked-up part about it is that nobody was out here helping us. "Can you motherfuckas call the police, please?" I screamed. I swear I'm about to lose it and I'm trying to keep it together, but I can't because this wasn't supposed to happen to her.

"Did any of you guys recognize those niggas?" Ketta asked. I damn near grew an extra neck. I looked at her like she was motherfuckin' crazy. How dare she ask us did we know them motherfuckas. If we did, they wouldn't have been able to kidnap my fuckin sister. I need Ketta to fuckin' think sometimes. Shit, her smart ass is a fuckin' nurse. How would we know them if they had on a fuckin' ski mask?

"Girl, if you don't shut the hell up," I sighed. Let me be quiet before I say some shit, I can't take fuckin' back. I know we've never been in this situation before, but we were trained to fuckin' go at any given time. Shit, we laid three of those niggas down. I don't know where the other two came from. My adrenaline was at an all-time high. I don't understand how them fuckin' niggas blindsided us. I swear I didn't see them coming. Damn, I should've been checking my surroundings. I don't like motherfuckas having one up on us.

"Damn Ketta and Barbie, that shit was crazy. Listen I asked her earlier when she picked me up was anything wrong? She played that shit off cool and I should've known better. I know Kaniya, so I knew something was up. I noticed she was dressed down.

I kept asking her was there anything I needed to know about. The only thing she asked me was if I was strapped," she explained. I wish Riley would've told me and Ketta about this earlier, so we could've been prepared. I would've probed Kaniya a little more about what was up earlier. I knew it was fishy that Kaniya wasn't dressed to impressed. Anytime we step on the scene, we're showing up and showing out.

We put on for the bitches in the back. I should've known something was up when she's normally dressed to impressed and the center of every niggas fuckin' attention. That was the first fuckin' red flag. I knew her and Lucky were trying to get back to who they used to be. So, I thought she didn't want the attention on her tonight. She always slayed for the occasion but tonight she chose to thug it out and dumb it down. Now I know why. I grabbed my phone to call Lucky and I said a quick prayer before the call connected. He answered on the second ring.

"Lucky, bruh, where are you? Somebody just ambushed us and kidnapped Kaniya in front of Magic City. Make your way up here now, please," I cried and screamed. I was nervous and so fuckin' shook, it's crazy. I hated to be the one to call Lucky. That's one call I didn't want to make because we don't see eye to eye. Ugh, just by his tone I could hear he was about to say something smart.

"Barbie, why are you calling my fuckin' phone? You know I don't fuck with you. If she went to go fuck with some nigga and you're covering for her, I'm killing both of y'all asses and I mean that shit," he yelled into the phone. I put the phone on speaker so Ketta and Riley could hear him. I raised my hand up to get their attention and flagged them over so they could listen to him.

"Barbie, I don't trust shit you have to say. I know you were the one that put Kaniya on to my infidelities previously. I want you to tell a motherfuckin lie and say it wasn't your motherfuckin' ass. I'm the last motherfucka you should've called." I looked at the phone and snarled my face up. This is the reason why I didn't want to call this motherfucka. I can't believe he just said all this shit. I'm calling about your woman and the only thing you should've said was that you're on your way.

"Lucky, that's not the fucking case. I shouldn't have called your stupid ass no motherfuckin way. I ain't got shit to do with her knowing about you cheating. Did I tell on you, Lucky? Yes, the fuck I did. What the fuck can you do about it?

Look, we're at Magic City right now. Bring yo motherfuckin ass on because arguing on the phone with you motherfucka, ain't bringing her back. Please, get the fuck up here quick. Stop being a fuckin' asshole. She wouldn't do no shit like that because for some reason she loves your stupid ass," I argued. I had to tell his ass off. I'm sick of him. He needs to stop blaming other people for his fuck ups. I know he could tell I was fuckin' irritated by my tone. I couldn't believe he just let that bullshit roll off his fuckin' tongue. He hung up the phone. Hopefully he was making his way up here.

"Barbie, I can't believe he said that shit. What the fuck is wrong with him?" Ketta asked. Her guess was about as good as mine. I don't know why he has it out for me but I'm not the one. If you were faithful you wouldn't have to worry about nothing, but you were doing some shit you shouldn't have. It's your fault you had to suffer the consequences.

"I wish I knew but I bit my tongue. I wanted to say I wish she had a nigga that wasn't you that I could call to help find her," I argued. I slapped hands with Ketta and Riley. Now wasn't the fuckin' time. I can't believe he falsely accused her of some bullshit. I need to call her parents and Julius. I need him to calm me down.

I can't believe this shit. Just an hour ago me and my little sister was making a fuckin' mess up in Magic City. We still had plenty of more ones to blow. Instead, we bodied some niggas and she got kidnapped in the process. It wasn't supposed to end like this. We were supposed to pull off and laugh about this shit at Waffle House or Denny's then kick it and shit. I knew Lucky was tripping. Hell, I was too.

I don't even know where to start to look for her. I can't stand him, but I know Kaniya loves his black ass. But damn, if he didn't kidnap her, who did and why? My sister wasn't beefing with anybody nor did she owe anybody shit. All the bitches that she was beefing with are six feet deep. I hope those niggas don't do shit to hurt her.

One of the voices sounded familiar. I knew him from somewhere. Kaniya was giving them niggas hell too. I couldn't believe the shit Lucky was saying. I'm not surprised though. He made it sound like I was lying and shit. I knew some private investigators. I'm going to have them investigate this.

Phil

Man shit just got real than a motherfucka. We just set it off in front of Magic City on the Fourth of July, ain't that about a bitch. I haven't done no hot ass shit like this since I was a fuckin' young nigga. The price went up because I'm pretty sure this shit is on fuckin' camera. Might as well make it count. I had to make these bitches feel me. I'm sure they thought they got the best of me. Nah bitch, not me those hoes better ask about me.

"AD turn this motherfuckin Denali around and lower the window so I can wet this motherfucka up and lay down one of these bitches since they laid down a few of mine," I argued and yelled. AD turned the Denali around and lowered the window. I pulled my ski-mask over my face. I had a devious grin in place. Shawty was looking at me crazy. She didn't want her girls to get touched. I cocked my gun back and she pushed me in the back of my head. I looked over my shoulders to see what she wanted.

"Aye bitch, you better keep your hands to your fuckin' self before I make a fuckin' example out of you," I argued. The bitches she was with started bussing back. AD whipped the Denali in a 360 and pulled off quick as fuck. Thank God this motherfucka was bullet proof. I don't know who this bitch thought I was, but I wasn't a fuckin' sucka. I don't give a fuck how fine she is. I'll kill her fuckin' ass.

"Look, my bitches ain't got shit to do with why the fuck you snatched me up. Leave them out of it," she argued.

"Boss, what you want me to do?" AD asked. I know he was ready to get to our destination. He was on parole and probably ready to get the fuck out of dodge. The last thing I need was for my nigga to get caught up because of me.

"Keep driving, AD. We got to hurry up and ditch this fuckin' Denali," I explained. To make matters worse this bitch was trying her fuckin' best to escape. I had to put a death grip on her ass and let her know I wasn't that fuckin' nigga. Boss Mayne didn't give us the heads up shawty and her girls was toting that motherfuckin iron and giving it up like that.

What are the odds of that? Licks always came easy, but we had to work hard as fuck for this one. We had our fuckin' work cut out for us. I thought we were about to snatch up shawty and keep it fuckin' moving. Boss Mayne was setting us up for the motherfuckin' kill.

It took everything in me not to push shawty and her girl's shit back. I had to remember that this was a fuckin' job. I live the life of sin and death is one of the chances that I take every fuckin' day. I ran my hands across my face. I had to get myself together because I'm liable to lose it and this bitch right here can get it and I'm not talking about these hands.

"Aye bitch shut the fuck up. You've been doing too much fuckin' talking. Lee duct tape and hog tie this bitch so she can shut the fuck up. AD drive this motherfuckin' Denali like you got some fuckin' sense. We just kidnapped a motherfucka in front of Magic City. Get Boss Mayne on the fuckin' phone and let that nigga know the price has gone up for this motherfucka. We put in too much work and I lost a few of my right hands in the fuckin' process, so that nigga has to pay for that," I argued and explained.

I don't know what this bitch did to my nigga, but he was adamant about not laying a hand on her. I don't know if I can keep that fuckin' promise, because I lost two of mine tonight and I don't like taking fuckin' losses. Lee ushered shawty to the back of the Denali. She was grilling the fuck out of me, mean while still fighting as she walked past.

I noticed he had duct taped her mouth shut, like I asked him to. I grabbed her shoulder and snatched the duct tape off her mouth. I knew that shit hurts, but I don't give a fuck. She asked for this shit since I couldn't shoot her.

"Aye bitch ass nigga, choose your motherfuckin' steps wisely, because I can guarantee you once my mother and father gets smoke of this, you won't live to see fuckin' Sunday, and that's on me PUSSY," she argued and spit in my fuckin' face. I wiped the spit off my face. I swear she's disrespectful as fuck. Lee and Ace were grilling me, pleading with their eyes, begging me not to fuck shawty up. I drew my hand back as if I was about to smack the shit out of her ass. Lee tossed me the duct tape and smacked that shit back on her lips. She tried to bite my hands.

Lee and Ace grabbed her and took her ass to the back. I smacked her on the ass. She tried to jump out their reach and I laughed at her ass. She was mad as fuck. "Sit your motherfuckin' ass down, I'm running this shit. I give you the orders. I'm not afraid, shawty. I live a dangerous ass life and death is always a possibility," I argued. My phone started ringing. I reached in my back pocket and pulled out my phone. It was Boss Mayne, just the nigga I needed to hear from.

"Talk to me, Phil. Did y'all get away with her?" He asked. I don't know what was up with Boss Mayne and this chick because if she's your bitch why in the fuck do you have to do all this shit. We almost got our ass blown off.

"Hell yeah, and that shit was DANGEROUS. Look MAYNE, I need a fuckin' BONUS," I laughed and explained.

"Damn, shawty wasn't that bad, was she?" He asked and chuckled? I couldn't even hold my laugh in if I wanted to. Boss Mayne knows that bitch required a lot of fuckin' work. I guess I had to work for this $100,000.

"Aye Lee and Ace, this motherfucka said shawty wasn't that fuckin' bad. Shit he a motherfuckin lie. She was the fuckin' worst. He sent us out, that's why he didn't fuckin' do it," I laughed. I'm sure Boss Mayne could hear Lee and Ace laughing, too.

"Aye, y'all get to the fuckin destination. I got you, Ace, and Lee. Y'all niggas rusty if y'all let my lil shawty get y'all worked up," he chuckled.

"Boss Mayne cut the shit man. You know I fucks with you the long way, but that wasn't no average fuckin' lick and you know that shit. Them bitches was like some fuckin' trained assassins. Boss Mayne, they were shooting first and not asking any fuckin' questions and your shawty gave them motherfuckas the call. She orchestrated the shit," I explained. I finished chopping it up was Boss Mayne after I explained everything. We had a long motherfuckin' ride. I looked over my shoulders and shawty was giving me an evil glare. I flipped her ass the bird. She ain't my bitch and I ain't beat for her shit.

Lucky

Who in the fuck would want to kidnap Kaniya? JD is dead so that only leaves Tariq's ass. I promise to God I'm at Sonja's house in the fuckin morning and I'm kicking in her fucking door. Nope, fuck that. I'm going to her house tonight. I want her to get her punk ass nephew on the motherfuckin phone. It's mighty funny that so many people that are close to me keep coming up missing or dead and Sonja is always smack dead in the middle of it.

I'm going to end up pushing her shit back if something happens to Kaniya. I can't blame Sonja for my father's death, but I can. From what I heard she told the nigga; she was the one that set him up and he damn near lost it after that. My dad's death is fuckin' with me something serious. I can't shake it for some reason and I'm not trying to lose Kaniya too.

I can promise you that and I put my life on it. I grabbed my phone to call Quan and Veno to see if they could ride out with me. Quan didn't answer the phone. Veno said he was about to pull up. If something happened to Kaniya I'll fuck around and lose it. This shit ain't adding up. I had a few of my workers pull up to Magic City to see what it was looking like, and they confirmed it was definitely a fuckin' crime scene. Who got at my baby and why? Who in the fuck is trying to risk their life behind mine?

Veno pulled up twenty minutes later. I slid in the whip with him and we pulled off. We dapped hands with each other. I sat my duffel bag on the floor and pulled out my Mac 11 and my 12 Gauge. I'm tired of playing with motherfuckas, period. Veno looked at me and gave me the side eye. I don't give a fuck.

"Damn Lucky, what are we about to do?" He asked while running his hands across his face. Veno already knew what time it was. A motherfucka can't touch mine and live to tell about it. No matter what we're going through. She was still mine no matter what and she was off limits. When motherfuckas kidnap people they're sending messages. I want a motherfucka to get my message too.

"We're about to handle some fuckin' business. They sent for me when they kidnapped Kaniya. Let me send for them and let them know they've kidnapped the wrong fuckin' one. Pull up to Magic City so I can see what's up," I explained. Killian and Kanan wasn't my favorite people right now but I had to make that call.

Chapter-2

Kaniya

"Who in the fuck wants to kidnap me? Aye, fuck boys, get your fuckin' boss on the phone and ask that bitch ass nigga or stupid ass bitch what the fuck they want with me?" I asked and yelled from the back seat. These motherfuckas had the nerve to duct tape, my mouth shut. I rubbed my face against the seat, and it pealed the tape off my lips. I'm confused who would want to kidnap me and why in the hell they couldn't at least bring my fuckin' friends with me.

"Do you ever get tired of talking, shit? Damn, I'm wondering why he kidnapped you myself. What the fuck does he want with your ass? You're fucking annoying," he explained. I'm sick of his stupid ass. I hate I was blindsided by him because if I wasn't, I would've shot his stupid ass in the fuckin' head and sent that bitch to his momma.

"Get that bitch ass boss of yours on the phone now and I'll ask the motherfucka myself what he wants with me. Trust me, I'm not willing to fuckin' be here. I have a nigga at home right now whose dick I was ready to jump on," I argued. He gave me a hateful look. I don't give a fuck. I made it very clear that I've become beyond frustrated at this point. Who is his fuckin' Boss? How does he know me and what does he want with me? I heard the motherfucka that was running the show grab his phone and call his boss.

"Boss, we have a fuckin' problem," he explained. I'm sure he's frustrated but so am I. I tried to be quiet because I wanted to know what his boss was saying. I wanted to hear his Boss' voice to see if I could recognize it.

"What's the fucking problem?" He asked. His boss didn't give him time to respond because it sounds like his boss said. "I'm trying to figure out what fuckin' problem y'all could have possibly run into?" I didn't really recognize the voice because I was sitting two fuckin' seats back and the music was on low.

"The subject will not fucking make it to you if she keeps on talking shit. I'm ready to off her ass right now," he argued and explained. He had his eyes trained on me and my eyes were trained on him. He can't fuckin' intimidate me. I'm sick and tired of his ass too. I don't give a fuck how annoyed he is. I know he's just a fuckin worker and not calling any fuckin' shots.

"You know that's not part of the fucking plan. I gave you strict instructions. Don't put a fuckin' scratch on her. She can talk shit all day," he argued. Who was his boss and what type of kidnapping is this?

"Aye, fuck nigga? Is that your boss on the phone? Let me speak to him now," I argued and yelled. I wanted whoever that was on the other end of the phone to hear me. I had some shit that I wanted to say.

"Boss mane, do you hear what the fuck I'm talking about? I don't want to hear that shit. She needs to shut the fuck up," he argued. I don't give a fuck how he may feel. His boss needs to let me fuckin go. I don't know what his boss was telling him on the other end of the phone, but he was handing me his phone and I shrugged my shoulders refusing to take his phone.

"Here, you wanted to speak to him to voice your fuckin' opinion, so take this motherfuckin' phone because he wants to speak to you," he argued and shoved the phone to my ear. I didn't say anything, I just listened. My mother always told me in a bullshit situation never let your opponent hear your emotions so I'm not going to say anything. I want them to speak first. "Talk your fuckin' shit, he's listening. Look, you got two fuckin' minutes to say what the fuck you need to say and give me my phone back." I swear I'm sick of his ass. The person on the other end of the phone was laughing. I swear to God I don't believe this shit.

"What the fuck do you want with me? That's all you can do is fuckin' laugh? I can't wait to see your ugly ass, too. Leave me the fuck alone. You been doing it. Kidnap the bitch that you were bragging about fuckin', remember that? Take me to this lame ass fuckin' nigga right fuckin' now. Just know TARIQ, Lucky is coming for your bitch ass too, nigga," I argued into the phone. I knew who was behind my kidnapping at this point. I can't believe Tariq. I tossed ole boy his phone back hoping to hit him in the head. I laid my head down on the seat. I used my arms for a pillow. I heard ole boy whispering to the two other niggas in the back.

"Aye, this shit is suspect. I'm riding with my nigga, right or wrong, but I never kidnapped a bitch before that didn't belong to me. To make matters worse, she's my cousin's bitch. I know for a fact this is not his girl. What's the real reason behind this shit? There's only one Lucky that everybody knows of. I can bet you any amount of money this is the Kaniya that Lucky talks about all the time. What does my boss want with her, though? He whispered and asked. I started to raise up and ask more questions. I played it cool. I wasn't supposed to hear that much. If Lucky knew Tariq kidnapped me, shit is about to get ugly as fuck.

Man, this shit is crazy! I recognized that laugh from anywhere. It's something that I could never forget. This nigga is going to fuck around and get me and him killed with these games he's playing. Oh lord, please let Lucky know that I'm not willing to be here by choice and I was forced.

This nigga here has been sitting in the background, hidden in the fuckin' shadows, lurking and plotting. I can't deal with him. If you had some shit you needed to say you could've very well said it and not do all this extra shit.

Who kidnaps a chick in front of Magic City? I still can't relax because I don't know where I'm going, but I know who they're taking me too. What did I ever do to this nigga for him to kidnap me? I don't see this shit working out well. Is he trying to kill me or some shit? I guess he was the creep that sent me the flowers with that bullshit ass card. He's crazy. I knew he was crazy but not this crazy.

Ketta

What the fuck just happened? I'm trying to keep it together, but I can't because if something was to happen to my best friend, I would lose my mind. I had to think positive because I know she can handle her own. I wish they would've taken me with her so she wouldn't be alone. I didn't want to wear my emotions on my sleeve because motherfuckas would play on that. I can't believe those motherfuckin' niggas snatched my girl up like that in front of Magic City.

The stupid bastard had the nerve to turn the vehicle around and act like he was about to shoot us. I bet he was surprised when we started bussing back. I wiped the loan tear that fell from the brim of my eyes. We were just having a ball and planned on doing the same shit again tomorrow. I caught my first body tonight. I don't have any feelings about it. It's either kill or be killed.

I was protecting myself. I just wish I could've killed the two motherfuckas that threw her in the Denali. I was able to get Kaniya's purse off the ground. I grabbed all the contents that came out of her purse and I noticed they took her fuckin' passport. Where are they fuckin' taking her? I hope they aren't using her for sex trafficking. How am I going to explain this shit to Don?

To make matters worse, Barbie refused to speak with the fuckin' police. I had to do all the talking since she acted as if she was foreign and didn't know English. A hot ass fuckin' mess, right? They took one look at her license and laughed. I gave the detectives that was handling the case as much information as possible. The murders were under investigation. It looks like we'll be in Atlanta for a couple of weeks longer than we expected.

The police advised us that they were going to pull the cameras from Greyhound and Magic City to make sure our stories lined up. I declined to be on the news due to my profession and former colleagues. I hope my girl is okay. My heart hurts so bad. I swear it's like I felt the impact when he placed the gun to the back of her head. I heard her wince in pain. I just pray she's okay and they don't do anything to her. I don't want to live without her. We've been through it all together.

Riley

Oh my gosh, what a night to remember. I can't believe this shit just happened to me. I swear if Kaniya would've told me this was going down; I probably would've kept my ass in the room. I swear my best friend is involved in too much bullshit that she doesn't care to share. Here I am, three hundred miles away from home. She knew those niggas were coming and she didn't want me to know. I knew it wasn't much I could do to help, but I was down to ride regardless.

We've come a long way and I never thought we would be getting down with a squad full of niggas catching bodies in front of a strip club. Especially not Magic City. We made the fuckin' news. FOX5 Atlanta was out here trying to interview us. Thank God this face was beat to the gods and my hair was still perfect. The only thing I wanted to do was come here for the 4th of July like I do every year and kick it with my girl, that's it. Leave it to Kaniya to set the 4th of July off in flames. My bitch always makes a fuckin' mess. Her pull up game was too strong.

Now, I'm in the middle of a damn murder investigation. I'm to fuckin' fine to be in prison. To make matters worse, the fuckin' ringleader who set this motherfucka off is nowhere to be found. Who would kidnap Kaniya and what has she done? Lucky didn't come up here at all. I knew why, though. I still have the keys to Kaniya's Corvette. Ketta tossed me the keys. I need to take it to her house. I can't wait to tell Tianna about this shit. I called her phone like five times already, but she didn't answer.

I knew Quan had her hemmed-up. Boss is going to be pissed once he finds out that I'll have too extend my stay in Atlanta because of a murder investigation. It was self-defense. Try explaining that shit to Boss, though. This night here is going down in the history books. I'll never forget this day long as I live. I hope my best friend is okay. I could always call Kaniya when I needed her and now, she's in a situation where she needed me the most. I got her back with every breath in me.

I caught a body tonight and my right hand got kidnapped. The life of hanging with Kaniya Miller, there's never a dull moment. I shot Boss a text to let him know what was going on. I didn't want to hear his voice when I gave him the rundown of what happened tonight. So hopefully this text will suffice.

Me - I'll have to extend my stay in Atlanta.

Soon as the text said delivered. He replied instantly. I could only imagine what he had to say.

Boss was so protective of me that it was crazy. He wanted to know my every move. Boss was a Henchman for one of the

Most Notorious Crime Families in Trinidad and Tobago, The Figueroa Cartel. He always had eyes on me because he had a lot of enemies and the last thing, he wanted was for something to happen to me because of him. I know from this alone he was about to go crazy.

HIM - For what???

God, I didn't want to type these next two words. Boss was involved in a lot of illegal stuff. It's one of the reasons we're able to live the life we live. I love him and I try to keep him as calm as possible because anything would set him off and he would be in straight beast mode.

ME - Murder Investigation.

HIM - Murder?? What the fuck happened?

I couldn't explain this through text. I'll have to face time him when I get back to my room. Everybody was out here looking. So, I wasn't about to call him out here. You never know who's out here listening and picking up information and running it back.

ME - Yes, it's too much to explain I'll call you in a minute.

HIM - I'm on my way

I knew he was coming without asking any questions. That's just the type of man he was. I wanted him here with me too. I hated being away from him. I felt so safe with him. The last thing I wanted was to go over to Tianna's and chill and see Veno's fuckin' ass. I'm glad Lucky didn't come because I'm sure his partner in crime would be right with him. I had a text from an unknown number.

770-268-3266 - I saw your fine ass posted up in front of Magic City. Let me find out you've been coming to the city and dodging me. Stop playing games. You know I know where to find you. Come see me or I'll come and see you. Veno

I wish he would leave me the fuck alone. I'm not beat for his shit. I hope Tianna didn't give him my phone number. I've changed my number twice to get rid of his ass. He doesn't want to come looking for me because I'm in a committed relationship. Something he knows nothing about. To avoid confusion, I sent him a text back.

Me - I'm in a relationship. Something that you don't take seriously. If so, your disrespectful ass wouldn't be on my line. Don't come looking for me because my MAN will kill you and that ain't a JOKE. If you want to live to continue to fuck Vanessa Monday through Sunday, you'll leave me alone.

I sent the text and waited awhile before I blocked his number because I wanted to see what he had to say. Veno and I both had an iPhone, so I knew he was responding back. I heard a car pull up fast and the tires screech.

I moved out the way quick because I didn't want to get hit. It was a black two door Maserati coupe that almost hit me. I walked toward Ketta and Barbie because I didn't know who it was. I was scared to look over my shoulders for all I know it could be the motherfuckas that grabbed Kaniya coming back to finish the job. Soon as I made it over to them, I felt a tap on my shoulder. I recognized his cologne from anywhere. It invaded my nostrils instantly. I refused to acknowledge him because I said what I had to say, and I meant that shit. He's married. What the fuck can he do for me. He stopped tapping me on my shoulder and stepped in front of me. I looked at everything but him and refused to get lost in his gaze.

"Riley, I need to holler at you for a minute," Veno's stated. His tone was stern. I knew he meant business but I'm not his business and he's not mine. Ketta and Barbie were both giving me the side eye. I hope they didn't think I was still fuckin' with him because I wasn't.

"I said what I had to say, and I don't have anything else to say," I sassed. The last thing I needed was one of Boss's muscle to see me standing out here talking to Veno and think that it's more than what it is. He grabbed my hand and instantly I jerked my arm away from him.

"Can you stop please and take what I said into consideration," I argued.

"Riley, you know I don't give a fuck about none of that shit you were spitting. I don't give a fuck about her right now. You're trying the fuck out of me and right about now I don't give a fuck about acting ignorant as you can see," he argued. Veno was so loud all eyes were on us. He knew I hated that shit. Barbie and Ketta looked at me telling me to go see what that nigga wanted.

I followed him to his car. He tried to grab my hand, but I refuse to touch him. He snatched my hand and led me to his car. He lifted me up and sat me on his hood. He made a gap in between my legs and stood in between them. I slid off the hood because he was doing to fuckin' much. I had a man and he had a wife.

"Veno stop, you're doing too much," I explained. The last thing I needed was for Boss to pull up and make this motherfucka a distant memory. Veno pushed me back on the hood of his car and closed the gap between us. My hands were rested on his chest pushing him off me. He grabbed my wrists with his free hands. I gazed up at him begging him not to do this. He let go of my wrist and removed the loose strands of hair out my face. He started stroking my cheek. I swatted his hands away.

"Can you please stop, Veno. I'm not trying to disrespect him by being in your presence and we're in a COMMITTED RELATIONSHIP. If you came here to bother me and disrupt my life, please leave. At the end of the day you married her and not me. You cheated on me with her. You lied and ended up marrying her. You chose her and not me, and to be honest I'm finally okay with that because I have HIM and you ain't HIM. I don't have to compete with any BITCH when it comes to HIM. I'm enough for HIM. I refuse to DISRESPECT HIM. Bye Veno, go home to her," I argued. I tried to walk away from him, but he ran up on me and grabbed me from behind. He wrapped his arms around my waist and bit the nape of my neck.

"What do I need to stop for, Riley. You know how I fuckin' feel about you. I know you fuckin' with Boss and giving that nigga something that belongs to me. I got a piece of you and you got a piece of me forever, so I don't give a fuck about the bullshit you're spitting. Fuck that nigga," he argued. My phone started ringing and it was Boss. Veno snatched my phone out of my hand and cleared Boss out. I wish he hadn't done that. Boss called right back and Veno cleared him out again. I'm livid at this point. Veno and I were tussling with my phone when Boss called back again. I hit the green button to answer. I was trying to catch my breath. Boss spoke before I did.

"Riley, you know I got fuckin' eyes on you. Whatever the fuck you and that nigga got going on dead that shit before I do," he argued. I heard the phone echo. I felt a pair of hands grab me and push me behind him. It was Boss. He was grilling me and Veno. I don't see this ending well at all.

My heart dropped instantly. I don't know how long he's been out here or what he saw. Boss wouldn't back down or fight. He'll just shoot Veno. It's crazy because Veno is the same way. I swallowed hard because I was nervous as fuck. Barbie and Ketta's eyes were focused on me because they didn't know what was going on. I pleaded with my eyes for them to come over and help defuse the situation. Thank God they ran over here.

"You got a problem with your motherfuckin' hands nigga? I'm trying to see the reason why you're all up in my woman's face. I know for a fact she told you that she's in a relationship. I need you to put some fuckin' respect on that because if not you and I got a motherfuckin' problem," he argued and yelled. Boss stroked his goatee a few times and wiped the brim of his head. Boss has shooters in position. I would hate for his bitch to be a widow because he couldn't leave me alone. I held my head down behind Boss because I told Veno to leave me alone. Veno stepped in Boss's personal space. I knew shit was about to get real. My heart was about to beat out my fuckin' chest.

"Yeah, I got a motherfuckin' problem and guess what my nigga? You ain't the one to fuckin' solve it. I heard she was your woman but that has nothing to do with me. She knows why I'm here. Y'all may be together and I respect that shit to a certain extent, but we have ties that's deeper than what you fuckin' see. Riley and I got a few issues that we need to address, and it has nothing to do with you. This was before your time my nigga so wherever I see her is where I'll address her," he argued and yelled. Why did Veno let that shit come out his mouth. I knew Boss was about to go in because he let a small chuckle escape his mouth. I knew whatever came from his mouth next I wouldn't like it.

"I'm trying to see what ties y'all have because she's with me and she doesn't have a kid with you, nor does she own any property with you. I'm far from a dumb ass nigga. I ain't like these pussy ass niggas that's running through this city. I'm a different breed. I know you want something that doesn't belong to you but partner I need you to move the fuck around before I move you around. Dead that issue or I'll dead it. When you see her don't even fuckin' look at her. Move on because she has. Riley let's go. Get your ass in the fuckin' car," he argued and yelled.

"Is that a threat?" He asked. I wish Veno would let it go. Boss looked over his shoulder and yelled.

"Let's go Riley. You heard what the fuck I said nigga. Take it how you want too." He didn't have to tell me twice. I tossed Kaniya's keys to Ketta and walked quickly to his car. I don't know how much he seen but I pray he didn't see me sitting on Veno's hood.

Tianna

If it's not one thing, it's something else. It's seems like our crew can't catch a break. I knew it was a reason I wasn't sleeping peacefully. I've been tossing and turning all night. I knew something happened, but I wasn't expecting it to be Kaniya. Quan woke me up out of my damn sleep. Lucky called and told him somebody kidnapped Kaniya in front of Magic City. What the fuck, man? I checked my phone to see if I had any missed calls. Well, I'll be damned. Riley had called me five times already. I'll hit her up in a minute once Quan calms down. I sleep with my phone on vibrate because I hate to hear my phone ring when I'm asleep. I called Riley to get the rundown. I couldn't believe this shit. They bodied a few niggas, Kaniya got kidnapped, and they're under investigation for murder, but it was self-defense.

That's one hell of a night. I wonder what the fuck Kaniya is into to get kidnapped. I hate I'm pregnant. Ugh, I'm missing out on all the action. First Miami, and now this. I hope my girl is okay. I know Lucky's going crazy. They were just about to get back together yesterday. He's in love with Kaniya and she's in love with him, too. I hate this happened to them. They can't catch a break. I locked myself in the bathroom and prayed nothing happens to her.

She's the strongest person I know, and she has the heart of a lion. I know she can make it through anything, but I hope and pray this situation doesn't make or break her physically or mentally. I know I haven't been the best friend to her lately because it's like I'm in the middle of her and Quan. I've tried my best to separate the two.

"Tianna, your girl got some shit with her tonight. I can't believe the shit Lucky just ran down to me about Kaniya," he explained and chuckled. I don't see what's funny because if anything happens to my friend, I'll stop fuckin' with him because I felt he preyed on her downfall. I don't care that I'm having his child. She doesn't have shit to do with what happened to Deuce. It's not good to believe everything you hear.

"I heard. Any lead on who kidnapped her?" I asked. I was curious as fuck. Did Lucky know something we didn't? Riley said he never showed up to the Crime scene. I don't give a fuck how many police were up there, he should've been on the scene, period.

I threw on some clothes and I was headed up to the crime scene. Quan tapped me on my shoulder. I wasn't sitting here in the house. I had to link up with my crew to see if we could find our girl.

"No, not yet. He's supposed to come through here in a few. Where are you going at this time of night? We can't catch a break for nothing. First my daddy, now this," he argued.

"I'm going to meet up with Riley and the girls. I can't sit here and wait on Lucky to do some shit I could be doing. Why wasn't he at the fuckin' crime scene to see about her? I know we've all been going through our shit Quan, but god damn, she gave him five years of her life despite what the fuck they went through," I argued and explained. Just hearing Riley say that bothers the fuck out of me. Do you not give a fuck because y'all ain't together how you would like it to be?

"It's to fuckin' late for you to be out, so you can dead that shit about leaving this house. Come on now Tianna, don't play my brother like that for real. He gives a fuck. Shit, he can't be on the crime scene of a murder. Come on, we're street niggas. Who do you think they're going to be looking at and taking in for questioning, HIM? So, to avoid all that he's playing the background," he explained.

"Quan, I'm grown, and I can handle myself. Trust me, I roll with some real bitches and I can handle my own. I don't need you telling me what I can and can't do because for Kaniya Miller I'm going to ride until I fuckin' die, and it ain't one motherfucka gone stop me. Not even you," I argued. I walked right past Quan and headed to the garage. I refused to go back and forth with him and wait on Lucky or anybody else to give me updates. I can update myself. Quan ran up behind me and grabbed my hand. I turned around to look at him. I knew he had some shit he wanted to say but I didn't want to hear it. I just wanted to find my best friend that's it. We already took one loss with Deuce. I wasn't trying to take another one with Kaniya.

"I feel where you're coming from Tianna, trust me, I do. I want you to ride for your girl no matter what, but shawty you're carrying something that belongs to me. If a nigga decides to get at you because you're looking for her and attempts to hurt, you to send a message to me and Lucky. Tianna, these motherfuckas don't want no fuckin' smoke. I swear these niggas don't want to see how stupid and fuckin' ignorant I am behind MINE," he explained. Quan pointed to my heart. I knew he cared about me. I never doubted that.

He grabbed the keys out of my hand and before I could put up a fight, he put his hands up to my mouth. "You want to ride out then let me drive you. We'll post up on the scene together, fuck you mean. Grab the bullet proof vests out the closet in case shit gets ugly," he explained. I did as I was told and tossed Quan his vest and I put mine on.

I loved Quan with everything in me. I'm glad he was able to put the bullshit aside and ride with me for my girl. If I had to choose, I was choosing her over him. I was hoping that it wouldn't come down to that. We've been through it all together. Quan grabbed my hand and he backed out of the garage. I closed my eyes and said another quick prayer for Kaniya hoping and praying for the best. My mind was in a million places. I knew Quan could tell because my legs were shaking. Damn, that's my girl. Why her? I've been trying to hold back my tears, but I couldn't. She was the realest bitch I had on my team. Losing Kaniya never came to mind. I swore we would grow old together. Quan grabbed my hand and handed me some tissue out the armrest. I wiped my face, but I couldn't stop crying.

"Tianna, baby, I need you to calm down and not get upset. Kaniya is going to be good, trust me. If this is too much for you, we can go back home. That's why I didn't want you to go by yourself because I knew this would happen," he explained. I understood where he was coming from but it's hard.

"I know, Quan." I sniffled. We finally made it to Magic City, and it was still thick outside. Ketta, Barbie and Riley were gone, and it was just the police casing the area. We couldn't even find anywhere to park.

"What do you want to do? Everybody is gone and I'm not trying to interfere with these cops," he asked and explained.

"I'm hungry. Do you want to get something to eat and then we can go home?" I asked.

"Cool, we can go home, and I'll cook us some breakfast. I don't want to be out here in these streets I'll get up with Lucky later and I should have some good news for you," he explained. I hope so.

Chapter-3

Don

I just got the craziest call from Ketta. Some shit isn't adding up. Whatever it was it had to be important. Julius and I were out handling some business. She called and told me to get to the house quickly, because she needed to tell me something and it couldn't be said over the phone. I noticed the nervousness and panic in her voice. I got to the house as quickly as I could. I didn't know what was going on, but I was for damn sure about to find out.

It took me about thirty minutes to get to our spot. When I pulled up, all the lights were on and that was a bit strange because it was almost 4:00 a.m. I patted my back pocket and grabbed my Glock. I cocked it back and made sure one was in the fuckin' chamber. I made my way toward the house to see what was up. Ketta left the front door open. If somebody ran up in my shit and touched my heart, I'm going to fuck some shit up.

"Babe, where are you? What the hell is going on," I yelled from downstairs. I combed my way through the house so far everything looks good. I made my way upstairs to see where she was so I could find out what was going on.

"I'm up here in the bedroom," she yelled. Why is she in the fuckin' bedroom and she left all the lights on and the front door open? I cut all the lights off. I grabbed Ketta her favorite juice and a kiwi. I locked the front door and made my way upstairs to see what she wanted. Ketta was sitting on the bed but she didn't look like herself.

I knew some shit was up and I'm dying to know what. I knelt in front of her to see what was up. I wrapped my arms around her waist. Her hands roamed through my waves. We locked eyes with each other. I knew Ketta had some shit she wanted to say. I just wanted her to say it.

"What's wrong babe, talk to me?" I asked. I'm curious as fuck. I couldn't read Ketta's facial expressions. I need to make sure that my baby was straight because she was cool before I left.

"Which do you want first, the good news or the bad news?" She asked and laughed. I cupped Ketta's chin forcing her to look at me. I knew she loved to fuck with me but it's late and I rushed over here because I thought something was wrong. She knew I would get mad and she hasn't said one thing but stare at me.

"Ketta, stop fucking playing and tell me. What the fuck you need to tell me? You know I hate that guessing shit," I argued. I don't know why she likes trying me. I wish she would stop that shit. I don't know why she thought it was cool to try a real nigga.

"Don, your just so sexy when you're mad," she beamed and smiled. I know she didn't rush me to get from securing our future just to tell me that. I pinched the bridge of my nose. "Kaniya got kidnapped and I caught my first body tonight. We can't leave Atlanta until they wrap this murder investigation up and we get cleared on it as self-defense," she explained and sighed. What the fuck. I know she didn't say what the fuck I thought she just said. I know my baby didn't just catch a body and she's just now calling me.

"Wait a damn minute. Please tell me you're lying?" I asked. I searched Ketta's face for a lie, but I didn't find one. My baby caught a body.

"I'm serious, baby. I wouldn't lie about something like this," she explained then sighed.

"Where did you catch a body at and where's the gun? Who kidnapped Kaniya?" I asked. I'm curious as fuck now? Ketta doesn't know the in's and out of killing somebody. My baby was to pure for that. It's my job to kill any motherfucka that brings her harm. Kaniya got kidnapped. Some shit isn't adding up.

"Don, stop worrying. Did you forget that I'm licensed to carry? I still have the gun. It was self-defense because we were ambushed. Whoever we killed were associates of whoever kidnapped Kaniya," she explained. I had to think for a minute. Yeah, Ketta was licensed to carry, but I still wanted to know who she killed because the last thing I need is for a motherfucka to come back for mine and I'm blindsided. I don't take losses, period.

"Who is we?" I asked. I wanted to know who she was with when she caught the body. Julius hasn't hit my line yet and I know for a fact he went home to Barbie.

"Barbie and Riley," she sassed. I don't know why she was catching an attitude. She should've called me the moment she dropped the fuckin' body. Not when she made it home. I would've pulled up to see what she dropped. I didn't know Riley though.

"Babe, what the fuck does Kaniya have going on this time that has my baby catching bodies and shit?" I asked. I needed to know what Kaniya was involved in. A shootout and a kidnapping in front of Magic City is to fucking hot. Whoever the fuck that was, they didn't give two fucks about the cameras. I knew for a fact Atlanta Police Department had them on that street and at the Marta Station.

"I don't know baby, something, but we won't know until she reappears and explains who took her and why," she explained.

"Are you sure Ketta, because I need to know whose body you caught and who they're affiliated with," I asked and explained.

"I don't know what Kaniya has going on. Don, I promise I'm trying to find out myself. It could be Melanie's family or some of JD's people coming back for revenge," she explained.

"Y'all are some fucking hot girls. How do you catch a body in front of Magic City? I know Lucky is going crazy because I would be. You're my good girl Ketta, and I need you to stay that way. I must holla at Julius about this shit. In the meantime, since you are bodying niggas and shit, let me shoot something up in you," I said. On some real shit, I knew Ketta knew how to handle hers, but I didn't want that for my baby. I wanted to keep her as innocent as possible. Somebody had to be following them to know they were at Magic City. This situation isn't a coincidence. I need to holla at Lucky, too. I wanted Ketta to have my shorty's though.

"Don, do you think we're ready to have kids? If you want me to have your child, since when did you need permission to bust in me? You've been doing it," she asked and explained? I slid Ketta's panties down her thick ass thighs. I don't know why she had these motherfuckas on anyway. I told her about that shit. I picked her up and tossed her on the bed. I had to get my pussy ready before I murdered it. "Don, you're not even listening to me," she pouted and moaned. "If you want me to have your child, why haven't you asked me? You think you're slick but I'm on to you," she explained. Ketta ran her hands through my waves and massaged my shoulders.

"I am listening. I want you to have my kids, Ketta. Shit, I want you to be my wife to, babe. I also want to hear what your pussy sounds like. Can I?" I asked. Ketta bit her bottom lip giving me the okay. She knew what time it was. I don't even know why she's tripping. The moment I come home from securing our bag every night. I take a shower and if she was asleep, I had plans to wake her up by diving in that pussy. I needed to feel the inside of her. She knew to be naked and ready. Ketta and I never fucked. I always made love to her because she was special to me. She widened the gap between her legs giving me access to slide in. She cupped my face in the palm of her hands and I gave her my undivided attention.

"Slow down, Don. It hurts, be gentle," she moaned and bit her bottom lip. Ketta was tight as fuck. It always took me a minute to open her up.

"Be patient, Babe. Give me a few minutes and I promise it'll feel better." I was serious about wanting her to be my wife. I wanted her to be the mother of my children. My father raised me to never shack with a woman. Don't get me wrong, I've had my share of women, but shit was different with Ketta. I loved everything about this woman.

Tariq

I know everyone has an opinion but I don't give a fuck. You can call it what you want, but a man must do what a man must do! The moment she heard me laugh, she knew what time it was. I love her ass something serious and she loves me too. The connection that we have is crazy and I know she can feel it. She was giving my man Phil hell and that shit was funny as hell. I know how Kaniya could be. My partner, AD, said that Phil's blood pressure was high fucking with my shawty. I knew it because he's called me to many fuckin' times.

I needed some alone time with her. Just the two of us with no interruptions. Fuck Lucky! It really pissed me off when she said he was coming for me. She knew that I didn't give a fuck, though. I can't wait until they bring her to me. It'll be a while before Lucky sees my future again. If I let her go back, which I doubt I will. My phone was ringing again, and it was Phil calling back.

"What's up, Phil? Talk to me," I argued. He was getting on my fuckin' nerves now.

"She's asleep now, nigga. About fucking time," he argued. I wanted to laugh. I knew Kaniya gave those motherfuckas a run for their money. Phil sounded like his blood pressure finally went down. I made sure those niggas worked for their money.

"Send me a picture, nigga." I was very curious. I've been missing her like crazy. It's been a while since I was able to get a glimpse of her sleeping.

"Hell no. You already sent me out to get this crazy ass girl. I promise you I have never met a chick so annoying. She can tote a pistol good, though. You know Lucky's my cousin, right? I don't want to be caught up in y'all shit," he argued. I don't give a fuck about Lucky. That nigga puts no fear in my heart. I heard Phil but I'm not tripping and I'm not fuckin' listening. I paid you to do a job and you went against your family for the bag, that's on you. Phil was trying to explain himself and make it clear if shit backfired, that's on him. If it backfired it's because he was sloppy as fuck and he told motherfuckas what he was up to.

"Word? It is what it is. Does she know that y'all are related? I'm not worried about him. I'm only worried about her, that's it," I explained. Fuck Lucky and I made it very clear that he's not an issue.

"No, I don't think so. This is my first time meeting her. I've only heard about her; she has no clue," he explained. This nigga was worried about Lucky way too much. He's worried about the wrong shit.

"We're good then. I don't want you caught up in my shit, but I'll see you when you pull up" I explained. He was good. I don't know why he was tripping. I can't wait until my queen arrives because we need some us time. I wonder what her reaction is going to be when she sees me. We have some shit we need to figure out.

If she would've kept her number the same or at least gave me her new number, we wouldn't be going through all this extra shit. I still wanted to take her out of her comfort zone to see how she would adapt. She wanted to cut off communication. I'll cut off all her communication and force her to communicate with only me.

She's been playing with me for too long. I'm tired of the games. She keeps running back to that nigga. What's that love shit about though anyway? I know she's feeling the kid; she's just scared to act on it. Damn, I can't wait until she gets here. I hate that Phil's partners got popped, but I heard those niggas were informants anyway. They just got cased up and haven't said a thing to Phil. He'll thank me later.

Chapter-4

Lucky

I'm tired of motherfuckers playing with me. I just don't understand why these niggas think this shit is a fuckin' game. I've been keeping shit cool since my father died but this cool shit was for the fuckin' birds. I'm not that fuckin' nigga and I don't want a motherfucka to get it confused and think I am. These niggas must have forgotten how I get down. I will wet some shit up in a fuckin' minute. The way I'm feeling, all these murders will make *The First 48*.

What better time to show these niggas how real this shit is about to really get? Like I said in the first place, I was going to Sonja's house first. She got me all the way fucked up and I'm kicking her door in. It didn't take me no time to pull up at Sonja's. I kicked her fuckin' door in and I didn't give a fuck.

"Sonja, get your ass out here right fucking now," I yelled. The last thing she wanted me to do was search this house for her because if I did, she may not make it to live to see tomorrow. I heard her coming downstairs.

"Lucky, what the fuck are you doing in my house? Why did you kick my door in?" She asked. I knew Sonja was nervous, but I don't give a fuck. If I couldn't sleep neither could she.

"Somebody took my heart," I argued.

"Your heart? What does that have to do with me?" She asked. She knew what the fuck I meant, and I wasn't talking about my fuckin' dad.

"Kaniya is missing and I know your bitch ass nephew has something to do with it. Get his bitch ass on the fucking phone, now," I argued. I grabbed my pistol from my waist. I wasn't playing with Sonja's motherfuckin' ass. I cocked that bitch back so she would know I was pissed.

"Are you serious, Lucky?" She asked and cried. I don't give a fuck about her crying and pretending like she was concerned.

"Look Sonja, quit fuckin' stalling and get his ass on the phone. I'm becoming impatient and my trigger finger is jumping. Look, I'm not playing no games. I'll kill you behind mine," I yelled. Sonja grabbed her house phone and called Tariq.

"Tariq, please tell me you didn't kidnap Kaniya," she cried and yelled. I heard Sonja mumble something under her breath. "He's stupid just like his damn momma. He's going to find himself dead just like her." I wonder what she meant by that. I knew Tariq kidnapped Kaniya. I just wanted that nigga to confirm it and when I kill him, he doesn't have to wonder why.

"Auntie, I do have her, and there isn't shit a nigga or a bitch can do about it," he explained. Sonja's facial expression change. She knew her nephew signed his fuckin' death certificate. He was very fuckin' nonchalant about the situation. I grabbed the phone out of Sonja's hand. I refused to listen to anything else this motherfucka has to say.

"Aye my nigga, you want my heart that bad that you're willing to die behind that shit? When I catch you, I'm going to bury you right next to your mammy, bitch, and that's on my fuckin' daddy. You're desperate as fuck. You have to kidnap a bitch to get some attention," I argued and yelled into the phone. I wish I could see Tariq right about now. I would really end his life today for pulling this fuck shit.

"Ha-ha. Lucky, that's your heart? That's how you feel, nigga? That's my heart too! A nigga once told me you either share the pussy or have, none. The day you fucked up and I found out, that shit was up for grabs, she was mine now. I staked my claim. Bitch I play for motherfuckin keeps" he argued and explained. I heard the call ended. *Click!* Tariq hung up the phone.

"Lucky, I don't have shit to do with that. I told Kaniya and Tariq to leave each other alone. Kaniya kept her end of the bargain," she explained. I don't believe that shit because he keeps giving me hints that he fucked her. This nigga is going out his fuckin' way to get her attention.

"I hear what you're saying and all, but your nephew has tried me for the last fuckin' time. He has an issue that I'm going to solve. He keeps coming for shit that doesn't belong to him. Get his fucking suit ready because when I catch him, it's lights out and that casket will be ready for him," I argued and explained. Sonja knew I wasn't bullshitting.

Some shit isn't adding up. I couldn't for the life of me click on Sonja like I wanted to. It's like I could feel the presence of my dad and he was telling me to chill out and take that shit up with Tariq. I planned to do just that, but why would this nigga kidnap her and think her pussy is his if she claimed that he hadn't had any?

That's the fucking question. Kaniya has some fucking explaining to do. The way he's acting has me thinking he's done more than ate her pussy. I can feel it. I could fucking kill her ass right now. For all I know she wasn't kidnapped. She could've ran off with the nigga. If I find out that Barbie fucking lied to me, I'm killing her ass too.

Tariq has started a war in these streets and Sonja isn't safe. I've spared him one to many times, but today was the last time. I needed to get a location on him asap. As far as Kaniya, she knows me and she knows how I think. She's guilty until proven innocent. Her pussy was supposed to forever be mine, and if Tariq touched it, she doesn't even want to know what will happen.

I need to call her mom though, and fill her in on what's going on. I'm not calling Killian after the fight we had, fuck him. He could've stopped me and been like that's my daughter. I was fucked up that night and didn't recognize him. He was right along with his brother when he killed my OG. He wanted to get some shit off his chest anyway. It's probably not meant for us to be together. On my daddy, it's a wrap if I find out anything else but the truth. I'm liable to hurt Kaniya for playing with me and playing me like I'm a sucker.

Veno dropped me off to my car. We slapped hands with each other promising to link up tomorrow. I couldn't believe this shit. I was ready to murk everything fuckin' moving behind her. Tariq kidnapped her and I know she fucked that nigga. I just want her to fuckin' admit it. I know I haven't been the best nigga to her but damn you gave my pussy up to the first nigga that fuckin' smiled at you. Barbie had the nerve to call me like some shit really popped off and this nigga is the one that fuckin' grabbed her?

Damn she must really think I'm a dumb ass nigga. It's a wrap. It ain't no more us and she had the nerve to call me and fake fuckin' cry. Her tears didn't fuckin' move me. I ain't tripping off Kaniya. That nigga wanted her so fuckin' bad he can fuckin' have her. Take her off my fuckin' hands. I'm tired of stressing behind her ass. I finally made it to my destination and the garage went up. I cut my fuckin' engine off. I didn't want to be bothered.

I made my way upstairs to her bedroom. She was sleeping peacefully, but I had plans to wake her up. I pulled the cover back and dragged her body toward the end of the bed. She was stirring in her sleep. I ran my tongue across her lips and raised her t-shirt over her head. I locked my teeth on her left nipple applying pressure to get her attention. She ran her hands across her face and opened her eyes and smiled at me.

"Lucky, what are you doing here?" She asked and moaned. My hands roamed every inch of her body. I finger fucked Yirah wet. It didn't take long for her to come on my fingers. She started grinding and rotating her hips on my fingers. I pulled my finger out and shoved it in her mouth. She licked her juices off my fingers.

"You know why I'm here. I want you in the worst fuckin' way," I whispered in her ear. She raised up and kissed me. This time I didn't object. Normally I wouldn't even kiss her but Yirah's a good girl. I knew I was the only nigga she was fuckin' and sucking, so why not. Kaniya and I aren't together.

"Baby, can you please put it in? I want you too and I missed you," she begged and moaned. I did as I was told. I took all my frustrations out on Yirah. I slammed my dick inside of her and started fuckin' her long deep and hard. She matched my rhythm stroke for stroke. We both had something to prove. She wanted me and I wanted her. Our bodies were both in sync with each other.

"Damn, I missed this pussy," I whispered in her ear.

"She missed you more," she moaned. Yirah ran her manicured nails across my chest. She already fucked my back up. The strokes of her nails sent chills through my body. She knew I hated that shit. I felt my nut rising to the tip of my dick. She had a sneaky ass grin on her face. She leaned up and started running her tongue across my chest intensifying the orgasm. I grabbed her face roughly.

"Bend over and arch that motherfuckin' back. You want me to fuckin' hurt you don't you," I moaned and grunted. I pulled out of Yirah so she can do what the fuck I told her to do.

I didn't have to creep with Yirah anymore. I could be out in the open with her and not give a fuck who saw us and who had something to say.

Sonja

I can't catch a break for nothing. I was minding my business the other day, headed to the hair salon to get my hair and lashes done. I was dressed to impress and clean and on the scene. I've been in a funk lately, so I decided to put some clothes on. I was cruising down Memorial Drive. when this dump truck rammed my Benz from the back. My car flew into the parking lot where **This Is It** was located. The truck kept ramming my car. This shit was intentional; I was being ambushed. The driver got out of his truck and shot my tires out. I had two flat tires now. He approached my driver's side door and opened it. I swear he was the last motherfucka I wanted to see. He was yelling in my face.

"Yeah, motherfucker, it's me! Please tell me you didn't think this shit was over between us. It's never fucking over when you are playing with Kanan Miller," he argued. He slammed the door so hard my window shattered. Is this nigga fucking crazy? Why would he run me off the road, shoot my tires out, and fuck my car up? To make matters worse, he fucked up my Mink vest. There was blood all over it. It was ruined.

I have a huge gash over my eye. Someone called the ambulance, but not the police. I just got out of Emory a forty-eight hours ago. I called Killian and told him to keep his brother away from me. Oh my God, this can't be my life right now! If it's not one thing, it's something else. Shit keeps getting worse by the minute. Deuce is gone and I still need to plan his funeral. Kanan is running around here acting crazy. I can't live like this. If he wanted to kill me, he had his chance in Miami. If not, please leave me the fuck alone, we are even. Also, this shit that Tariq has going on will be the death of me.

Out of all the women out here, he chose Kaniya. I told him she was off limits. He's a grown ass man. I can't fight his battles or protect him from everything, so he's on his own. I hate that it must be this way, but what else can I say? May the best man win. I'm going to beat Kaniya's ass when I catch her hot ass. I told those two.

Let me give Killian a call so he won't start to panic. I know Killian and I aren't going to see eye to eye because of what happened between Deuce and Kanan. I rather him hear it from me than anyone else.

I wish Tariq wouldn't have done that because it's a lot of tension in the family already. Kidnapping Kaniya is only going to make shit worse and the last motherfuckas I need at my neck is KANAN and KILLIAN.

Tariq

It didn't take long for Lucky to make that call. He should've known by now my heart doesn't pump Kool-Aid. If I want something, trust me, I'm going to get it. I wanted Kaniya. I always have and I always will, no matter what. Nigga, I play for keeps when it comes to that one! He called me talking about I took his heart. Nigga, if the shit were that serious, you would've never fucked up in the first place. Kaniya is mine for the keeping. Me and my heart are on our way to Jamaica.

I have a one-way flight booked. No phones allowed. I've been thinking about her like crazy these past few weeks. I had a few flicks of me and Kaniya in my phone. Our pictures got a nigga mesmerized. I always visualized us being together. I knew we were meant to be together because we have to many odds stacked against us. I've been back and forth to Miami. When I stepped foot back in Atlanta, shit I rode past her house a few times. I noticed she was never there.

I put something in her mailbox, and it was full, which mean she hasn't been home in a few weeks. I put the word out a few weeks ago to my partners if they were to see her grab her. I rode by yesterday and I saw Lucky's car in the driveway, and it pissed me off. I knew she was fuckin' off with him. That's why I grabbed her. She shouldn't even be doing that. She deserves better and I want to give her that.

We really need some alone time so we can get this shit right. I needed to see where her head is to see if I'm really where she needs to be. I refuse to let her take Lucky back after all the shit he's done to her. I think she needs to give us a fair shot and take a chance with a real nigga and see where it can go.

Did she think she could fuck me and leave and there would be no consequences? It doesn't work like that. We were building something. She let Shaela fuck up what we were building and Shaela already knew how I felt about her. Shaela was pregnant by John, anyway. It's time for us to rekindle and get back to what we were planning. She was my lil shawty. I have a soft spot for her. I can't wait to see her.

Chapter-5

Killian

I promise you I can't even fuckin' relax if I wanted to. If it's not Kanan, it's Kaniya. I promise you I think Kaniya is Kanan's child. She's just like his ass. The two of them both are going to be the death of me. I swear I think they're trying to kill me. Sonja called me two days ago and said that she was in the hospital. I was confused as to why she was calling me. Sonja and I were always cool but the nigga that she was engaged to tried my fuckin' life so I couldn't rock with that.

I wanted to hear what she had to say. When she told me that Kanan ran her off the road and shot her tires out. I just shook my head because he hasn't even been out that long and he's doing some hot ass shit fuckin' with Sonja. I knew he loved her, and he's hurt, but damn you ain't got to come at her like that. I felt bad for her. She just called me a few minutes ago and said her nephew kidnapped my daughter and not to panic because he's in love with her. Fuck that. Love don't make you kidnap a woman. This is what the fuck I'm talking about.

What would make him kidnap my daughter? Kaniya just came back to Atlanta not too long ago. I never knew she was involved with him. I would've been nipped that shit in the bud. Where the fuck was Lucky at when my daughter got kidnapped? I hope that he's in the streets looking for her. I needed to have a conversation with Tariq asap. He can't fuck with my daughter, period. I'm not signing off on that.

He's probably crazy like his momma. Bitch showed up at my house years ago and confronted Kaisha about me. She fucked up my home and my wife left me. Kaisha never looked back. I need to understand his motive. I'll have too call Sonja back. I need to call Kaisha's ass, too. She's going to chew me a new asshole when she finds out her hardheaded ass daughter has been kidnapped.

Let's not forget its Tyra's son, Tariq. She's going to go freaking nuts. She's already crazy. It's only going to make shit worse than what it already is. I'll never stop hearing her mouth and it's late. I'm not even trying to go there with her. I'll text Killany and tell her to tell her mother. I can't deal with my ex because we haven't seen eye to eye in years.

Me - Sweetheart I know it's late. Can you do me a favor?

I know it's late so I may be pushing it, but Killany always answer the phone whenever I call. I don't have that problem with her.

Killany - Yes daddy. Is everything okay??

Killany knew her mother and I weren't on good terms because of some things that went down a few weeks ago. I knew she wouldn't mind relaying the message.

Me - Yes and No. Kaniya got kidnapped. You wouldn't know anything about her and Tariq seeing each other? He's the one that kidnapped her.

I knew Killany would tell me everything she knew. Our relationship is good. She tells me everything.

Killany - I knew she was seeing him daddy, but she isn't anymore. Is she okay?

Kaniya had no business seeing him. She should've run that shit by me first because I would've made her end that shit immediately. I can hear Kaisha's mouth now as soon as she finds out it's Tyra's son. She's going to start bringing up old shit that I'm not trying to hear or relive.

Me - She BETTER BE. Get some rest sweetheart I'll call you in the morning.

I need a number and location on Tariq because he had no fuckin' business running down on my daughter like that and kidnapping her. I'm not feeling that shit at all. If you like her cool but you can't fuckin' make her be with you by doing that. I don't respect that shit at all.

Killany

Kaniya, Kaniya, oh my, the infamous Kaniya. My father just woke me up out of my sleep to tell me that my sister has been kidnapped by her secret lover, Tariq. This shit is comical to me. She just left my house four days ago. Kaniya must have some good ass pussy or some fire ass mouth because these niggas are going fuckin' crazy. I thought bitches were playing for keeps, but I see these niggas are playing for keeps as well. I want her to be with Tariq, though. I like his demeanor. I love how she talks about him. It's a glow that she has and it's a good look for her. I don't know why everybody was against their relationship. You can't help who you love. Love will find you when you least expect it.

Kaniya can't blame anybody but herself. She got herself into this mess and she'll have to get herself out. If anything happens to my sister, then all bets are fucking off. They think the Millers fucked Miami up and made a mess, Atlanta is not fuckin' ready. I think Kaniya will be okay. She was calling Tariq's name out in her sleep. She was having withdrawals and shit. I recorded her ass too. She was yearning for him. Kaniya says that it's lusts between her and Tariq, but that's a lie. She loves him, and I can see and hear it.

I must call my mom and let her know that Kaniya has been kidnapped because of the pussy she was giving up. My mom is overdramatic. Kaniya is her favorite. She'll die tonight. Even though I was sleepy I still wanted to get my mother's blood pressure high. I know it's wrong, but I don't care. She's probably still mad at me about our little run in a few weeks ago. I apologized to my mom. She's crazy and I love her to death, but Kaniya is just like her. She bodied a bitch in my house in the room right next to me with no silencer.

She's too old to still be bodying bitches behind my dad. I think it's cute my dad is still in love with my mom. She's in love with him too, but she just won't admit it. Every nigga that she thought she would be with my dad killed them. I wish they would grow up and be together. Lord, let me prepare for this conversation because my mom is over the top. I dialed my mother's number and she answered on the first ring.

"What is it Killany Denise? Why are you calling my phone this late at night?" She asked. I rolled my eyes. She wasn't even asleep. She was moving around, and I could hear the music in the background.

"Ma, can you talk? Are you busy?" I asked and sassed? My mother is so extra. I knew she was still mad at me but I'm a daddy's girl. I can't help it.

"I answered the phone, Killany. What's up, what's going on?" She asked.

"Daddy wanted me to call you and let you know that Kaniya's been kidnapped," I sighed. She started snapping instantly. I had to throw my phone on mute to stop from laughing.

"Who kidnapped my fuckin' daughter and why the fuck your pussy ass daddy couldn't fuckin' call me? Where was she Killany? I'm about to catch a flight. They fucked up and kidnapped the wrong fuckin' one," she argued. I had to hold my laughter in. I knew she was going to fuckin' lose it.

"Ma calm down she was in Atlanta. Tariq kidnapped her. She's okay," I explained. I knew I shouldn't have called her. I hate to hear her speak so negative about my daddy. I wish she would stop doing it.

"I don't give a fuck who it is, Killany. Kidnapping. That shit doesn't sit right with me. He took my child involuntarily. Tariq who, please tell me it wasn't Sonja's nephew?" She argued. I swear my dad owes me big time for this. He set me up. I already know what I want for putting up with this.

"Ma, yes it's Tariq, Sonja's nephew," I sighed.

"Killany, you know what? Stop letting your father send you out because that motherfucka knows he couldn't tell me this for that reason alone. Pack your shit and meet me in Atlanta, so we can find your sister," she argued. I wasn't going to look for Kaniya because she's fine.

"Ma, I'm not meeting you in Atlanta to look for Kaniya because she's fine. He loves her and she loves him too. I know he won't hurt her. That's what happens when you give your pussy up to crazy motherfuckas," I sassed and explained. I wasn't looking for Kaniya. She's fine and I can feel it. If we get a call from her saying something else, then I'm catching a flight.

"Are you fuckin' serious right now? Just because she gave him the pussy a few times it gives him the right to kidnap her? So that's cool with you? Since you're enlightening me on who's fuckin' who, who are you fuckin' Killany? Because you're not as innocent as your father thinks you are.

At least Kaniya is real about her shit. She's not sugar coating nothing," she argued and explained. I wasn't about to go back and forth with her about who I'm doing and why.

"Good night, Ma. I'll talk to you soon," I laughed. I hung up before she could say anything else. I knew she was on one and I'm dealing with it. Let me call my grandmother and give her this tea. My grandmother was always up at night. She claims she doesn't dabble in my father and uncles drug business anymore, but I don't believe it.

"Sweetheart, what are you doing up this late at night?" She asked and smiled through the phone. I'm my grandmother's favorite. My grandmother answered on the first ring like I knew she would.

"I can't sleep, grandma. Daddy called and woke me up out my sleep and told me that Kaniya was kidnapped," I yawned and pouted. I was laying it on thick. I knew my grandmother wanted to know more about what's going on.

"Hold up, Killany. Did you get the money that I put in your account this morning? Say what now, Kaniya got kidnapped? I talked to your father a few hours ago and he didn't say anything. It must have something to do with that nigga she's dealing with. What's his name Luck or damn Shamrock or whatever the fuck y'all call him. I know that nigga has some shit with him. Does he beat on Kaniya, Killany?" She asked. I had to throw my phone on mute again. I didn't want her to hear me laughing. I swear she's crazy.

"Yes, I got it. Thank you! No grandma it's not Lucky. They're not together anymore from what I was told. It's the new guy she was seeing and stop seeing him suddenly. Tariq is his name. You remember Sonja the one Uncle Kanan was dating? It's her nephew," I asked and laughed. I knew my grandmother didn't like Sonja, that's why I asked her.

"She must be giving up her cootie cat to him, for him to do some shit like that. I ain't surprised, Killany. She gets that shit from your mother. She always had to have one up on a nigga and put miles on her pussy. You know I ain't never liked Sonja or her fuckin' mammy. Don't mention that bitches name to me. You know Sonja's sister used to mess with your daddy. That's why your momma and Sonja fell out, but you didn't hear that shit from me," she explained. My grandmother was always dropping dimes, but she never cared to give more detail. I knew I wouldn't get the tea from my mother.

"She was, grandma. I guess he got tired of her playing with his feelings and he took matters into his own hands and kidnapped her. I'm sure she's okay," I laughed. If Tariq kidnapped Kaniya he wasn't about to do any harm to her because he loves her.

"I figured as much. I blessed y'all with dead man's pussy. Once a nigga gets in, he ain't gonna want to get out of it. I guess your mother got a little bit of that too, because your father is so far up her ass it's crazy. The two of them both are playing dangerous games.

Your father told me about what your mother did a few weeks ago. I knew she still wanted him," she laughed and explained. My grandma could talk. I know she didn't care for my mother, but I still wasn't going to let her dog her out. I finished talking to my grandma making promises to speak with her tomorrow. Kaitlyn Miller is off the chain. I wouldn't trade her for nothing in this world. I need to lay down for a few hours and say a quick prayer for Kaniya.

Kanan

Tariq's young ass has kidnapped my niece? What the fuck does he know about kidnapping? I taught that nigga everything he knows. I damn near raised him. Shit, I did. If my niece has a scratch on her, I will kill that lil nigga and I mean that. I don't play about kidnapping, period. Sonja isn't his lifeline when it comes to my niece. I really must pay Sonja's ass some extra visits now. She already knows I don't play about my fucking niece. Last I knew, she was dating Lucky. Where in the hell did Tariq come from? If Sonja was letting her nephew fuck my niece behind my back, it's two shots to her dome.

Killian called my phone sounding like a little bitch! I had to remove my phone away from my ear. His daughters and their mother were his weakness. I know my niece can handle her own, so I'm not tripping but still, what's the motive behind this shit? I think I'll go bust up in Sonja's shit now. She shouldn't have any niggas over there. I need to speak with Tariq now, and it can't wait. If you wanted to get at my niece, you should've asked for my permission.

I would've gladly declined. I know Kaisha won't be happy about this shit. She hated Tyra, Tariq's momma. I knew Sonja killed Yasmine. I watched her do it. She left my sons motherless and I'm not even pissed about it because she handled something that needed to be handled. That's cool because I'm packing their shit up now and dropping them off to Sonja so she can raise them. I wish she would fuckin' object. She has life fucked up.

Yasmine wasn't raising them anyway. She started to get them when she heard I was out and started trying to play the mother roll, but it was too late. I knew that shit was a front because my ears were always to the street. It was too late for her to try to be a mother to them. They were already 15 about to be 16. If they weren't with Killian, my mother had them. It was late as fuck. Kanan and Yashir tried to play like they were sleep but I was on their motherfuckin' ass. It was late and in the middle of the summer, I told them to grab some clothes because we had a few runs to make.

You killed their momma, so it makes you their new fuckin' momma. You should give it all you fuckin' got to avoid me busting a cap in your motherfuckin' ass. I got her ass now, right where I fuckin' want her. Kanan and Yashir haven't asked about their mother and she's been gone for a few weeks. Yasmine wasn't raising them anyway since she's been out of jail.

She had been living her life and not thinking about my fuckin' sons. She still wanted to be young and a hoe. I swear I regret sticking my dick in her, but I don't regret my sons at all.

"Aye, wake y'all motherfuckin' ass' up and pack y'all shit up. I mean every fuckin' thing. Y'all are moving out of here this summer. I got some heavy shit going on and I need a motherfucka to watch y'all ass'. Don't say my mother can because she already said y'all can't go back over there. The two of y'all have been driving her crazy. Beat y'all feet before I beat y'all ass'," I argued and chuckled. Kanan Jr. was more like me and Yashir was just like Killian but when he got mad you see me.

"Old man, we don't need a babysitter. We can watch our self. We've been raising ourselves for as long as we can remember. Whatever heat you got going on in the streets we can assist you. Ask Uncle Black and Uncle Killian," he explained. Kanan Jr. always had something to say. Yashir nodded his head in agreement. I'm not the type of father that would tell my son's not to be in the streets.

I wanted my sons to do their own thing, but I know Black and Kanan have been showing them the ropes because I don't want to do this shit forever. When I decide to retire, I'm passing my portion of the business to them. Kaniya and Killany will handle Killian's fraction. Black's son will handle his.

"Old, Kanan Jr., watch your fuckin' mouth. Ain't shit old about me. You heard what the fuck I said and it ain't up for debate. I know what the two of you can do. I know what you've been doing. Follow my lead and I'll never steer you wrong," I explained. Kanan and Yashir started packing their stuff up. I heard them little motherfuckas mumbling some shit up under their breath while packing their shit up. I needed them to keep an eye on Sonja to see what the fuck she had going on. They needed to get to know her anyway because we would be living together soon. Black sent me a text stating Sonja had movement at her house.

Chapter-6

Kaisha

Killian is so full of shit. Ugh, I can't believe once upon a time I loved him. I hate I'm still fuckin' married to him. He could've had the decency to call and let me know that my daughter has been kidnapped by that motherfucka. He already knew how I would react. He knew he was going to hear my motherfuckin' mouth. Why did I have to hear it from Killany? I fucked him and made Killany. It wasn't the other way around. To make matters worse, it was his baby momma's son that kidnapped her. I swear that's a slap in the fuckin' face.

Killian is a fake ass motherfucka. That's why I left his ass. A bitch you used to fuck; son kidnapped my fuckin' daughter. He knew that shit wouldn't sit well with me. He couldn't even tell his kids they have another sister out here, but he signed the child's birth certificate. Yes, I swabbed the child's mouth, that's how I know she's his. Sonja is fake as fuck.

That bitch knew her sister was fucking with my man and she smiled up in my fuckin' face the whole fuckin' time. She smiles up in my daughter's face and all I hear is Sonja this and Sonja that. Well, when in the fuck can she tell my daughter that her niece is her fucking sister. I don't play any games about my kids at all. I'll see a motherfucka period, about mine.

Tyra tried me. That bitch got besides herself on a numerous occasion. I had to let that bitch know I wasn't the fuckin' one. I knew what Killian was doing. Did I need that shit on my doorstep? No, but if it ever touched my doorstep, I was going to air that bitch out. I was doing me, too. The moment that bitch decided to knock on my fucking door asking me about my husband she signed her fuckin' death certificate. The bitch couldn't have known about me.

I caught that hoe slipping one morning right after she had just got done fuckin' Killian. I followed her and bodied that hoe. I beat her senseless. Killian knew I did that shit. I wanted the motherfucka to know. What the fuck was he going to do about it?

A bitch will never come to my house and pop off and live to tell a bitch about it. You can never play me, but you can pay me. If Kaniya is fuckin' Tariq, she can dead that shit now because he will be joining his mammy.

I know stepping back in Atlanta will open some old wounds, but I promised my baby I would be here for about two months like she asked me to. I should dig Tyra's ass up and throw her corpse on Killian's porch. Call me petty, but yeah, I'm that bitch. I hope and pray that nigga doesn't hurt my baby. I'll wipe out his whole bloodline, starting with Sonja. I need to find out who his father is. Where was Lucky? That nigga was calling my phone every fuckin' day begging like Keith Sweat when Kaniya left his ass.

She gets it from her momma. Kaniya's just like me. She's not sneaky. It is what is with her. Hate or love it. Killany, on the other hand, is like Killian all day. Now that's another story for another fuckin' day. Ugh, I can't stand it, yuck. She's his favorite. He worships the ground she walks on. He swears she's perfect and can't do any wrong. Killany is sneaky as fuck, just like her daddy. She loves to call me and gossip about Kaniya. I had to tell her we're not going to do that, heifer. What do you think you're doing? I told Kaniya to stop telling her business to Killany a long time ago.

At least Kaniya can keep it real about what the fuck she does. Tell me what it is that you do again, Killany? She's on mute every time, but I ask that question. Exactly, just like a thought. She's a sneaky fuck, get that shit off your tongue. You're sneaky just like your daddy. That gets her every time. I'm catching a flight to Atlanta later. I planned on helping Kaniya with her temp service. I know people wonder why I don't spend as much time with Killany in Virginia. I have my reasons. Killany is boring and

I'm not welcomed at her house anymore. I was there last month with her sneaky ass. I popped up and Killian was there with some bitch, and they were having dinner like one big happy family.

I didn't even tell Kaniya because I didn't want her to feel some type of way. I'm minding my own business. I opted out of dinner, so I came back to the loft about 1:00 a.m. Killian is still a petty and salty ass nigga. I assumed he was gone, but he was still here. I showered and got ready for bed. The room him and his bitch were occupying was right next to mine. I made my way to the room. See, Killian's the type of nigga that would never lay up in anybody's home but his own.

So, I knew he was there just to fuck with me. He's barking up the wrong tree. Don't come for me unless I send for you. He's still mad I was the one that got away after all these years. Baby, when I say good black don't crack. I was still snatched! He knows he can never even breathe on this pussy again. So Suddenly, I hear noises and they get louder and louder.

He decides to fuck his bitch while I'm next door. It was cool, I wasn't tripping but this bitch had the nerve to tell this nigga "Fuck me better than you ever fucked that bitch next door" and to drop some twins in her. She was disrespectful, both were. He was wrong for entertaining the shit. Mind you, he was laughing too.

She didn't know me and I didn't know her. He should've stopped that bitch in her tracks and corrected her. What you won't do is disrespect me and think I won't check your ass. Bitch, you better ask about Kaisha in these motherfuckin' streets. Ask your nigga about me, bitch. I kicked the fuckin' door open in the room they were in.

I asked the bitch, "you want this nigga to fuck you better than he ever fucked me? Speak up, bitch. Keep my name out of your fuckin' mouth. If you want to keep breathing, that's how you better tread. Don't ever call me a bitch unless you're prepared to meet the baddest bitch that ever graced your presence." That hoe popped slick at the mouth. Why did she do that?

I didn't ask any questions or do too much talking. I pray for patience on a daily. I pulled the gun out from the back of my pajamas. I shot that bitch dead in her head and told Killian that bitch could never be me. He was hollering and shit talking about I was still crazy. Kaniya acts just like me. I told that bitch ass nigga to stop acting like a bitch and get a real one. Killany woke up out of her sleep and the first thing she said was 'Daddy, what's wrong?' and he explained what happened.

This motherfucka had the nerve to tell me 'mom, you must go. That shit is not cool, you could've killed my dad.' Can you believe this lil bitch? I politely told her I was glad to leave. I'll never be somewhere I'm not wanted. I'm not fuckin' with Killany right now because of that but because she tried me, and she shouldn't have.

Her father provoked me, and he already knew how it would end up. He knew I wasn't going. I should've shot his ass too for playing with me. I want my divorce. That's all I want at this point. I don't know why he's still holding on to me.

THREE DAYS LATER

Ketta

Thank you Jesus, we finally got cleared for the murder investigation. The Atlanta Police Department checked our stories out. They were able to pull the camera feed and saw the whole ambush unfold. The video showed Kaniya being ambushed and ushered into the black Denali. There's still not a lead on Kaniya. Barbie had tried to call Lucky and he didn't answer. I called Riley to let her know that we'd been cleared, and she was free to return home.

I've been calling Mrs. Kaisha, but she hasn't answered her phone. I left several messages. I just hoped and prayed that nothing foul happened to Kaniya and they didn't hurt her. Where is she and what did she do? I mean, damn, is anybody looking for her seriously. This shit is making my nerves bad. I've been tripping on Don because my friend is still missing. I didn't mean to, but my nerves are fuckin' bad. I wasn't comfortable going back to New York and she's still missing. My phone rung and it was Barbie. I answered on the second ring to see what she was up to. We were supposed to meet up with Tianna and Riley for a massage later.

"Hey Ketta, what's up? Girl I got some good news and some bad news. Which one do you want first?" She asked. Barbie's voice was chipper. Whatever she had to say couldn't be too bad.

"Spill it girl, it doesn't matter to me," I sighed. I couldn't take any more bad news.

"Girl, Mrs. Kaisha called me back this morning. She said she was going to call you, too. You wouldn't believe who kidnapped Kaniya's motherfuckin' ass. Tariq bitch, and Lucky talked to him. Tariq told his ass it was him," she laughed.

"Bitch, you motherfuckin' lying. You know it's about to go down when they see each other. Damn, Kaniya should've never gave that nigga the pussy. He done lost his fuckin' mind," I laughed. Barbie and I finished talking and I couldn't believe this shit. At least my mind is finally at ease. I couldn't wait to meet up with her later so I could get the details. I knew Mrs. Kaisha would call back.

Barbie

I'm all over the place. My feelings are a wreck. My mind has been idle for a few days because there were to many what if's and the thought of losing my partner in crime was fuckin' with me mentally. If I couldn't count on anybody in this world, I knew I could count on Kaniya. I didn't want to lose that. It's safe to say I haven't slept in a few days because she was missing and heavy on my mind. I don't even pray but I pray every night that she's okay.

I'm finally able to relax just a little bit since I heard from Mrs. Kaisha, but I wanted to hear from Kaniya that she was okay. I know how she feels about Tariq. I didn't personally see her face, but I could hear she was feeling him, and he was feeling her too. I planned a spa day for me and the girls. We needed it. Damn I wish she was here so we could talk about this shit.

JeJu Spa is about thirty minutes from Julius' loft. I wanted to go home and relax in my spot while we're here, but Julius wasn't having that. I haven't been in a relationship in years, so this experience was new to me. I'm crushing hard on Julius. I swear I was at the right place at the right time. I know we linked up that night because of Kaniya.

If she wouldn't have went out to catch Lucky. Ketta and I wouldn't have been chilling. I guess some things happen for a reason. A small smiled appeared on my face. Julius walked up behind me and wrapped his arms around my waist. His hands roamed every inch of my body. He bit the crook of my neck. He smelled so good.

"Baby, can you please stop. I'll never be able to leave because you're starting something that I can't finish," I moaned. I tried to break free from his embrace, but it wasn't working. I hated it when he did that.

"Ma, where are you headed this afternoon," he asked and placed kisses along my collar bone. A soft moan escaped my lips. It felt so good. Things with Julius was different. I've dated a lot of men and although we're moving fast, he's taking the time to get to know me and my body.

"I have a spa date," I moaned. I haven't even gotten dressed yet. The only thing I had on was my bra and panties. Julius was pulling them down trying to get a quickie in before I left. I wouldn't make it to the spa. I would be lying up with him until him and Don had a few moves to make.

"Oh, yeah. I could've given you a full body massage, all you had to do was ask," he explained. Julius started massaging my shoulders and thighs. His hands caressed my pussy a few times. He knew what the fuck he was doing. I looked up at him, he gave me a devilish grin. I swatted his hands away. Julius knew exactly what to do. I was always mesmerized by his appearance but to be in a relationship with him was amazing. He's the perfect boyfriend. I'm proud to call him mine.

"I know, I'll take you up on that offer tonight," I moaned and beamed. Julius slid me his black card. I looked at him with wide eyes and shook my head. I slid it back in his hand. He cupped my chin forcing me to look at him. I ran my tongue across my lips.

"I gave you the card because I want you to have it. I want you to use it when you need to if I'm not around. I'm giving you access to my money because I trust you and I like this shit we got going on. If we're together Barbie, it's my job to handle all your needs and wants. Do you understand?" He explained and asked. Our lips were touching, and I could smell the mint on his breath. I wanted to slide my tongue in his mouth. I swear he was turning me on in the worse way. Julius is everything I ever wanted and needed in a man. I swear it feels like I'm dreaming. These past two months he's been taking very good care of me. I can't even complain but I didn't want him to think that I was a gold digger because I wasn't.

"I know baby, but I got it. Since I met you, you've been spoiling me like crazy. I appreciate you Julius so much. Can I spoil you?" I asked.

"No, you can't spoil me. I'm a grown ass man and I'm a provider. It's my job to take care of you and spoil you. You can continue to cater to my needs. I'll gladly let you do that," he explained. He placed his Black card between my bra and kissed me on my forehead. I slid my jeans on. Julius wrapped his arms around my waist and pulled me in for a kiss.

"Thank you, Julius, for everything," I beamed and smiled. I threw my wife beater on and slid my feet in my sandals. I grabbed my Chanel tote and keys. I'm already running late fooling with Julius.

I finally made it to the JeJu. I'm twenty minutes late and traffic was fucked up. There were a few accidents. Ketta and Riley called me a few times and stated they were waiting on me. The moment I stepped through the door all eyes were on me. I sucked my teeth before I spoke.

"Hey y'all, I'm sorry I'm late. Julius had me tied up a little," I beamed and smiled. "Thank me later because our spa date it's on him." I pulled out Julius Black card and paid for massages and facials. We decided to do the sauna first and that was perfect. We had time to talk before the massages put us to sleep.

"Riley and Tianna, I heard from Mrs. Kaisha this morning. She said she heard from Kaniya and Tariq was the one that kidnapped her," I laughed. It wasn't funny but it was. He had us killing niggas because he wanted to get at her. He's going crazy behind that pussy. Kaniya had to be riding his dick real fuckin' dirty for him to show out like that. I wish I could've been a fly on the wall or saw Lucky's reaction when he heard that.

"Barbie, I know you motherfuckin' lying, Tariq did that shit? I don't give a fuck what y'all say or what Kaniya says, she gave that nigga the pussy. The moment that nigga pulled down on her I knew he was trouble. Quan ain't said shit about that. I guess Lucky don't want a motherfucka to know Tariq swooped in and grabbed Kaniya," Tianna explained. I knew Kaniya and Tariq made love but if she hadn't told them then I wasn't. I'm sure she told Riley, but she was a little on the edge about telling Tianna because of Quan.

"I'm not going to be the one to air out Kaniya's dirty laundry because she's not here to defend herself BUT I hope she fucks him. I'm not a fan of Lucky at all. Especially after he accused her of going off with another nigga, but hey maybe he knew something we didn't," I sassed and sucked my teeth. Riley looked at me with a smile which means she was aware. Lucky knows Kaniya fucked that nigga. That's what the fuck he gets.

"I'm with you Barbie, I hope she puts that pussy on that nigga. I'm not a fan of Lucky, but Tariq is smooth as fuck. They're feeling each other and I've witnessed the chemistry between the two of them. He's drawn to her like a moth in a flame. He sampled the pussy, he had too," Tianna laughed and explained.

"I like Tariq for Kaniya although I haven't met him, but kidnapping is another level of crazy. I can't fuck with that, period. If he wanted her attention, I don't think doing that was the right way to go about it," Ketta argued and explained.

I felt where Ketta was coming from because the cops were involved. I'm not a fan of the police. Tianna and Kaniya were close but Kaniya told me a few weeks ago that she hasn't been acting herself. My lips are tight but since Kaniya's been gone she's been in the loop with us every day being the concerned friend she should've been. Maybe it's the pregnancy and not the nigga.

"I feel where you're coming from Ketta but enough about Kaniya. Let's enjoy our spa date. I'm sure she's enjoying her vacation with her bae. I want front row seats for what's about to go down when Lucky and Tariq see each other," I laughed. Ketta, Riley, Tianna, and I slapped hands with each other, agreeing that we wanted to see that. Our masseuses started on our massages. I said a quick prayer for Kaniya hoping she would call or FaceTime me soon.

Chapter-7

Kaniya

I still haven't made it to my destination. I don't even know what fuckin' day it is. It seems like we've been driving forever. I know we're no longer in Atlanta. I swear to God when I see Tariq, I'm going to fuck him up. I just want to go fuckin' home, take a hot shower, and relax. What would make him want to do this to me? I have shit to do unlike the other bitches he's used to fuckin' with. I don't know what he has in store for me and if this was a few months ago maybe I would've been smiling. The last time we saw each other he made it his business to let me know he was fuckin' someone else. Did it hurt? Yes, the fuck it did because I gave myself to him on multiple occasions. One of the reasons why I killed Shaela was because of him. I hated that bitch and I was sick of him entertaining her whenever he fuckin' wanted to.

"Fuck boy, get Tariq's bitch ass on the phone," I argued. I hated this, Phil motherfucka. I always gave him a fuckin' attitude. He doesn't like me, and I don't like him. I don't appreciate him getting a free feel of my ass. I haven't kick boxed in a while. I wish I would've kicked his ass in the balls, but he'll get his.

"My name isn't, fuck boy," he argued and explained. He heard what the fuck I said. If it wasn't his name and he wasn't a fuck boy, then he wouldn't have responded. I don't like him, and I don't trust his ass for some reason. He just rubs me the wrong way. He should thank God that I didn't have a gun or else I would've shot his ass dead.

"I don't give a fuck what your name is. I'm running the show. Get Tariq on the motherfuckin' phone now, before you end up like your niggas on the street," I argued. I didn't give a fuck how disrespectful I was. I wasn't bull shitting either. I might not have a gun, but I would tag his ass in his chest a few fuckin' time and kill his ass.

"Lil buddy, you got a lot of mouth," he argued. I knew he was disgusted with my mouth and attitude at this point. I don't give a fuck, now I'm his buddy all sudden. I just wanted to talk to Tariq to see if we can talk about this and possibly take me back home.

"Look, lil buddy, get Tariq on the phone," I argued and stated. I tried to be very calm, but I don't know how long it would last. I need to brush my teeth and wash my ass. I'm beyond fuckin' frustrated at this point because I needed to soak in the tub.

"Tariq, she wants you bruh, and she's getting on my last nerve," he stated. I don't care about him being annoyed with me or my attitude. He shouldn't have kidnapped me in the first place.

"Yeah baby, what's up?" He answered calmly, not knowing what type of mood I was in. I don't want to be fuckin' kidnapped, period. I want to be at home in my bed and laid up with Lucky, that's it. What Tariq and I had been over and it's nothing we could do about it. We crossed that line and we shouldn't have.

"Don't yeah baby, me. Why are you doing this shit? When you were with Jasper, you weren't coming at me this hard. You were disrespectful. Do you remember that shit?" I asked him with a vengeance. I remember it like it was yesterday and I'll probably never forget it.

"I want to talk and kick it for a few days, that's it." He chuckled and explained. I don't want to do any of that. We could've talked in Atlanta, but it wasn't going to be any kicking it at all.

"You had to kidnap me and get some niggas killed in the process?" I asked. I'm curious as fuck. It's many ways he could've got in touch with me without kidnapping me. I've dropped plenty of bodies before, but my girls haven't. I can only imagine what they're going through just because this nigga wanted to play a game with me.

"Why are you acting surprised? You know how I come when I'm coming for you. Kaniya Miller I play for keeps! I'm serious about you, baby." He explained. I don't care about none of what Tariq was saying. I knew he cared about me and I know he wanted me to know how he truly felt about me. I'm surprised because I had no clue that he would do this.

"What are you trying to prove, though?" I asked because I needed to know the motive. I could hear Tariq debating on what he wanted to say but he needs to choose his fuckin' words wisely.

"I'm that nigga and you should be with me," he shot back at me.

"I'm sorry but it's a little too late for that." I looked at the phone because I know he didn't say what I thought he said. He must come better than that because judging by his actions he's not.

He couldn't wait to hurt me because I hurt him, but I didn't mean to. I've caught him with Shaela and the other chick. It was just too much for me.

"I need to call Lucky and let him know that I'm not willing to be here. Second, you know we can't be together." I had to remind him. I hate we even explored each other.

"Lucky knows where you are! He called me already and I let that nigga know. Why can't we be together, Kaniya? You scared you are going to love a nigga that much? I'll never hurt you. I love you and I'm tired of playing these games with you. That's why I kidnapped your ass," he revealed. *Click!* He hung up the phone in my face. My heart dropped instantly when he revealed that Lucky knew I was with him.

"I hope I never run across no pussy like that," Phil laughed. He thought the shit was hilarious and it wasn't. He could never fuck a bitch like me even if he was fuckin' paying.

"Can I use your phone? I need to call Lucky and my mom, then you can get your phone back?" I asked and sucked my teeth. I'm irritated as fuck. My whole attitude had changed once I found out Lucky knew Tariq had kidnapped me. This is one phone call that I wished I didn't have to make. I know he's going to think the worst but I'm praying for the best.

"You're good! You shouldn't have put that pussy on that nigga, you stuck now. You're going to get somebody killed. I pray I never run across a woman that'll make me do this shit," he explained and laughed. I know he was being real about the situation at hand. I brushed him off because I wasn't hearing nothing he had to say. I dialed Lucky's number. If he knew who kidnapped me, then when the fuck was, he coming to get me.

"Lucky, baby, where are you? When are you coming to get me? I don't want to fuckin' be here," I yelled and cried. Tears were pouring down my eyes. I was very sad and emotional at this point. All I wanted was him. I needed him. I don't know what to do. I've made a lot of mistakes. I don't regret them, but I wish I hadn't done them.

"Don't Lucky baby me, you know you ran off with that nigga. I don't believe shit you have to say. I know you fucked him and let him sample the pussy. It doesn't make any sense that he's doing all of this for you if you claimed the only thing, he has done was eat your pussy," he argued.

"Excuse me," I argued and cried. He cut me off before I could say anything else.

"The best thing that you can do for me is leave me the fuck alone. I'm cool on you. Go be with that nigga that you ran off with," he argued. Lucky hung up the phone on me. I can't believe this nigga. He was dead serious. I shook my head.

That's all the confirmation I needed to move on with my fuckin' life. I don't feel bad at all. I had some shit I wanted to say, too. I heard him and now it's time for him to hear me. I called his phone back and he answered on the first ring and he didn't say anything.

"Lucky you ain't never got to worry about me no more. If I wanted to be here with him, I wouldn't have even called you. Why would I? Did you think about that before you jumped to fuckin' conclusions? I would rather be with you than with him, but I guess you're with someone else. Fuck you Lucky, and I mean that shit. Live your fuckin' life. If we ever see each other again don't say shit to me. I guess I mean as much to you as the five years we spent together, NOTHING.

I don't even know why I'm explaining myself to you because you don't even deserve that much," I argued and cried. I hung up the phone on him. I can't believe his ass, but I'm not even surprised. I should've expected that from him.

"I'm calling my mom and you can have your phone back," I sighed. Mommy, please answer the phone. I need you. She answered on the first ring. Thank God she did because I really needed to talk to her. She normally doesn't answer for numbers that she doesn't know.

"Hey baby, how are you?" she answered. How did she know it was me? I guess she was waiting for my call. I missed my mommy. I don't think that I could live in this world without her.

"Mommy, what are you doing? I miss you," I beamed and cried. I tried my best to mask my pain, but I couldn't. Lucky's words alone fucked me up. I was so happy to hear her voice.

"I'm thinking about you, my sweet baby," she beamed and smiled. I could tell that she was excited to hear from me. I knew she was worried sick.

"I'm ready to come home. I'm not with this shit," I sighed and sniffled. Tariq took shit way to fuckin' far.

"You have a dilemma, baby. What are you going to do? You know I'm always here if you need any advice. Have you heard from Tariq?" She asked and laughed. I wiped my tears. I wonder how she knew it was him.

"How do you know that Tariq kidnapped me?" I asked her. My mother knew everything. I wasn't surprised she knew that. I knew it wouldn't be long before she came looking for me.

"Girl, everybody knows. Your father didn't even have the decency to call and tell me, Killany did," she explained. I'm not surprised. My mother and father have been at odds lately. I'm sure Killany is telling everybody my business.

"Oh Lord, mommy. I hate to hear his mouth. This will be another thing he will go on and on about," I sighed. My mother knew how hard my father could be. I wish Killany wouldn't have told him. My father is probably wondering why Tariq kidnapped me. I knew he would never approve of me being with him.

"Listen Kaniya, don't feel bad about any of this, because you had no control over this. At least your kidnapper is sexy, so I've heard. You'll have to take the good with the bad, baby. Fuck your daddy. I'm tired of him always having something to say about you anyway. You're the spitting image of me. He's harder on you because you remind him of me. That nigga isn't what he says he is either. He's got some skeletons in his closet and I'll be glad to air out his dirty laundry." She explained. What did my mother have on him? At least I feel better about the situation.

"Momma, really?" I asked. I'm curious to know what my dad had going on. He's the realest man that I know. I don't want to believe anything that will taint the image I have of him.

"Yes, Kaniya, Momma's the realest on your team. I got some tea for you that can't be spilled on the phone. I'll be at your house waiting for you until you get back from your baecation! I love you. I will see you soon," she laughed and beamed. Oh lord. What does my momma have on my daddy? I need this tea. I love my momma. She's so damn crazy. My momma has my back no matter what. She doesn't mind going to war with my dad for me. I'm ready for this tea!

Tariq

I had to hang up on Kaniya ass. She just pissed me off for real with her questions and attitude. She got me fucked up. I'm not scared of Lucky. That nigga doesn't put any fear in my fuckin' heart. My heart pumps just like his. I'm not a pussy. Never have I ever been that. I had to look at the phone for a minute to make sure I wasn't tripping. I asked myself was she crazy. I knew she was, but we love each other. Love is a motherfucker and I know I love her. I can't deny it if I wanted to. I can tell you that much. I'm doing shit that I thought I would never do.

Kaniya has my nose wide fuckin' open. I've been trying to shake her from my mind but it's not happening. She had the nerve to question me about why I was doing this shit now. She knew why. It's because of her and I'm tired of her playing with me. The Jassity shit fucked her up and I'm sorry for that. I need to apologize and make it up to her. She tried me when she fucked Lucky on the bus and lied. We were just fuckin' around and you know it.

It's so easy for her to forgive Lucky, but she holds everything against me. Maybe she really doesn't want this like she said she did. It's too late for the excuses now, we're going to work on a solution. She's given me mixed signals the whole time regarding us. I just don't get that shit. One strike and I'm out. She is too weak for him, and he's constantly fuckin' up, but she'll boss up on me quick. I'm laying down the law when we get to our destination.

I understand they have history and we do too. All I'm asking is for her to give me a fair shot. I promise I would never make her regret taking a chance on me. I wish she would forget about Lucky's ass. I'm tired of competing with that nigga. He's not any competition because I'm in a league of my own. She can love me, or I'm going to leave her ass for good, though. I can't wait to snatch her ass up. She'll leave Jamaica when I'm ready for her to leave.

She better not even think about escaping. Yes, I'm holding her against her will, so what. Nobody can stop me. She knows what it is with us and I'm tired of hiding it to spare the next motherfuckas feelings. They've never spared mine.

Lucky

"Baby who was that?" she moaned and asked. I had to put my hand over Yirah's mouth because I couldn't let Kaniya know I was fuckin' a bitch while she was on the phone with me trying to plead her fuckin' case. Yirah knew who the fuck it was calling me. She just wanted me to confirm it but that's not her business. Kaniya would call me when I was knee deep swimming in some pussy. I hated to be mean to Kaniya, but I had to. What the fuck did she expect?

Tariq kidnapped her and I'm supposed to be happy about that shit? She wants to call me acting all sad and shit, cut that shit out. She should've never entertained the nigga and she would be here right now with me. That's what happens when you go against the grain. To make matters worse, the fact that he gave her $100,000 to put up while he was away still fucked with me. Why would you give my lady money and not your own? I knew it was more to them than what she claimed it was.

Kaniya has some explaining to do. Until then, I'm going to do me. She should understand where I'm coming from. When I told her, I knew she fucked that nigga, she didn't object or stop me in my tracks. I wanted to know when and where. I should've asked if she was okay, but I already knew the answer to that. He wouldn't hurt her because that nigga loved her. He fucked up by falling in love because he signed his fuckin' death certificate. Tariq and I couldn't coexist because Kaniya belongs to me. The sooner he understands that, the better he will be.

The only thing I would have to worry about that would drive me crazy is the two of them fuckin'. When I catch him, he'll wish he never laid eyes on her. He thinks this shit is easy to fuck a bitch that you knew was mine and it ain't no consequences. His death will be hard. Can't no nigga kidnap my bitch and think that I'm supposed to be cool with this shit. What niggas do you know kidnap females for pleasure? No sucker free shit over here partner.

Just like I bodied JD's ass and she had to watch, I'm going to do Tariq's ass the same way and she'll watch. I'll make her dispose of his body since it's her fault I had to kill him. Keep playing with a real nigga and watch how real this shit gets. I'm done talking about what I'll do to his ass; when I see him, it's on. I don't give a fuck where we're at. I'm seriously done with Kaniya this time. Tariq took the cake with the kidnapping.

Chapter-8

Kaisha

My baby called me! I was so happy and glad to hear her voice. I'm glad she's okay. I hated to hear her voice crack at the mention of Killian and what he would think. Bitch ass nigga don't you ever in your fuckin' life make my daughter feel some type of way. He knows I will come and see about his ass. Kaniya looks up to him. He's wrong for that shit. He worships the ground Killany walks on. Don't get me wrong, I love Killany to death also, but she does shit also. Her shit stinks as well. They're equal so he needs to stop doing that shit.

I wanted to call and cuss his ass out, but he's not worth it. What I will say is that he will hear my mouth. I'm sick of him and his shit. I should've killed his ass when I killed his dusty bitch, but his twins saved him. Kaniya could live without Killian but Killany couldn't. That's the only reason his shitty breath ass is still breathing! Bad breath ass bitch!! I should leave a bag of peppermints on his fucking porch.

My daughters are my weakness but Kaniya, she's my everything. I guess it's because she's spent the most time with me. When Killian and I split I took Kaniya with me and Killian had Killany. I should've never done that. He was an asshole just because we weren't together. He wanted to make my life hell. Him and his mother. Kaniya and I made the best out of it. He was the worst at co-parenting. He would only let me get Killany on the weekends and majority of the time he wouldn't do that. He always wanted to be at my house to make sure I didn't have any men around his daughters. He knew me better than that. I called it bullshit.

When Kaniya hurts, I hurt. I feel it too. We're just bonded like that. I knew despite the circumstances she was worried about what her father and Lucky thought. I don't give a damn how old she is, it's not a motherfucka walking this earth that I'll let cause her any harm, and I mean that shit. Her heart is so big and it's going to get her in trouble. I hate that because she always sees the best in a motherfucka without looking at their faults. I hope Tariq's intentions are good for her because she needs a break after everything, she's been through these past few weeks.

Sonja

I've been sitting in my living room all night long drinking on Cîroc Peach with a few cherry's and a Sprite. I'm trying to get my head together. A lot has happened in the past few weeks. I swear this felt like a bad dream that I was dying to wake up from. I was good until Lucky popped up with this extra bullshit. I'm totally lost. I couldn't focus on Kaniya and Tariq right now. I still needed to have a memorial service for Deuce. I owe him that much. I just didn't want to accept that it was true, and he was really gone. DNA confirmed it was him.

I'm so lost, it's crazy. I don't know if I'm going or coming. Life without Deuce these past few weeks have been crazy. I'm so used to him doing everything for me and waking up next to him. Reality set in that I no longer had that. I had to call Chelle up here. I needed her more than she would ever know. I hope and prayed I made the right decision. I didn't want to risk her running into Black, but I needed my right hand here with me to get through this shit. I don't think I can take anymore. I swear I feel like giving up and throwing in the fuckin' towel. Deuce was everything to me. He was so loving and so fuckin' affectionate, that it's crazy.

My life was perfect before I met Kanan. I swear it was. I was dating doctors and lawyers. Hell, even NBA players. I knew I was going to be the wife of a Drug Lord. I couldn't stay away from East Atlanta if I wanted to, because something or someone was always pulling me back. I never knew things would've ended up this way. Kanan and I were together for over twenty years. I always took the good with the bad. It came with the life we chose to live. It came with the territory. I was born into a family of strong independent women who were about their business.

My mother and aunties were some real fuckin' hustlers. They got that cash all day. I didn't want to be like them. I just wanted fast cash. "Only the strong survive and the weak will die. Never give up and keep trying and never fall victim to a crime. Get it how you live and get this cash by any means. Pussy is power!" My mother and auntie Yvette would say. That was their motto for everybody and anybody! They instilled this in my head every day. I still live by it.

The ones who wanted to listen to what she was saying prospered. The ones that didn't listen; they're not here to tell about it. I did what I had to do to survive and keep my family's legacy alive. I hooked up with Kanan when I was about twenty or twenty-one.

My mother already put me up on game. I knew what to do to keep him. I knew what I had to do to satisfy his needs and his wants. He was deep in the drug game and he wasn't a corner boy. He had a seat at the fuckin' table. I had more to offer him besides pussy. I was an asset, not just a piece of ass.

My mother taught me how to cook dope, weigh up coke and make the best fuckin' X pills Atlanta has seen. It made us a force to be reckoned with in these streets. I'm the definition of a true ride or die bitch. I was with him from the beginning, but he had to go and fuck up what we built for that bitch Yasmine. I couldn't believe he done that shit, he stepped out on me for a bitch that wasn't even weighing up to me.

He had the nerve to let that hoe ass bitch have two sons by him; twins at that. It hurt my fuckin' soul. I was depressed and embarrassed. Everybody was laughing and talking about me. I kept my cool because I knew I was going to get Kanan back. He wasn't man enough to come to me and tell me, so they hid that shit for the longest, but that bitch kept trying me on the low. I noticed her whole attitude would change when he would come around. She wanted me to know she was fuckin' him, but she never had the balls to come out and say it. I could feel the hate rolling off her.

I wanted her to because I had plans to kill that bitch in the TRAP just to let any other bitch that wanted to fuck him know how I was giving it up. I ended up following them one day way before they got caught up and caught their case. I just played it off like I didn't know about his kids until that day, but I knew.

I'm sorry, but I wasn't keeping his kids that I never knew about. I really got the shock of my life when I followed them to the Mall of Georgia, and they were shopping for the boys. My heart dropped when I saw that shit because those boys were the spitting image of their father. To say I was hurt was an understatement. I was livid and I wanted to run their ass off the fuckin road that day. I kept my cool for a long time and played that shit raw. I stopped cooking and fucking that nigga.

That's why I stole all his money. Nigga, you can never play me, but you can pay me. I taxed his ass. I shouldn't have told him what I did and got Deuce killed. Oh well, he deserved that shit. That was my get back. I had something for Kanan's ass. He had Black's dumb ass in on that bullshit the other day and ran me off the road. They awakened a sleeping beast. Stop fuckin' with me. I'm ruthless, too. That's why I'm going to shoot up his mammy's house. I hated Kaitlyn's old bitter ass.

I hope I hit that miserable old bitch. She never liked me, and the feeling was mutual. He took Deuce from me and I'll take his mammy from him. Just the thought of that opened some old wounds. I was ready to close them for good and put behind me. I needed to live my life and be free of bullshit. Now play with it if you want to because I'm ready for a fuckin' war at this point.

Kanan

I've been sitting outside of Sonja's house for over an hour debating on how I wanted to drop these kids off. I know she's at home because the living room light is on. I guess it's only one way to do it and that's to bust up in this motherfucka and drop them off. Sonja knows she doesn't want to fuck with me or object. I knew she was still salty about the shit that happened a few days ago but oh well. What doesn't kill you makes you stronger. She knew how I was coming. I don't even know why she was fuckin' surprised. She should've expected it because this shit is far from over.

"OG, where are we? I'm tired and whose house is this?" Yashir asked. I knew he was tired. He was sleep but Kanan Jr. was up to some shit. I know it was getting late and they wanted to get back to sleep or whatever teenagers do. I needed to head back home and meet up with Black and Killian. I'm asking the questions not them.

"A friend of mine, why?" I asked. They were nosey as fuck. I don't like to be questioned about anything. Especially by some got damn teenagers. I looked at them and stroked my beard. I let out a soft chuckle. I'm the fuckin' boss. I don't know what Black and Killian were letting them do but I'm not the one. I don't know who those young niggas thought they were talking to but it's time I let them know a few things. I paid my dues to be the boss that I am. The only motherfucka I answer to is Kaitlyn Miller.

"Are we going in or what? I'm tired of sitting in the car," Yashir asked. He was aggravated as fuck and ready to make a move. Its levels to this shit and I move when I feel good and god damn ready not just because a kid is fuckin' ready, and my kid at that. Yashir may have been sleep but you can sleep when you die. If y'all want to live to take over my shit, y'all must move how I see fit. When it's go time, it's fuckin' go time. Everybody wants to put in work but not fuckin' work. It didn't work like that when you're affiliated with The Miller Mob.

"All right grab your damn bags. Let's go!" I argued and yelled. These are some impatient ass niggas, putting pressure on my ass. I got something for their asses, and I meant that shit.

"Dad, do you want me to kick the door in? I think I'm ready," Kanan Jr. asked. He was ready to get this show on the road. He was a hot head like me and I had to be careful with his ass because he would trip instantly. He's the type that doesn't think before he does shit.

He can't move like me. You're ready when I say you're ready. I know he wanted to show off. I already know him and Yashir was into some hot shit, so the two of them kicking in doors was nothing to me.

"Sure, go ahead. Let's see what the fuck you got young bull," I chuckled. Me, Yashir, and Kanan Jr. made our way up toward Sonja's house. She should be glad I didn't set this bitch on fire because it was fuckin' tempting. I know she has an attitude and I have one too. I knew he was strong, but I wanted to witness it. He kicked the knob off that bitch. He looked over his shoulder to see if I saw that. I wasn't surprised at his strength because he gets that shit from me.

"Who sent you motherfuckers," she yelled and argued. I laughed because Sonja wasn't fuckin' scaring me. I don't give a damn how much authority her voice held. She's fuckin' up because she should've been shooting first and asking questions later as soon as her door was kicked open. She wanted to lay up with a pussy ass nigga that she let her guard down.

"What are you going to do with that shit, Sonja? Get that shit out of my kid's fuckin' face before I train that motherfucka on you!" I argued and yelled. I stepped in Sonja's personal fuckin' space daring her to say the wrong fuckin' thing. She couldn't even look at me. I was breathing down her neck. She took two steps back and I took two steps up. I could hear her breathing heavy and her heart beating fast as hell. Sonja knew I was a crazy ass motherfucka and she knew I didn't give a fuck. The only reason she's still breathing is because I love her ass. The love I have for her trumps all the bull shit, we've been through. I know I haven't been the best man to her in the past and I'm sorry for that.

"Why are you here in my house and kicking my door in? Should I call the cops? You're trespassing," she argued and explained. I cupped her face and started laughing. I'm sure she could smell the mint on my breath. I wish she would call the fuckin police on me. I don't give a fuck how tired she was of this shit. Try me if she wants to and her ass would be in jail for stealing my fuckin' money.

"I wanted you to meet your new roommates! It seems like you need some fuckin' protection. Kanan and Yashir, go find you a room. Pick anyone you want and make yourself at fuckin' home and let me talk to Sonja in private," I explained. Kanan and Yashir did as they were told. Sonja gave me an icy glare and I grilled the fuck out of her.

"What the fuck is going on, Kanan? I want you out of my house now, and your kids aren't staying here," she argued and sassed. "Kanan I'm serious, your kids aren't moving in my home." Sonja's hands were rested on her thick ass hips. Her breasts were sitting up begging me to suck them.

"My kids are going to stay here because you killed their fucking mammy, so that makes you their new momma. Pick up your fucking loose ass lips, snitch. You're going to do what the fuck I tell you to do. I'll drop money by once a week. Everything you need for school and shit, they have it with them. My money bought this spot, right? See you soon! Don't have no niggas around my fuckin kids or in my house," I argued. I told Sonja what it was, and my word is fuckin' law.

My sons were moving in rather she wanted them to or not. No wasn't an option. I left out the same way he came in. Sonja watched my every move. I stopped in front of the door before I left and turned around and looked at her. She had a snarl on her face.

She knew her little fuckin' play time was over since I was fuckin' home. "You ain't got to watch me leave. Watch fuckin' TV or read one of those books you used to read. I know I'm the shit. I know you want to hop on this dick and ride this big motherfucka like you use to," I chuckled. Sonja threw her glass at me and I ducked. She should be glad that motherfucka didn't hit me because if it did, I would've reached out and touched her ass.

"I fuckin' hate you. Leave me the fuck alone. Your money didn't pay for shit. The last time I checked you were behind bars when I was running up a fuckin' check. Take your ass back to fuckin' East Lake and stake claim to that motherfucka. I don't want you. REMEMBER I LEFT YOU."

"Is that what you think Sonja? You think you fuckin' left me? It ain't no breaking up and you know that. If you really felt like that you should've pulled the trigger," I argued.

Sonja

I don't know who in the fuck Kanan thought he was? I'm sick of him I swear to God I am. He's always trying to intimidate some fuckin' body. I wish the glass would've bust him in his shit. I don't care what his money has bought. It ain't like he gave me shit for free. I still had to fuckin' work. He had the nerve to bring these bad ass kids to my house. I said what the fuck I said. He just wanted to clock my fuckin' moves. It had to be Kanan Jr. that kicked my door in.

I'm not being bothered with these bad ass kids. He told them to pick a room; bitch, not over here. He had the nerve to tell me since I killed their mammy, I'm their new momma. Bitch, no I'm not! I'm putting this house up for sale. I don't need him popping up at my shit. Damn, Kanan looked good as fuck, though. He had the nerve to say I wish I could ride his dick. He wanted me to ride his dick but I'm good.

That man knows he is getting finer with time. Jail does a body good. He knows he still wants me. He can't resist Sonja the Body! He'll be mad when he sees me with another nigga and it's coming. He was all up in my fuckin' personal space. I must call Chelle. I know it's late, but damn I had to tell her about this crazy ass nigga. I couldn't wait until tomorrow.

"What's up, lady? What happened, are you okay? Are you back in the hospital?" She asked. I knew Chelle was concerned because she knew Kanan was crazy and it's no telling what he could've did to me this time.

"Girl shut the hell up! No, I'm not in the damn hospital. You will not believe this shit. Are you sitting down?" I asked. I had to tell Chelle what happened because she wouldn't believe the stunt that nigga just pulled. What would make him think it was okay for his kids to stay here? His kids are the reason we're not together and you want to rub them in my face, opening some old wounds that I shouldn't even be dealing with.

"What? Spill it," she laughed. Chelle was anxious as a motherfucka to hear what was going on. She already knew Kanan was so fuckin' extra.

"Kanan, just kicked my door in and dropped his boys off. These grown lil niggas brought their suitcases with them. He just forced me to keep them. Bitch, I'm not keeping these kids so you and Black can run the streets and entertain hoes! His old ass momma could've kept them. Who do I look like? Bitch, I'm too fine for this shit," I argued and explained. I swear he pissed me off with that. Kanan was wrong as fuck for doing this shit; I wasn't up for raising his boys, and I don't know why he thought it was cool to force it on me.

"Sonja, are you fuckin' serious? What would make his ass think that shit was okay? I guess some shit never fuckin' changes. Kanan needs to grow up. Why would he do that shit? He's still moving around like he's fuckin' twenty-five years old and he fuckin' ain't. Old ass motherfucka. I'm with you, why couldn't Kaitlyn keep his fuckin' kids? It's not your fault that bitch is dead. If he would've kept his ass in Atlanta we wouldn't even be going through this shit, but that's too much like for a nigga like him. He can't stand to lose. That's why he should've kept his dick in his pants," she argued and explained.

"I agree," I sighed.

"That nigga is still crazy! How does he know where you live? I'm not sure if I want to stay at your house. I don't want to run into Black. I guess he told you. I'll be there tomorrow. My flight arrives at 1:45 p.m.," she explained. I knew Chelle was nervous about staying at my house. It's possible that she would run into Black since Kanan was out. I didn't want to tell her that I've been seeing him lately because she wouldn't come. I knew she was really second guessing coming to Atlanta now.

"Who the fuck is Black?" Couture asked and argued. He was crazy, too. Chelle sure does know how to pick them. I knew it was time to get off the phone now. He didn't want Chelle discussing another man while she was talking on the phone. I understood that.

"Girl, I have to go, you hear Couture's nosey ass in the background," she explained. I knew Chelle wanted to hurry up and hang up the phone. She had said to much already and let Black's name roll off her tongue.

"Alright, I'll see you tomorrow," I laughed. I knew how extra Couture could be. I swear this shit is awkward as fuck. Kanan is fuckin' nuts. He really brought his fuckin' kids here.

Kanan

I had to give Sonja the fuckin' business. She knows I don't play no fuckin' games, period. What's understood doesn't need to be explained. You do what the fuck I say do! It's not the other way around. I'm not Deuce. I'm fuckin' Kanan. I slang good pipe. I whip great fuckin' white! I beat the pussy out the frame. I was shocked that she was up. I thought she would be in bed sleeping. I had plans to do more than that. She was wide awake. I hope she wasn't waiting on a nigga to come over. She knows I don't play that shit. It's a fuckin' wrap. Any nigga she thinks she can bring to the table will meet the same fate as Deuce death.

I guess you could say that we are even. I killed Deuce and she killed Yasmine. I could've let my mom get them, but that would require me going to her house every day and I'm not about to do that. I wish Kaniya were here because she would've looked after them with no questions asked. That reminds me, I need to call Kaisha back. She called me talking shit about Killian and I hung up in her face. I wasn't trying to hear that shit. That's a crazy motherfucker right there.

Kaisha will give a nigga hell; do you hear me? I called her back to see what the fuck she wanted. I wasn't about to sit on the phone with her while she pops her shit about my brother. They need to fuck and make up. Killian is better than me because Sonja would never pull the shit Kaisha does. If I'm living, ain't no fuckin' way. I guess he picked the right fuckin' one.

"What Kaisha? What did you want earlier? You should be calling Killian instead of me, that's still your husband remember?" I asked. I was already fuckin' annoyed at this point. I didn't need her to add to it because I knew how extra and over the top she could be. I knew she was ready to go in. I heard her suck her fuckin' teeth.

"Who pissed in your Cheerios, Kanan? Look, you, old ass motherfucka, tell Killian's shitty breath ass I heard from our daughter. When I called his phone, he picked up the phone on purpose. He wanted me to hear some bitch that he was fuckin' moaning in the background. Tell that motherfucka the bitch he was fuckin' pussy must have been dry because all I heard was him out of breath and shit.

If the pussy was that good, he would've never answered the fuckin' phone. I don't give a fuck who he fucks. Ask that motherfuckas how my ass tastes when you hear from his shitty breath ass," she argued and sassed. All I heard was *Click!* She hung up the phone in my face.

I had to laugh because she knew I couldn't wait to run it back and tell Killian what she said. Kaisha's ass was crazy as fuck, but that's my girl, though. I wished her and Killian would've worked out. He loves to call me childish, but he has a little bullshit going on with him, too.

Let me call shitty breath up. Kaisha is crazy as hell. I swear I needed that motherfuckin laugh! I dialed Killian's number and he answered on the first ring. I could tell he was still knee deep in some pussy. I heard the bed rocking. He's a disrespectful ass motherfucka. This nigga put me on speaker. I see why Kaisha was fuckin' mad. This nigga didn't give a fuck.

"Kanan, if you called me to hear me fuck a bitch, I'm hanging up now. Go find you some pussy to swim in. What the fuck do you want? Why are you calling my phone this time of night?" He asked and grunted. Killian was with the shits for real. Let me say what the fuck I got to say and hang up because I'm not beat for his shit either.

"Take me off speaker phone. I don't want to hear you stroking that dry ass pussy with your weak dick!" I argued and yelled. I knew Killian was mad. I heard him tell old girl to raise up.

"Ain't shit weak about my dick, nigga. What the fuck you want?" He argued. I knew Killian was mad because I made him come up out the pussy, he was in. If it was that good, he would've never answered the phone. Shit couldn't have been snatching if he answered the phone twice.

"Kaisha called me and told me to tell you that Kaniya called her," I chuckled. I tried to keep it together. I can't because that shit was to fuckin' funny. I didn't take him to be an ass licker. "She also told me to ask you what her ass taste like because that's the only thing you're good at SHITTY BREATH."

"You tell that motherfucka-," I hung up in Killian's face before he could say anything else. I don't have time to be passing messages back and forth between the two of them. If he got some shit he needs to say, he knows where to find her. I wish they fuck and make-up and move on. That shit happened over twenty years ago. If Sonja thought about hanging with Kaisha and doing the shit, they used to, it was a fuckin' wrap. I was killing all that shit. Kaisha didn't give a fuck. She got a thrill out of trying Killian. That nigga lost plenty of sleep fuckin' with her. Sonja knew she could never play me like that.

Chapter-9

Killian

Motherfuckas should stop fuckin' with me after hours and I mean that shit. Kanan called me laughing, telling me about the hot ass shit Kaisha was spitting. What the fuck was she calling my phone for this late at night anyway? She should've sent a fuckin' text. Yep, I sure did pick up the phone so she could hear me laying pipe. I'm petty just like her motherfuckin ass! Why are you calling me after twelve anyway? The only things that are open after twelve for me are legs, and I had some wide the fuck open.

She wants me and she knows that shit too. She can front for whoever. That chick is crazy. That's why Kaniya is so fuckin' wild. She gets it from her mother and it's nothing I can do about it right now. It's to fuckin' late. She's too far gone. I'm glad I kept Killany. I think I need to pay Kaisha a visit. Let me head over to Kaniya's house quick. I knew she was in town, that's why she was calling this fuckin' late. She's bored and want me to put her ass to sleep.

I'm tired of her ass talking shit all the time. She just wanted me to come and see her, that's all. Kaniya didn't even think to fuckin' call me, but she called her momma. This is the shit I'm talking about. Kaisha is crazy as fuck. She's killed two of my bitches. I don't have proof that she killed Tyra, but I know she did. I used to ask Sonja all the time what happened to Tyra's daughter and she would never tell me. I should've asked Tariq. In my heart I knew she was mine; I just didn't want Kaisha to know. I never had the chance to do a DNA test for her daughter. I wanted to though.

"Who was that Killian and where are you going this time of night?" Caryn asked. I looked over my shoulder and pulled my pants up. She knew better than to ask me where the fuck I was going. I slid my shoes on my feet, and threw my shirt on, and headed out the door.

"Killian, baby, where is you going? We weren't finished," she cooed and pouted. Caryn already knew the drill. I don't even know why she was questioning my fuckin' moves. I already told her what it was with us. I slammed the door on my way out.

Kaniya didn't stay to far from here. I was forty-five minutes away. Kaisha sent for me. She knew I was fuckin' coming. I want her to back up all that shit she was talking. I have a key to Kaniya's, so I don't even have to knock. I finally made my way over to Kaniya's and used my key. I locked the door back and I started combing through the house to look for her. I searched Kaniya's room first and she's not in there. I checked the guest room and she was sprawled out across the bed. She knew what the fuck she was doing. Look at her, laying butt ass naked. She knew I would come over here.

Damn, Kaisha is still beautiful, and her body is still right. She doesn't look like she carried two twins for me! She was always screaming Good black don't crack! She's tempting as fuck and I don't have shit to lose. I'm going to try her. I just want to suck on it. I'll eat her ass too since she told Kanan to ask me what ass tastes like. I listened to her moaning in her fuckin' sleep. I got her right where I want her. I stripped out of my clothes and down to my boxers.

Kaisha always slept naked. I threw her legs over my shoulder. I wanted to marinate the pussy before I tasted it. Damn, she's wet as fuck and still tastes like pineapples! I tongued fuck Kaisha wet. She gripped my shoulders and started bucking her hips wildly. I applied some pressure to her nub, and she came on my tongue more than once. I put that pressure on her pussy. I wanted her to wake up and to see who's the man behind the mic.

I had to laugh because I knew Kaisha would freak the fuck out once she saw me between her legs. That's what she gets. My intentions were to wake her up and fuck up her world. I don't give a fuck how long it's been; she still belongs to me. I know her body like the back of my hand. Kaisha and I still wanted each other. Twenty years later and she's still playing hard to get.

Kaisha

I must be dreaming, and since I am I ain't waking up. I don't know who's this niggas face, I'm riding but he knew WHAT the FUCK TO DO. I couldn't stop these orgasms that were coming from my body if I wanted to. It feels amazing. I haven't had my pussy eaten like this in a while. I'm so wet it feels like I've pissed on myself. Damn this man right here is eating me like he's in a pie-eating contest. I just want to smack the back of his head. I didn't want to call out any names because I have a couple of cats on my team. I didn't invite anybody over.

I opened my eyes. I had to smack my face to make sure I wasn't tripping. I noticed that big ass Kaisha tattoo on his back. I smacked my face again. I was nervous at this point. I know he didn't fuckin' try me like this. It's only one nigga with a Kaisha tattoo on his back. I jumped up instantly. He had a fuckin' death grip on my legs.

"Get the fuck off me Killian," I argued and yelled. I swear and I put it on my life he was never supposed to get this close to me again let alone touch me. He knew he couldn't do that to me if I was awake. I hate my body responded to him.

"Yeah, it's me Kaisha, in the flesh. You wanted me to come and suck and fuck on you, right? You wanted me to eat your ass. Bend over so I can get fuckin' to it. That's what you told Kanan, huh? That's why you called me after twelve. You wanted me to put in some work. You wanted me to stretch your pussy wide open and bless you with a few more of my kids?

That's why you were laying here naked. You knew I would come. I had you moaning and shaking some odd years ago. I still have you moaning and shaking now. I'm still that nigga and you know it. Turn around Kaisha so I can eat your ass. I'm not going to tell you twice," he argued and commanded. I don't give a fuck how good his tongue felt and how many times he made me cum it ain't fuckin' happening. I wanted him, though. Motherfucka, please.

"I'm good, Killian! I hate that you even tried me in my fuckin' sleep. I would never let you suck on me long as I'm living. You still a nasty ass nigga! You just got done fucking and sucking on God knows who and you want to put your nasty ass mouth on me. The best thing you can do is get the fuck up out of here right now. I feel violated," I argued. Apart of me still wanted him, but I would never tell him that.

"For the record Kaisha and understand me when I fuckin' speak. I don't eat everybody's pussy! I've only ate yours! Pick up your fuckin' mouth, you heard what the fuck I said. I don't eat everybody's ass. I only ate yours because you carried my seeds. I'm far from a nasty nigga. I have a clean bill of health, do you? I don't smash everything moving. That pussy still Grade A though!

It tasted good as fuck and that motherfucka got wet for a nigga like it used too. You still bitter, though KAISHA. Let that shit go! I can't change the past, but I can change the future. I still love you. Ain't shit changed, you know that," he explained. Killian was putting his feelings out there. He wanted me to know how he felt. His eyes were piercing through my soul. I looked at everything but him. I just want to be happy. I'm tired of him killing every nigga I dated.

Damn Killian had me in my feelings! I'm glad he kept it real but why now though? I know it's because I'm back in Atlanta for a while and he wanted to keep tabs on me. I still had feelings for him too, but we could never be. He destroyed us when he had a child on me. He's still an old hoe. He shouldn't have come over here. He knows I sleep naked. I appreciated the head. Boy, that nigga's tongue game was still the fuckin' truth. I had to stop him, though. I didn't want him catching feelings at all. I never backtrack. He's in my past for a reason.

He didn't make it to the future because he fucked up. I gave Killian all of me. When he cheated with Tyra and blessed her with a child that shit hurt my soul. For that reason alone, I had to let him go. I couldn't circle back this time. I don't care how good he made my body feel, not me. He's the reason that we're not together. We're still married, but only because he refuses to sign those papers. I stopped pressing the issue and continued to live my life. I never wanted to get married again after everything we went through.

Killian

Kaisha knows she's too old to be playing these ghetto ass games. She should be glad I got my rocks off earlier or else I would've taken it. I'm not lying. She was to fuckin' wet. Her pussy was begging me to take it. Each time my tongued sucked her nub she got wetter. I would've beat that pussy out the frame too. I don't give a fuck. She likes it rough anyway. She knows that she still belongs to me anyway. I had to test her when we were in Virginia to see if she was still about that life. I didn't know that she was going to push old girl's shit back. May she rest in peace. I told her my ex was crazy. She didn't believe me, so she had to find out the hard way.

Killany was wrong for putting her mom out. I provoked that situation. It was funny, though. Kaisha bust in that room so fuckin' sexy in some panties and no bra. She knew what the fuck she was doing. Women are a trip, I tell you. She didn't have to kill her, but she was making a statement. I didn't want Kaisha's big head ass to leave that night, but she insisted on it. I gave Killany's ass the business too. No one is to come before her mother, especially some random bitch that she just met. I'll be back though.

I'll make Kaisha come on down with that soaker between her legs. I love her, I promise you I do. I wish I never cheated on her because she was the one that got away. She was my rider. Kaisha had my back out here in these streets. She was my fuckin' muscle. She was the realest nigga on my team. Kaniya reminds me so much of her mother that it's crazy. I guess that's why I'm so hard on her.

I really wish me, and Kaisha would've worked out because Kaniya wouldn't be exposed to so much shit. Killany is more relaxed and chill. I hated that Kaniya was a part of that shit back in Miami. I was proud of Kaniya, though. I need to tell her that more often and maybe she would come to me about stuff more often. If I wasn't there, I believe she would've killed Kanan. I know she would've. If I could turn back the hands of time, I would do a lot of shit differently.

Chapter-10

Tariq

P hil, AD, Ace and Lee finally made it to the undisclosed location. I've been waiting on those niggas for a few days. I know some shit came up in the process but that was a part of the transport anyway. AD popped the trunk and opened the door. I've been waiting on Kaniya to bring her ass out for a minute now. I'm ready to get this show on the road. I've been missing her ass like crazy and I don't think that I can take it, and she's only a few feet away from me. A nigga has run out of patience. I heard a commotion going on, so I stepped in the Denali to see what the fuck was going on. I heard Phil talking shit to Kaniya. I hired him to do a job and that doesn't fuckin' mean to talk to her like that. I don't give a fuck how he may feel but it's not going down like that.

"Lil buddy wake your tired ass the fuck up. You have arrived to your fuckin' destination!" He argued and yelled. I heard Kaniya suck her teeth. I knew she was about to spit some fly ass shit out her mouth. She's already been giving Phil hell.

"I don't give a fuck where I'm at. I didn't ask to fuckin' come here. I told you that shit already. Take me back to where the fuck you picked me up from. Fuck you and your boss, pussy ass nigga," she argued. I knew Kaniya was sleepy and tired and that wasn't a good combination. I already knew she was about to go in on my ass.

"Girl, get your ass out this fuckin' truck and stop playing so damn much before I put my hands on you!" He argued and yelled. I knew Phil was acting as if he was about to put his hands on Kaniya because the moment he did I was going to drop that motherfucka right here and let AD, Ace and Lee split his fuckin' bread.

"I wish the fuck you would, bitch ass nigga. I will kickbox your ass so motherfuckin' quick," she argued and explained. Kaniya was alert now and ready for whatever. I swear my lil shawty mouth is reckless as fuck. I got to do something about that. Phil ran his hands across his face. I could see Kaniya was wearing him thin as fuck.

"Tariq come on and get her ass up out this truck before I hurt her smart mouth ass," he argued. Phil was ready. He wanted to smack her ass one good time, but I would never let that shit happen. I made my way back to the seat where Kaniya was sitting. I slapped hands with Phil. Kaniya refused to look at me.

"Bring your stubborn ass on and stop fuckin' playing. I'm tired of you and these childish ass games you play," I argued and explained. I approached Kaniya and stepped all in her fuckin' personal space. I wanted her to talk that tough ass shit she was spitting on the phone earlier. I could hear her breathing heavy. I watched as her chest was heaving up and down. Her cheeks were red.

"Watch how the fuck you talk to me! Did I ask to come wherever the fuck we are? No, I didn't. I was chilling, minding my business, not yours," she argued. I knew she was annoyed and didn't really want to be bothered with me. I'm done with the games. I just want to focus on her. I knew she was thinking about Lucky. I knew he was on her mind heavy and her heart was aching for him but fuck him. He doesn't deserve her and soon she'll see.

"I don't give a fuck what you were doing. You'll do what I tell you, and what I want you to do!" I argued and yelled. I put extra base in my voice, I was trying to scare Kaniya.

"Keep thinking that," she sassed and sucked her teeth. Kaniya was trying to act like she was unfazed by me and my tone. She's so fucking hardheaded. It doesn't make any sense. I guess I'll pick her big head ass up and carry her on the plane. I picked

Kaniya up and threw her over my shoulders. My hands roamed every inch of her body. She was punching me in my back.

"Come on, you can walk. I'll put your motherfuckin' ass down," I argued. She's pissing me off. I'm getting angry as fuck. Kaniya was putting me through all of this when I just want to spend some fuckin' time with her ass.

"I'm not going anywhere with you," she argued. I'm sick of her fuckin' attitude and I'm dead ass serious. I hope she wasn't still tripping off Lucky. Fuck that bitch ass nigga.

"Oh, you not? Okay, I got you," I argued. I grabbed a handful of her ass and squeezed it with so much fuckin' force. She tried to knee me.

"That shit doesn't fuckin' hurt." I chuckled. I knew she was pissed but I don't give a fuck. She wanted me to rough her motherfuckin ass up.

"Put me down," she yelled. I knew she was angry. She tried to pry my hands off her. It was something about her touch that sent chills to my dick. It was magnetic. I know she felt it too. I felt her body tense up.

"If you wanted Daddy to pick you up and feel on your ass, that's all you had to say. Cat got your tongue now, huh," I whispered and bit her ear. I loved teasing her. I could tell she was beginning to relax because she wasn't going anywhere.

"Where are we going?" She asked. I knew she was curious but it's a surprise. I carried her onto the private jet and sat her in my lap. I'm surprised that she didn't object. "What kind of tricks do you have up your sleeve?" If she only knew what I had up my sleeve. She'll find out.

"You like giving me a hard time, don't you? You want me to chase you, huh? I owe you for all that lil bullshit you've been sending my way," I explained. Kaniya looked at me with wide eyes. She knew I wasn't fuckin' lying.

"Whatever, Tariq. I haven't done anything to you. If I have, I'm sorry. Can you take me home?" She asked sincerely. It wasn't happening, though. I wanted my time, and nobody was about to come in between that. Not even the nigga she was dying to get back home to see.

"You're really in love with that nigga, huh? I have a new home for you. You'll go home when I want you to go home. That nigga can dog you out to your face and you'll run right back to him like shit ain't happened," I argued. I know I shouldn't wear my heart on my sleeve, but I do because I want her to know how I feel. I'm pissed because I knew she was trying to rush back to Lucky.

"That's how you feel, Tariq? Last I checked, I never ran behind no nigga. They were running up behind me. You kidnapped me for what? Stop running up behind me since you have an issue," she argued. Kaniya got up and walked off. At this point, I knew she didn't want to be anywhere near me. I made my way toward the back where she was headed. I know she's angry, but she doesn't have a reason to be. I got her and she knows that. I know she's acting like this because of him. Why else would she act like this? We've already crossed that line.

"Baby. Kaniya, don't walk away from me," I begged and pleaded. I wrapped my arms around her waist making sure I held her in place. I turned her around so she could face me. I cupped her face and put her lips toward mine. "I'm sorry, Kaniya. I miss you. Can I kiss you?"

I tried to soften the mood. I wanted to kiss her, morning breath and all, I don't care. If she was here, that's all that mattered to me. I did a lot to get to this point and I'm trying to cherish it. I've been missing her like crazy.

"No, you can't," she pouted. I grabbed the back of her head and forced my tongue in her mouth. I was praying she didn't stop me. It's been a minute since we've been this comfortable with each other. She's been hiding from me and I finally caught up with her ass.

"You're just going to make me kiss you, huh?" She asked. My eyes were trained on her. Being with her felt so right. Nothing was wrong about it. I felt her heart beating. Our hearts were beating the same tune. I hope she didn't think it was wrong. I wanted to kiss her. I couldn't help myself. She was tempting as fuck. I forced my tongue in her mouth and she didn't stop me.

"I asked you first because I always get what I want. You miss this, don't you? Why can't you be with me?" I asked. I wanted to know why we couldn't be together because she never left my mind. The last time we were together before shit went left, us being together was in the making.

"Why won't you let me be, Tariq?" She asked. She knew how I felt about her.

"Because I love you, and I want you to give us a fair chance. I understand that you're scared, but I will never hurt you. Can I love you? Will you let me do that much?" I asked. I put my feelings out there once again.

"Go on with that shit, Tariq! Let me keep it real with you because you deserve that much. Yes, I'm scared. I know you're that nigga and you're more than worth it to take that chance with. I have very strong feelings for you that I can't shake, and you won't let me shake them. Under the current circumstances, it's hard for us to be together and take it there," she explained. She put some of her feelings on the line. She was still holding back.

"What circumstances? Nobody can stop me from being with you but you. I don't live for anybody. I live for me. I go for what I want. You're worried about Sonja and Lucky? Sonja can't say anything. When she told me about Deuce, I didn't object? Deuce is dead now, so what! As far as Lucky, when he was entertaining old girl, you killed her in her sleep. Yeah, I saw you. The question is was he thinking about you or your feelings?" I asked.

"I hear you! I don't live for nobody. I live for me," she explained. I knew she was hot that I saw her kill Melanie and threw that shit up in her face.

"Prove it! Actions speak louder than words. I heard everything you said, but damn, Kaniya, show me. That's all I ask. Please, show me. I had to do all of this just for you to finally tell me how you feel." I explained. I practically begged her for the chance for us to be together.

"I truly wanted this more than you would ever know Tariq. I prayed for this," she sniffled and pointed at me. She tried to turn her back so I wouldn't see the tears in her eyes. I tapped her on her shoulder making her face me. "I wanted to tell you this for the longest, the time just never presented itself. Why are you doing this to me? I can't take it and I don't want you to hurt me."

"What's wrong, Kaniya? Why are you crying? I promise you I'm not going to do that. I will be mad at myself. I don't want to do that. It will never happen," I explained.

"I don't want to hurt you, Tariq or get hurt in the process. When you care for someone as much as I care for you, it would hurt too bad if we crossed that line and it doesn't work out," she explained.

"I'm a man and I can handle whatever comes my way. I want this, Kaniya." I had to let her know at this point. I didn't care, I still wanted to take that chance and be with her. I knew that she was the one for me.

"Where's the shower? I need to freshen up since I've been held against my will," she sassed. The jet was loaded with everything she needed to soak and think about our situation. I pointed toward the bathroom.

"Can I join you?" I asked. I'm ready to get shit popping. I've been wanting to see her naked again for the longest. I couldn't wait to dive in that pussy again.

"Hell no!" she shouted. We locked eyes with each other. She offered me a faint smile. I bit my bottom lip. She wasn't talking about shit. She knew I was coming in the shower with her rather she wanted me to or not. I've been waiting on this moment for a minute now and it was time for me to seize the fuckin' moment.

I gave her a few minutes and the moment I heard the water turn on and I heard her head go under the shower it was on from there. I knew she was comfortable, so I stepped in the bathroom myself and started undressing myself. I pulled the glass back and climbed in right behind her. She looked over her shoulder and wanted to object.

Kaniya

So, Tariq kidnapped me and decided to take me to Ocho Rios, Jamaica for a few weeks. I needed a vacation but damn he could've given me the heads up, so I could've been prepared. I've never been to Ocho Rios, Jamaica before so that was a surprise within itself. I've really gotten myself into some shit this time. I'm woman enough to admit that. The moment the private jet took off and I stepped in the shower, this man couldn't keep his hands off me. I wanted to shower alone he knew that. He let me shower alone only for a few minutes.

Soon as he opened the door, we locked eyes with each other. He just stood there for a minute and watched me. I continued to shower because the water felt so good. My mind was in a million places. I heard the glass pull back to the shower and it was him. He stepped in behind me and his hands roamed every inch of my body. I swatted his hands away immediately. I feel so bad engaging in this knowing that Lucky was heavy on my mind. I shouldn't even be thinking about him reflecting on how he fuckin' spoke to me.

He's the last person's feelings I should be considering. Last I checked he hasn't been considering mine. I couldn't keep my hands-off Tariq either. We stood up under the shower for a minute and took each other in. He cupped my face with his free hand. He ran his index finger across my heart. I'm sure he could feel it beating out my chest.

"Tariq, we shouldn't be doing this," I moaned. We haven't even worked past the issues that we had. He cupped my chin forcing me to look at him. I didn't want to get lost in his gaze at all. I knew where this would lead to. I wasn't ready because sex only complicates things.

"Why shouldn't we?" He asked. Tariq's stare was intense. I wanted him bad and we're already complicated. The two of us having sex would only complicate us even more. I don't think neither one of us are ready for that.

"We just shouldn't Tariq, please don't fight me on this," I begged and pleaded. He wasn't hearing me at all. He leaned in and kissed me and stroked the side of my neck. I wrapped my arms around his neck. We stared at each other for a minute. I kissed him back. I couldn't help myself. I've been yearning for his touch for a while now. I'm feenin' for the twelve inches in his pants that God blessed him with.

I've been waiting for this moment for so long. I craved and wanted it. He was always so rough but gentle and passionate with me. Tariq knew my body better than I thought he did. I loved it extra rough. He was rough in a passionate kind of way. He lifted me up and pressed my body up against the base of the shower. I bit my bottom lip. I knew it was about to go down, but I wasn't ready.

"Tariq, we need to strap up," I moaned. He put me down and went to retrieve a condom. He put the condom on. He lifted me back up and I wrapped my arms around his neck. He tried to slide his dick in, but I was way too tight. Finally, we were able to explore each other. We've fucked in so many positions. He was doing pushups in this pussy. Our sex session started in the shower and ended where are seats were.

I knew the pilot was looking from the cockpit. I could feel it. I missed Tariq's twelve inches of hardwood. I fucked him like I missed him because I did. There weren't many positions that we could do because we were on a jet. I wasn't fucking on the floor. The seats were bucket and oversized, so we reclined them all the way back. Tariq had positioned himself in the seat so I could squat and ride. He loved the way I rode him. For some reason, that's all he ever wanted me to do.

He said that he loved the way my eyes looked when I was on top. Sex with him was always so rough, passionate, and wild. I loved every minute of it. He knew my body very well. He knew that my breasts and nipples were my sensitive spot because they're pierced. He would suck them extra hard because he knew I would get an orgasm instantly from it. He dug his nails into my ass and sank his teeth into my neck.

He was plunging his dick into my pussy so hard, I wanted to scream. He was the biggest I ever had. His hands covered my mouth. It was hard to get used to. Tears started forming in my eyes. He licked my tears. I was sore and I would need to soak in some Epsom salt. Tariq took all his frustrations out on me.

Tariq

Kaniya just didn't know what her body did to me. I wanted her to get those fuckin' Lucky Charms covered up on the side of her rib cage. I've wanted to make love to her ass for a minute now, but she's been missing in action. We haven't made love to each other in a while. I've fucked a few females here and there, but they didn't mean shit to me. I had to apply pressure on her pussy. I had some shit to prove and I wanted her to feel me. I didn't want to make her cry. I hated to see her tear up in the process.

Love hurt sometimes and I learned that shit the hard way fuckin' with her back and forth ass. I hope she knows it ain't no going back from this. I'll be the last man to dig deep in her. I can promise you that. I wanted to fuck her in one last position. I picked her up and threw her up against the window in the jet. I placed her hands above her head and bit her nipples so she could feel the pressure of my teeth. Her pussy was still soaking wet and smelled like Aquafina water.

Her juices were running down my legs. I had to really give her the business. I owed her every stroke and thrust. I made sure I was giving her some act right with this pound game so she would never forget this long as she lives.

I watched her fuck Lucky on the bus. I wanted to kill her ass that day and she was very nonchalant about that shit. Also, the JD situation. I wanted her to feel my pain. I had to beat this pussy up so she would know who was running shit. I didn't give a fuck about the tears. I hit her spot extra hard when I noticed the tears. I decided to take it a little slower and take it easy on her. I grabbed her face and forced my tongue into her mouth.

Kaniya's tongue game was serious. She could make me nut off her kisses alone. We both had something to prove during this lovemaking session. We missed each other so much so that with each thrust and pound nobody wanted to tap out. She squeezed her pussy muscles on my dick so I could bust first. Guess what? I emptied all my seeds in her ass. We were rudely interrupted when the pilot came and told us we were about to land. I didn't want him looking at her at all.

"I got mine, I hope you got yours."

"I can't take any more dick. Tariq, you were extra rough with my body; I don't appreciate that shit at all. I guess you got something else on your mind," she moaned. I'm sure she noticed my eyes and facial expressions. I was pissed about some shit and I refused to share. It has nothing to do with what we just done. I did some shit also and I know she was waiting for an apology.

Chapter-11

Tianna

It's been so much going on these past few weeks since Kaniya's been gone. I don't know what to do. It feels like I'm losing my fuckin' mind. I know she's with Tariq but that doesn't mean shit to me. I haven't heard from her to confirm that she's okay. Riley, Ketta and Barbie were still here in Atlanta. We've been kicking it tough lately since our glue is gone. They confirmed they weren't going back to New York until her feet touches Georgia soil.

I'm glad and Riley decided to stay also. I decided to throw a little Kickback at my house. I invited Ketta, Barbie, Riley and their significant others. Of course, Quan was inviting Lucky and Veno and a few of their other business associates. I warned Lucky if he had the balls to bring a bitch to my house again, he wouldn't like the outcome. He tried me with Melanie, but he wouldn't try me again. If he wants to be mad at me and in his feelings because Tariq kidnapped Kaniya, that has nothing to do with her and everything to do with him. If he wouldn't have cheated, we wouldn't even be in this predicament.

Veno already knows how I felt about his wife. She wasn't welcomed to my home and I wasn't welcomed to hers. Riley and Veno met while they were broken up. Kaniya met Lucky through Riley and Veno. Vanessa's Best friend used to date Lucky. It was just a mess. LaRoya wasn't tripping because she knew what it was but Vanessa for some reason didn't get it. The Kickback was scheduled to start at 6:00 p.m. I made a few fruit trays. I called Julissa's to get the food catered. It's a cool little spot down by Piedmont Journee owns. I know it was last minute but Thank God she came through. Quan and I ate breakfast there every Saturday. I ordered 3 dozen of her hushpuppies, 300 wings, and 60 pieces of fish. Journee's wings and fish are the best.

I can drop my own fries. I made some nachos and Rotel dip. Journee just left. She sat up everything in the warmers. The Rotel dip and nacho cheese dip were on low simmering. I had about thirty minutes to spare before everybody came. Quan walked up behind me and wrapped his arms around my waist. I was barely showing so I was still able to dress cute. Quan bit down on my neck. I tried to move from his embrace. He had me in a tight bear hug.

"Baby, stop." I moaned. I wish he would stop. I'm trying to get everything ready before our company comes. I would love to get it in before everybody came but lately after we have sex I fall right to sleep.

"Stop for what Tianna, you know you belong to me. What do I have to stop for? You know I got an issue with you. Why did you talk to my brother and Veno like that? I know you run shit, but damn baby, you don't have to be so fuckin' cold," he explained. I pushed Quan off me and turned around to face him.

"It's not about being cold, Quan. It's about my loyalty to MY best friend. I know your loyalty is with your brother and I expected that, but since Lucky has been exposed with his cheating, he won't do that shit in front of me. If he does, I'm telling it. Had I known Melanie wasn't your Motherfuckin cousin I would've said something then, but I didn't. I'm not giving your brother a fuckin' pass. He wouldn't give me one," I argued and explained.

"Tianna chill out. What Lucky and Kaniya got going on ain't got nothing to do with us. If Tariq kidnapped Kaniya or whatever it's something deeper going on between the two of them. Kaniya doesn't care to share, and it ain't got nothing to do with him eating her pussy. My brother ain't fuckin' stupid. Everything a motherfucka does in the dark will come to the light. Veno and Vanessa are married. Come on Tianna, you're tripping for real," he argued.

"I don't give a fuck, Quan. You want us to stay out of their business but you're in it. Fuck, Vanessa, that bitch don't like me, and I don't like her. She probably got a bitch in the stash somewhere that you're fuckin' with. Lucky thought Kaniya showed her ass! Motherfucka, you don't want me to show MINE," I argued. I meant that shit. I don't like bitches like Vanessa. I know her kind to well. Riley is in love with Boss but for some odd reason she thinks she still wants Veno. She hates that Kaniya is with Lucky. Bitch focus on your own fuckin' relationship. You're about to kill yourself worried about the next motherfucka. I walked off from Quan and headed upstairs to our room. Quan ran up on me and grabbed my shoulders. I turned around to face him and gave him an evil scowl.

"Tianna, are you really doing this?" He asked and argued.

"Are you doing this? Last I checked, you were the one that fuckin' started it, not me. We don't have to do anything. You said stay out their business. Practice what you preach," I sassed.

Vanessa

I've been pacing the floor in my home for that past few hours. I'm expecting and I've been sleeping more due to morning sickness. For some odd reason it's lasting all day. He was using that as an advantage to stay gone. Veno left the house around 6:00 p.m. and he said he'll be back before 9:00 p.m. I looked at my watch and it was after 11:00 p.m. I grabbed my phone instantly to see if I had any missed calls. I don't know what's going on, but Veno hasn't been acting himself lately. We've been married for a little over two years and we're expecting our first child.

I know a baby can't keep a man, but I thought he would be a little more attentive to my needs. The last time he strayed off for a few months is when we broke up about three years ago when I was away at school. The long-distance thing wasn't working for me. So, we decided to call it quits. Veno was stressing me out bad. Every other week someone from back home was calling me and telling me what he was doing. I couldn't take it.

During us breaking up he started messing with Riley. I thought it was just a little fling, but I started seeing more pictures of them on social media. I started following her. I knew she was feeling him. I wasn't having it. I put in too much time with him to give it to someone else. I transferred back home to get my man back. Did I regret it? Yes, because I missed living on campus. I did it for love. Ugh I despised that bitch. Veno and I were together during high school. Riley was Kaniya's best friend. Lucky met Kaniya through Riley. Those two motherfuckas were double dating.

Kaniya was missing. Veno mentioned it, but I didn't care because she wasn't my bitch. I know a few days ago Lucky and Veno went looking for her. Kaniya wasn't my girl, LaRoya was. Riley was her girl, so I didn't care to be in her company and I'm sure she didn't care to be in mine. We never crossed paths or done any double dating together. Occasionally when LaRoya comes to town we all link up at my house and chill. I know Lucky still cares about her. I can tell by the way they look at each other. Lucky knew how I felt about that. I think he should've waited on her because she went away to college to do something positive.

I'll always root for him and LaRoya! I'm sorry, but I'm not a Kaniya fan. I couldn't be because my loyalty lies with LaRoya and I'm sure hers lies with Riley. Lucky and LaRoya dated all throughout high school.

Lucky and Veno were always in the streets heavy so going to college was never a part of the plan. LaRoya and I knew they wouldn't follow us. I kind of hoped they would but that was wishful thinking. I wiped the sleep out the corner of my eyes and a small yawn escaped my lips. I swear this baby is taking all my energy. Veno and I find out what we're having in a few weeks. I climbed out my bed and grabbed my cell phone off the nightstand. I hit the FaceTime button to call Veno. He kept clearing me out. A small scowl appeared on my face. I'm irritated and pregnant. Anything could be wrong with me. I don't know what that was about.

Veno wasn't a cheater anymore to my knowledge. He shouldn't be because if he was, I'll fuck around and strangle his ass in his sleep. I went through a lot with him and Riley when I moved back home, and I wasn't for none of his shit now. Veno always had a wandering eye. I called back one more time and he did the same thing. A text came through and he said he was in a meeting. What kind of meeting are you in at this time of night?

Veno was in the streets heavy if he wasn't at the club or the studio him and Lucky had. It sums it up that he's with someone else. He took advantage of my morning sickness and was playing on that. I didn't reply to the text because that was the first red flag. Veno got me fucked up. The moment we said I do he should've been done with the games and shit. I made him choose me over her. It shouldn't be a fuckin' her period. I'm playing for keeps behind him.

I enabled the share my location app on Veno's phone and he had no clue. I wanted to keep it that way. His location was already shared with me. I logged into the App and he was at a house I didn't know in John's Creek. He got me fucked up. I knew Kaniya stayed in Johns Creek and Lucky's house wasn't too far from hers, but I didn't recognize the street address.

I was only three months pregnant, so I wasn't showing that much, but I had a small pudge. I walked over to my closet to find something cute to put on. I found a cute summer dress. I jumped in the shower to handle my hygiene. I applied Bath and Body Works French Lavender lotion. I brushed my hair into a knot ponytail. I hate that I'm even doing this, but I knew he was up to something. I could feel it because he never not answers the phone for me.

I slid my bikini and bra on and slid into my dress. I slid my feet into my sandals. I grabbed my phone off the counter and my clutch. I pray Veno isn't doing nothing that he shouldn't be.

Riley

Tianna and Quan were throwing a little kickback at their house today. I was going to go, but Boss made a run to Florida. He had some business he needed to handle. I declined the invitation earlier because it was a couple's thing. My man was running up a check, so I didn't want to sit around and watch other couples. I wanted to lounge around in the suite and maybe do a little shopping. Boss told me to find a house out here since we're here so much. I like Atlanta but I never wanted to live here. Cali and Miami are more up to my speed. I'm cool with the suite, but I understood where he was coming from. It was running $6,000.00 a month.

The only reason why I knew my way around is because I went to school at Georgia State. Tianna invited everybody, Barbie, Ketta, Julius and Don. Lucky didn't come and I find that odd. I was surprised when Veno came through and Vanessa wasn't with him. I mentally prepared myself to not beat her ass and fuck her up at Tianna's house. I didn't want Veno talking to me after the stunt he pulled a few weeks ago. Boss and I never argue but that night we went at it for hours. I felt where he was coming from because I was in a position that I shouldn't have been.

It's late and it's time for me to clear it. I helped Tianna clean her kitchen and put the leftovers away. Ketta and Barbie said their goodbyes. I grabbed my clutch so I could head out too. It was almost 1:00 a.m. and way past my bedtime. Tianna walked me to the door. Quan and Veno were in the living room smoking. Quan said bye and I chucked up my deuces at him. I could feel Veno's eyes staring a hole in me. I paid it no mind. I'm positive after his encounter with Boss he wouldn't be speaking to me. The moment I exited out the door. I heard him get up and slap hands with Quan. I walked to my car quick. I could hear him jogging trying to catch up with me. I hit the unlock on my car and attempted to get in. He slammed my car door shut. I swear I wasn't beat for Veno's shit. I opened my door again and he slammed it shut.

"Move and get out my way," I sassed and sucked my teeth. I'm ready to get to my suite. I don't have time to be arguing with him about shit that doesn't even fuckin' matter. He started breathing down my neck. I could feel his lips touch my skin. "What do you want?" His hands touched the forearms of my shoulders. I swatted his hands away. I turned around to face him. I had a scowl on my face. He gave me that smile I hated so much.

"Riley, you know what I want. You've been tripping and you know I don't give a fuck," he argued. I swear I don't get

Veno but guess what he's not for me to get, because he married her and not me. He left me and went back to her. I'm not the type of woman that would beg a man to stay with me. He has that with her. I refused to run up behind any man. I guess that's what he was used to, but he'll never get that with me.

"Veno, I've told you once and I don't want to tell you again. It's over between us. It's been over for a few years now. You made your bed so lay in it. You're a married man and I want you to stay that way. Please stop running up behind me because you're causing problems in my home. I'm in a committed relationship and unlike yourself I'm in love with the one I'm with.

I don't want to disrespect him by having conversations with you about shit we shouldn't because last time I checked you said I DO. The only thing you need to do is get up out my face," I argued and explained. Veno had an evil look on his face. I'm sure he didn't like what I said but oh well, I said it.

"Riley, you're so full of shit. You always have been. I didn't come out here to talk about me. I came out here to talk about us. I know what the fuck you got going on and I know what I got going on so what's understood doesn't need to be explained. I care about Vanessa. I'm not going to lie but I got a special place in my heart for you too. I love you and no matter what you think I cared about you too. You ruined us when you decided to kill my child because we weren't together.

No matter what, I was going to fuckin' take care of you and mine and you know that. I may be a lot of things, but I've never been an ain't shit nigga," he argued and explained. I knew I shouldn't have come here, and I don't want to talk about this. I turned around and tried to open my car door and he slammed it shut. "Stop fuckin' running because we're going to talk about this shit rather you like it or not." I shoved him out my way because I wasn't doing this with him. He grabbed me and held me.

"Veno, can we not do this please. It is what it is. Just let it be," I cried and broke down in his arms. I didn't even realize I started crying. I don't want to talk about my abortion. He started whispering in my ear.

"Stop crying. I got you Riley and I'm not trying to upset you, but you should've given me the option to choose. I wanted our child. You should've consulted with me first," he argued and explained. I understood where he was coming from, but he wasn't in my shoes. I couldn't stop the tears from falling even if I wanted too.

"Don't say that, Veno. I did what was best for me because I wasn't dealing with you and your EX, period. I've come along way," I cried. I couldn't even catch my breath. I had to count to ten. "I will never say her fuckin' name. She tried me one to many fuckin' times. I wasn't dealing with that. I didn't have to ask you because you've always coddled her and never corrected her when she was wrong, so you made your choice then. Veno, you didn't have to say it because your actions spoke for you," I cried. I swear I don't want to relive this shit.

"Riley, my actions don't mean a motherfuckin' thing. You don't know what the fuck I've done so don't say that. It should've been a WE decision not YOUR fuckin' decision. You know I wanted you to have my child because we were trying to have a baby. Nothing about US was a fuckin' mistake," he argued and explained. Veno was in his feelings and I was in mine too. I was still wrapped in his arms trying to break free from his embrace, but he wouldn't let me.

"Goodbye, Veno." I sighed and sobbed.

"I love you Riley, and I still do," he whispered in my ear. I wasn't about to say it back because I'm in love with Boss. It took me a minute to get him out my system and I wanted to keep it that way. Veno was temptation but I couldn't feed into it.

"I knew it was a reason you were fuckin' clearing me out, Veno. It's still HER and we're MARRIED and EXPECTING OUR FIRST CHILD. How was the meeting looking at the two of you? I guess it went well. Let me ask you a question, RILEY? Bitch, how does it feel to be number TWO to a MARRIED MAN that would never want you?" She asked, argued and explained.

I had to count to ten because I'm liable to kill this bitch pregnant or not. Address him and not me. Veno wasn't even about to say shit. I pushed him off me because at the end of the day I don't owe her any explanation, he does. "Just like I thought a coward ass bitch to push up on a MARRIED MAN, run and not say shit." I slammed my car door shut and stepped in her fuckin' face. Veno grabbed me. I pushed him off me. I saw Tianna and Quan coming down the driveway.

"Vanessa, take your motherfuckin' ass home. What the fuck are you doing out here anyway? I know you got that app on my fuckin' phone. I ain't as stupid as you think I am. I ain't got shit to hide that's why I don't give a fuck about showing you my location," he argued. I don't care about none of that.

"I'm not going to be to many more of your bitches. You and I both know I'll treat you like a bitch if you want me to? Try me. Keep your fuckin' husband away from me. If I were you, I would choose my words fuckin' wisely. I would hate to have to make you eat those words. ADDRESS your HUSBAND and not me BITCH. Do I make myself fuckin' clear?" I argued. I'm about two seconds from slapping fire from this bitch. I just want to get out of here before I do something that I'll regret later.

"Riley, what's going on out here? Is everything okay?" she asked. Tianna knew that shit wasn't okay. I gave her a look to let her know that shit was about to go up. I just shook my head because I just wanted to leave and go to my suite to take a hot shower. I knew it was about to be some shit. I knew it was too good to be true. I knew this bitch was somewhere lurking in the shadows. I should've trusted my first instinct and stayed at home because I knew this would happen. She's pregnant but you're so worried about the child that I didn't fuckin' have. I wasn't dealing with this bitch, period.

"Oh, I see what the fuck this is? The four of y'all where on a fuckin' date. Tianna, I can't fuckin' believe you, bitch. You know I'm married to Veno. I'm HIS fuckin' WIFE and he's my fuckin' husband. Y'all got me fucked up. The only thing that's stopping me from beating y'all ass is the child I'm carrying," she argued. This bitch was crazy as fuck. She still hasn't addressed him. He's holding me back and not her. Quan couldn't even hold Tianna back because she was all up in Vanessa's face.

"Guess what, bitch? I'm pregnant too and I don't give a fuck about beating your ass. I ain't never gonna let a bitch get a pass just off the strength of the disrespect your giving. Vanessa what you won't fuckin' do is come to my house talking loud and waking up my fuckin' neighbors. This is my shit. Quan and I take care of all this. Do trust, if they call the fuckin' police you're going to jail for trespassing. Veno, I don't give a fuck about this bitch being your wife.

Don't ever come to my fuckin' house assuming shit. I ain't got to hook up nann motherfucka with your husband. As you can see, he can hook his fuckin' self-up. God don't like ugly Vanessa. What goes around comes around.

I know you don't like me and that's cool, but bitch you gone fuckin' respect me when you step foot on my premises. A bitch always told me the same way you gain a man is how you lose him. If the shoe fits, bitch, wear it. We know all about you trying to push LaRoya back on Lucky with the double dates. We peeped all your slick disses on the internet but bitch, if it ain't directed it ain't respected. Next time at us bitch.

I'm speaking for Kaniya since she's not here. I'm speaking for Riley since I invited her here. We got that COME BACK PUSSY. They always come back. No matter how hard you try to push your bitch into the arms of a nigga that don't want her. It's always KANIYA no matter what. No matter how hard you try to put on and throw your marriage up in a motherfuckas face. We're not impressed. If you got to brag about it, it ain't about shit. It's always RILEY, BITCH. You should thank her for allowing him to come back to your desperate ass, BITCH. Now get the fuck off my property before I use my hands on your face, BITCH," she argued. Tianna tossed her shoe at Vanessa and I almost died.

Thank God Tianna gave her the business. I was done with the talking a few minutes ago when she let word bitch slip from her lips. I swear this bitch is crazier than I thought. I knew all about her throwing slugs on INSTAGRAM and shit. Kaniya and Tianna always shared the screenshots in our group messages. I'm glad she pulled up because she saved me time and tears. I didn't want to explain to him anymore about what I did and why I did it.

I wasn't dealing with that shit. Vanessa and I fought once over him. I had no clue she was back in town, but she knew I was with him. My parents sent me to Atlanta to get an education. Not to be fighting bitches or out here fighting over him because his EX can't get the clue. Judging by his wife actions I did the right thing. Finally, I was able to hop in my car and pull off. Veno and Vanessa were arguing at her car when I pulled off. We locked eyes with each other, and I just shook my head. My phone was ringing, and it was Tianna. The Bluetooth was on automatic answer.

"Bitch, you know I had to call you. I couldn't believe that bitch pulled that shit at my fuckin' spot. I'm sorry for even bringing you over here. I thought everything was cool," she sighed.

"I'm not surprised. I should've trusted my instincts and stayed at home. I can't come to your house anymore Tianna. I'm not trying to run into Veno anymore," I sighed. Tianna and I finished talking. I couldn't do it and I refuse to. I had a lot of things on my mind. I shouldn't even allow him to get that close to me. Veno bringing up my abortion was a touchy subject for me. Do I regret? In some ways I do but dealing with Vanessa wasn't an option. I've moved on and I'm not trying to relive nothing that I went through with him.

I think God is punishing me for my abortion. Boss and I have been trying to have a child for a few months and it hasn't happened yet. Either way I was going to be punished because taking her life was an option too. She didn't know when to ease up. She was coming hard for no reason. I loved Veno and I can't even front like I didn't because once upon a time he was my everything. We created a child together, but Vanessa ruined that. I knew my worth then and I know it now. It's best that I stay away from him because I'm not trying to ruin what Boss and I have. Especially after our last encounter when Boss pulled up. I couldn't have that on me. I didn't get any sleep that night. Boss has eyes, on me all the time. I don't want to get caught slipping.

Vanessa is stupid as fuck. I'll fuck around and do life in prison for killing her ass. I'm done giving out passes. She can keep that nigga because I don't fuckin' want him. If I did, I would've never returned him back to her. She's stupid as fuck. Not one time did, she confront him. Everything was directed toward me. She wanted me to know that she was pregnant. Baby, I'm not bothered by it.

Veno chose her and she chose him. She's pregnant with his child and he needs to focus on that instead of running down on me every time he fuckin' sees me. I knew him being quiet and not saying anything to me was too good to be true. He was waiting on the perfect time. Why now, though? I wanted to stay in Atlanta until Kaniya came back, but I can't. I'm taking my ass home. I don't like pops ups and running into motherfuckas I don't like to see. It took me a long time to get to this point and I refused to let a miserable bitch take me back.

Vanessa

☆

"Vanessa let me holla at you for a minute," he argued. I didn't want to hear shit Veno had to say. I caught him in the arms of another woman. He was guilty as fuck. How can he explain that? Even after I caught him, he was still holding her back and trying to stop her from getting at me. He grabbed my hand and I pushed him off me. "Vanessa are you going to fuckin' stop or do I need to stop? You came here to find me so, why leave after shit hits the fuckin' fan?" I stopped in my tracks and turned around to face him. I hated he even got the chance to witness my tears. I wiped my eyes with the back of my hands. I pointed me finger in his face.

"Veno, what the fuck do you want from me? Can you explain to me why I caught her in your arms? Can you fuckin' explain to me why you cleared me out and acted like you were at a meeting? Why her, Veno? Why do you want to have me out her looking like a fuckin fool?" I argued and cried. I couldn't hold it in even if I wanted too. He wrapped his arms around me. I broke down in his arms.

"Look, Vanessa I'm sorry. I love you and I'm not out here cheating on you, but Riley and I have some unfinished business. I needed to get some shit off my chest. I shouldn't have been that close to her, but I needed closure," he explained.

"Veno, what do you need closure for if we're married? You blamed me for months because she killed your child? Did it ever occur to you Veno, that her child may have not been yours anyway? How do you think I feel as your wife to witness that? It hurt me to see that, Veno. I guess you don't give a fuck about hurting me and upsetting me. I pregnant with your child. I could lose our child because of the position and the stress you're putting me in," I argued and cried.

"Come on, Vanessa, don't say that shit. Watch your fuckin' mouth. What Riley and I had doesn't have shit to do with you. I know her child was mine because I was her first. I wanted her to have my child, but she killed my child because of you Vanessa.

I CHOSE you and the only thing you had to fuckin' do is mind your business and not fuckin' mine. You and I were together. Regardless, I wanted my child. Killing one of mine is never the FUCKIN' option. IF THE POLICE IS KILLING US, and WE'RE KILLING US.

IT WON'T BE NO MORE US. Yes, I was comforting her Vanessa, because I wanted to know why. I needed to know why and now I know," he argued and pointed his finger at my forehead.

"I hear what you're saying, Veno. I love you but it hurts. I had to witness and see the love that you share with someone else is still there. I'm your wife so, why do I have to compete with that? Sometimes you should just let that shit go but I can see you're still holding on. You lied to me and said you were in a meeting. You were in a meeting but here you are meeting another woman. When are you ever going to consider my fuckin' feelings? Leave her alone or I'm leaving YOU, and I'm taking my child with me. I'm all cried out. I guess I should kill my baby too," I cried and lied. I was laying it on real thick. Veno got me fucked up. He can either get rid of Riley or I'll do it myself.

"Vanessa don't fuckin' play with me. Kill my child if you want and motherfucka I'll bury you and shawty. I'm not fuckin' playing because I see what you're trying to do. Pull that stunt if you want to prove a point with me and I swear to God you'll fuckin' regret it. I DARE YOU, Vanessa. Go ahead if that's what you want to do. Take your motherfuckin' ass home. I'll meet you there," he argued and explained. He pushed me in my car and slammed the door. I looked at him with wide eyes.

"Veno, why are you doing this to me?" I cried.

"Vanessa, you heard what the fuck I said. Take your ass home now and don't let me beat you there because it'll be some motherfuckin problems," he argued. I raised the window up. My hands were rested on the steering wheel while tears poured down my face. My vision was so fuckin' clouded it was ridiculous. My heart was beating out my chest because he handled me like that. Once again, he's made a fool out of me. I can't believe VENO done that shit to me. I couldn't stop the tears from falling even if I wanted too.

Damn Veno, why would you do this to me? I came here because I love you and to show you how much you mean to me. I'm married to you. You and I both said I DO. I'm about to have our first child, too. You didn't explain shit to me, you left my heart EMPTY. I stopped for a minute to get myself together. I had to do something because I wasn't losing Veno to Riley for a second time. It wasn't happening.

I finally got the courage to leave. I looked in my rearview mirror to see if Veno was following me and he wasn't. My heart was hurting for him because I don't know where our relationship stood.

Chapter-12

Kaniya

Tariq Harris. I bit my bottom lip and smiled just thinking about him. I was infatuated with him. He was so fuckin' fine. I swear this man has been spoiling me from the moment our feet touched the pavement in Jamaica. I needed a vacation bad. I've been through a lot these past few months and let's just say, Tariq's been making up for that in more ways than one. I've been making the best of it no matter what has been thrown at me. Even despite the circumstances on how I got here. I deserved it and I've been having fun. Too much fuckin' fun. I deserve to let my hair down and enjoy what's going on around me.

I miss home, but I'm not ready to go back yet. Even though Lucky and I had our disagreement over the phone, I know once we see it's each other it's going to be a mess. I'm not prepared for that because it wouldn't end well. Lucky and I would have to shoot it out. He can dish it, but he can't take it. Men want to cheat and expect women not to cheat back. I didn't cheat because we weren't together when I bounced on Tariq a few times. I knew we would never be together after this. I think our relationship has ran its course.

I took a loss and he can take one too. He wanted what he wanted, and I wanted what I wanted. If I was alone with Tariq on an Island, he knew we fucked. I don't know why I was scared to tell him, but I was. I guess it's because I loved him so much. He knew Tariq and I had sex. He's been trying to figure it out for a long time. No matter how much he's hurt and fucked over me. I care about his feelings. I guess that's just who I am. I hooked up with Tariq on some get back shit, but I knew I could be with Tariq. It wasn't about the pussy with him, it's deeper than that.

I can point the finger at Lucky, but I wanted to give myself to Tariq. I'm sure once we see each other again he's going to ask. I'll have to be honest. I just don't understand why he wants to know so bad. I knew the night I spent the night at his house it was about to go down. We wanted each other bad. We've been wanting each other but we just never had the chance to act on it.

We were both single and the opportunity presented itself. The thing about sampling some new dick, is that you'll have to make sure that you don't like it, but I was gone off Tariq. He had my nose wide the fuck open. He knew what the fuck he was doing to me. He took his time with me. He learned my body and wanted to touch every spot. He wanted me climbing the walls stroke for stroke. I see why Shaela was crazy if he was giving it up like that.

He wanted me and I wanted him. The reason I wasn't trying to be in a relationship with Lucky is because I wanted to explore Tariq some more. I wanted to ride his dick until I couldn't ride that motherfucka no more without any strings attached or feeling bad about what Lucky would think. My summer has been super lit. I swear my life is like a fuckin' movie. If a motherfucka would've told me three months ago this shit would've popped off I wouldn't have believed them. I knew the summer was mine after Lucky cheated. Who would've known one fuck up would lead to all this?

I wanted to do something special for Tariq tonight because he's been doing special things for me every night. I love this little Villa that we've been staying in. I could get use to this. I haven't thought about using a phone one time since we've been here. Tariq and I went scuba diving earlier and before we made it back home, I made him stop by the local market.

I grabbed two lobster tails, a pound of shrimp, two T-bone steaks, potatoes, scallops and oysters. I grabbed a few ingredients to make a salad. I've never cooked for Tariq before, so I wanted to pull out a few stops tonight and put on a little bit for him. He deserved it because he earned it. We've been eating out every day, so tonight I wanted to cook us a nice dinner. I also wanted to setup a cozy spot for us on the beach, so we can watch the sunset. I wanted to take advantage of the scenery. Tariq was still asleep, so I decided to go ahead and take a bath. After that I'll get our dinner started before, he wakes up. Before I hopped in the shower, I placed a few soft kisses on his lips. He grabbed the back of my head and started kissing me.

"Come lay with me," he requested and yawned. I wanted to so bad, but I couldn't because if I did. I wouldn't go through with my plans.

"I can't because I'm trying to do a few things, but I will later," I sighed

"What are you trying to do?" He asked.

"You'll see," I smiled.

Tariq

I've been tossing and turning for a minute. I was tired as fuck since Kaniya and I touched down. We've been moving around like crazy. I can't think of the last time I was able to get this much sleep. My hands roamed the bed and I thought I would've been felt Kaniya by now, but she wasn't in bed. So, where the fuck was, she? I could've sworn I told her to lay with me. I rolled over on my stomach to check the time on the clock and it was a little after 6:00 p.m. I can't believe she let me sleep this long.

I inhaled the smell of food and whatever it was, was smelling good. I felt my stomach growl instantly. I hopped out the bed and went to the bathroom to brush my teeth. I grabbed a face towel to wash my face and take a piss. I went searching for Kaniya in the living room and she wasn't in there. She was in the kitchen moving around. I walked up behind her and wrapped my arms around her waist. I rested my face in the nape of her neck. She was cooking. Who told her to do that?

"About time you woke up. I was just about to wake you," she smiled and looked up at me. Her hair was in its natural state. She had on a pair of thongs with the matching bra. Her ass was doing the pair of thongs she had on so dirty. I pulled her thongs down and unfastened her bra. I started massaging her nipples. A soft moan escaped her lips.

"Bend over and arch that motherfuckin' back. I want you to sit on this motherfuckin' dick," I commanded. I wanted her in the worst way, and she knew that shit. She was being disobedient as fuck, more of the reason why I'm about to punish her ass. I picked her up and sat her on the island. She looked at me with wide eyes as I threw her legs over my shoulder. I wanted to taste her pussy because she was looking good as fuck.

"Tariq stop you're ruining our moment," she pouted and whined. She swatted my hands away and tried to raise up, but I wasn't having that. I had her penned in the perfect position. I wasn't about to let her move at all. I don't know why she was trying to move.

"What moment because you're ruining mine? I'm trying to see if that pussy taste as good as you smelled." She turned around to face me. She cupped my face and brought her lips closer to mine. We stood still and took each other in for a minute.

"Tariq, can you please just stop for a minute. I want you as bad as you want me. I'm trying to do something nice for you. Can I show you how I appreciate you and then we can get to it?

Go take a shower and get dressed and meet me outside in thirty minutes and bring that dick with you," she sassed and grabbed my dick.

"Alright but keep your hands to yourself before I fold your ass up and show you how much I appreciate you," I explained.

"You're not playing fair. Tariq, please go and take a shower and meet me outside. I promise you it's something that you'll never forget," she pouted and whined. Kaniya had something up her sleeve and I'm wondering what it is. She's going hard, so I guess I'll ease up.

"I got you," I sighed. I kissed Kaniya on her forehead and headed back to our room. The only reason why I decided to comply was because she was persistent about what she was trying to do. So, I went ahead and gave in. I've had my share of females, but I've only felt something about two of them. Tamia Raye was my first love and I fucked that up chasing some pussy that wasn't even worth it in the end. Tamia was a good girl too. She probably could've been my wife. I always wondered how she was doing.

I love Kaniya too. I always had. Since the moment we met we were connected. I knew she was meant for me. I wanted her to be mine a long time ago. I wasn't a hoe, but I've been with a slew of women. She was special to me, real fuckin' special. I cared about shawty for real and she knew that. She held a nigga down while I was away doing my bid and I appreciate her for that. Just off the strength of her flipping my money while I was away spoke volumes. She didn't have to do that, but she did, and that shit came in handy for an investment that I just made.

It's one of the reasons why I went so fuckin' hard. She got a special place in my heart, and I just wanted to show her that. I wanted to see what she was up to. I want her to have my kids on some real shit. I've been wanting kids for a minute. I've been trying to knock her up since we've been here, so hopefully I succeeded.

Kaniya

I swear Tariq was doing the most. I hated it because he was stubborn as fuck and persistent. He just wanted what he wanted. Ugh, now I'm hot and bothered. I had a tsunami between my legs. My juices were begging to be freed. He was the only one that could free them. I had to count to ten to get myself together. I just wanted to surprise him, that's it. Good food and some bomb ass sex afterwards. The food was done already. I just had to setup outside on the balcony. I decided to not setup on the beach because I didn't want our food to be cold. I like everything cook to serve and so does he. Tariq and I were chilling inside tonight.

I wanted to go out for a late-night swim, but we'll see if that would happen. I had the table set up real nice. The tablecloth was white and draped in candles with gold candle holders. I picked a few fresh flowers and placed them inside of the vase. I had to go inside to find Tariq before I brought the food and wine out. I was still in the bathroom flexing in the mirror. I stood by the door and admired him for a minute. I guess he felt me looking at him because he turned around and faced me.

"Come here. Why are you looking at me like that?" He asked. My feet weren't moving, and his eyes were trained on me.

"I like what I see. Is that a crime, Tariq? I told you to meet me outside in thirty minutes and you're running late," I sassed and sucked my teeth. I exited the room. I heard him say something. I didn't bother to look over my shoulders because I knew he was coming. He ran up on me from behind and picked me up. "Put me down Tariq, please."

"Nah, I can't do that because I asked you a question and you kept walking. Why you got an attitude and a nigga ain't did shit to you?" He asked.

"Put me down, Tariq. I don't have an attitude. I made plans and your late," I sassed. He put me down and backed me up against the wall. Our lips were touching. He slid his tongue in my mouth. We exchanged a kiss. He slid his hands behind my back and gripped my ass.

"Stop playing with me, Kaniya," he explained. He grabbed my hand and I led the way outside to the balcony. He took a seat at the table and he pulled me onto his lap. "Is this for me?" He asked and bit my ear.

"Yep, sit tight so I can get our food. What are you drinking tonight, White Hennessy or Wine?" I asked. I'm taking it easy tonight no hard liquor for me.

"I'm drinking you tonight," he chuckled. I swear he plays too much. I popped him and headed back in the kitchen and I grabbed our plates.

"Tariq," I yelled. He opened the balcony door. I slid his plate in front of him and I took a seat in front of him. He smiled at me and stroked his goatee. No words were spoken between us. I just wanted to eat and enjoy the sunset and listen to the ocean. I could feel him catching glances at me in between eating his food. I wouldn't look up and acknowledge his presence for nothing. I stood up from my chair to go and use the bathroom. I couldn't even get to the bathroom because he stood up and blocked me from going to the bathroom. I looked at him and turned my face up.

"Tariq, I have to use the bathroom. Can I do that, please?" I asked. He moved out of my way and followed me to the bathroom. Damn, I can't even piss in peace. I slammed the door in his face. I used the bathroom, wiped myself clean and washed my hands. The moment I opened the door. He was right there smiling at me. He backed me into the bathroom, lifted me up, and sat my ass on the sink. I rested my hands on his chest. I wrapped my legs around his waist. He cupped my chin forcing me to look at him.

"I know you felt me looking at you while we were eating. Dinner, what's up with that?" He asked. I was being petty, and I was hoping that he didn't feed into it. I just wanted to eat without any questions.

"Nothing, I was just fuckin' with you," I smiled. He leaned in and gave me a kiss. It was so passionate and intense. I couldn't even catch my breath. He broke the kiss. I cupped his face bringing his lips closer to mine. I wanted to finish what he started.

"Kaniya, you know I care about you. I appreciate you for cooking dinner for us. I didn't know you could throw down like that. Let me know when you're ready for me to wife you. Come on, let's get out of here. We got plenty of time to feel each other," he explained. Tariq grabbed my hand and led me back outside toward the balcony. He grabbed the champagne flutes and filled them to the brim.

"Let's take a walk on the beach." I took a sip out of my glass. He grabbed my hand and led me to the beach. Every few steps he took he would look at me and smile. We found a spot right by the ocean. I slid my sandals off. I raised my sundress over my head and tossed it in the sand. I had my swimsuit underneath. He pulled me into his arms and wrapped them around my waist. He buried his face in the crook of my neck and started whispering sweet nothings in my ear.

"I love you, Kaniya," he stated. I love Tariq too, more than he would ever know. I loved him for as long as I could remember. I wasn't in love with him, but I loved him. If I allowed myself to, I could fall in love with him.

"How do you know, Tariq?" I asked. I wanted to know how did, he know that he loved me.

"I know because I always tell you that and I mean that shit. I feel it and you do too. I need you to stop holding back. We could be something great if you tell me how you feel and what you want. I don't want to play any games with you. I want you and I want us," he explained.

"I love you too, Tariq and I mean that shit. I want us also, but we need to continue to go with the flow and get to know each other some more. I don't want to rush us. I know we could be something great but let's gradually get there," I explained.

"I'm holding you to that, Kaniya." He stripped down to his swim trunks, picked me up, and carried me out to the ocean. I swear this vacation was everything to me.

Chapter-13

Yirah

I've never been the one to step on any females toes, but I had to try my hand with Lucky. It was something about him and I was drawn to him. My heart and mind both kept telling me to go for it. I don't know what he saw in Melanie. Kaniya was beautiful but she didn't deserve him. Lucky had Kaniya on a pedestal, but she's been fuckin' with Tariq for a long time.

I could tell by the look in his eyes at his party that night. He loved her and the love he had for her didn't happen overnight. It took some time and work for them to get there. I saw it in her eyes too that she loved him. I knew Lucky and Kaniya were together but for some odd reason I didn't care because I wanted him. He was made for me. Whenever we saw each other we both exchanged lustful stares. We wanted each other but we never acted on it until a few months ago.

Lately shit was a lot different with Lucky since Kaniya's been gone. He's free game and I'm the only woman in the race. I'm the one that told Tariq to kidnap her ass if he wanted her. It was a joke and I never thought he would act on it. I can't wait to thank him for helping me out. I've been crushing on Lucky for a long time and I'm finally able to get in where I fit in.

Melanie was gone so it was just me. Lately things between Lucky and I were looking up. We were together in public and not behind closed doors. Everybody wanted to know what was up with us. I wanted to know too. Let's just say my bed was a permanent place for him. I wanted more from him than being in between my legs every night. I wanted it all. I wanted his heart because he had mine in his pocket. I wanted to go with the flow, but I just had to know where we stood.

Lucky was still in my bed every morning. I woke him up with head for breakfast. My mouth was a fool. I knew I had him when I felt him grab a fist full of my hair. He started fuckin' my face roughly. His dick was touching the back of my throat. I gagged a little bit, but I swallowed him whole. He dug his nails in my ass cheeks and started finger fuckin' me wet.

"Yirah, get up here and ride this dick," he yelled. He didn't have to tell me twice. Riding his dick was the only place I wanted to be. He cupped my breasts with both his hands. He started sucking each of my nipples and stroking me long, deep, and hard. My eyes rolled in the back of my head.

Tears were threatening to seep through the corner of my eyes. Sex with Lucky was so amazing. He took his time with me confirming that I was more than just a fuck. We went at it for about another thirty minutes before we both tapped out.

I came all on his dick. I'm sure he blessed my insides with a kid of his. He flipped me on my backside and just smiled at me. He went in the bathroom and I heard the water running. I assumed he was getting a towel to clean our mess. He walked back into my bedroom. He stood in front of me and gave me the smile that I loved and adored so much. I bit my bottom lip. God, I love this man. He wiped my pussy clean and kept his eyes trained on me.

"Tell me what's on your mind, Yirah. Talk to me," he demanded. I guess it was now or never. I might as well speak up since he sees that something is on my mind. He tossed the washcloth in the laundry hamper and cupped my chin. "What's wrong? Are you going to talk to me and let that shit out?"

"I just want to know where we stand. What are we?" I asked. Lucky gave me a stern look. I could tell he was choosing his words wisely.

"Yirah, lil mama, you know I care about you and I'm feeling the shit out of you. I just got out of a relationship and I'm not in a rush to jump back in one yet. That's the best thing for me and you right now. You're the only female I'm kicking it with right now. I come home to you every night and wake up to you every morning. If that's too much for you right now let a nigga know something and I'll fall back," he explained. I was hoping for more than that. I understood where he was coming from. I took a minute to respond. My feelings were hurt because I wanted more than that. He's been cheating in his relationship.

"Okay," I sighed. I guess Lucky didn't like my answer. He hovered over my body and started placing soft kisses all over me. I closed my eyes because I didn't want to look at him. He cupped my chin and bit my bottom lip.

"Yirah, don't do that. It's me and not you. I'm being honest with you. A nigga ain't ready. What, you want me to string you along? I'm not trying to do that. Here's your key and I'll see you when I see you," he argued.

"You can leave but how is it fair to me. Why do I have to wait? I've been waiting and I can't do this because I'm falling in love with you," I cried.

Vanessa

My marriage has been in shambles lately. It's killing me to the point where it's starting to stress me out. I love Veno with all my heart and I don't want to love another. I can't take it. I'm pregnant and I shouldn't be going through this. I could lose our child because of this. I've lost fifteen pounds in the past two weeks. I don't know what I've done wrong. He won't even talk to me. Veno hasn't been treating me right since the night I caught him with Riley in an awkward situation. I'm his wife, what the fuck did he expect?

I hope he didn't think that I would just be quiet and not say anything. He knew I wasn't built like that. It's been tension with us ever since. He won't even sleep in the bed we share and he's barely home. The last time he was here I was crying in the bed while he laid next to me. He didn't even console me. He acted as if I didn't exist and that shit hurt me to my fuckin' core. I didn't deserve any of the shit he was putting me through.

Lucky told me that he's been staying at his condo in the city. I know things between Veno, and I have taken a turn for the worst if he left our home to go stay somewhere else. I'm miserable without my husband. If he's laid up with Riley somewhere crying and getting closure about a kid that probably wasn't his, I swear he's going to regret it. I'm glad she killed his baby. I couldn't allow her to have his first child.

It wasn't going down like that, so yes, I made her life miserable giving her plenty of reasons why she should've never fucked with a man that was mine. I've cried my last tears over Veno and Riley. LaRoya always told me don't worry about what I can't control. But guess what, I can control my husband and make sure he'll never fuck with that bitch. I hired a motherfuckin' hitman to take that bitch away from him.

She can join her baby in hell and watch me and my husband ride off into the sunset. I have a meeting with the Hitman at 5:00 p.m. It's a little after 3:00 p.m. I knew it would take me over an hour to get there. I was supposed to meet with LaRoya later, but I told her I needed to meet up with her later. LaRoya was my best friend but I wouldn't dare tell her what the fuck I was up too.

I put in way too much time with Veno to let the next bitch reap the benefits of my hard work. My cousins on my father side of the family are well connected. They knew some people who put me in touch with a Hitman. I'm meeting him in a little small town outside of Georgia in Chattanooga, Tennessee. I dressed casually. I stole a few pictures off Riley's Instagram account so I could give the hitman a nice picture of her. My ride was outside blowing like they lost their fuckin' mind. I had to make sure I had all my stuff and the cash I grabbed from Veno's safe. I was coming. Sometimes men are so inconsiderate, and my cousins weren't excluded.

My cousins Eric and Sam were escorting me to meet up with the Hitman. Sam and Eric didn't know that Veno and I were having problems. I didn't want to tell them because I know they would intervene. The last thing I needed was for Veno and my family to be at each other's necks. We finally made it to our location. Before I stepped foot out the car, Sam and Eric both grilled me.

"Vanessa, I know you don't want to tell us what's going on but please don't write a check that you can't cash. This nigga is the real deal so make sure you have everything lined up to avoid any casualties," he argued. I knew what I was doing. I don't need Eric and Sam to school me on shit. The moment they pulled up at this abandoned warehouse, chills ran across my body and I could feel the hairs raise up off the back of my neck.

Eric and Sam escorted me into the warehouse. The security patted me down. I swear it felt like he was getting a few free feels. They emptied out the contents of my purse and snatched my cell phone and powered it off. Eric and Sam slapped hands with each other and took a seat in the corner. The security escorted me to a room.

I locked eyes with one of the sexiest human beings I ever laid eyes on. He was tall, dark and handsome. His skin was the color of a Hershey chocolate bar. He has a clean cut too. Deep waves adorned his head. His lips were nice and plump, and his teeth were white as snow.

"I'm Haus, what brings you by? How can I be of assistance to you?" He asked. He extended his hand out for me to shake it.

"Hi, I'm Vanessa. It's nice to meet you too, Haus. I have a problem and I wanted to use your services," I beamed and smiled.

"You're too beautiful to have a problem and to need my services. I'm a killer baby, and I don't rough nann motherfucka up. I shoot first and never ask any fuckin' questions, you feel me. Make sure this is what you want," he asked.

"I know what you do and the only thing I want you to do is shoot and don't ask any fuckin' questions. What's the price?" I asked. My mind was made up a few weeks ago. I knew I wanted this bitch dead the moment I caught her in my husband arms.

"$100.000 for a body. No face no case," he snarled trying to intimidate me. I sucked my teeth because I hate being underestimated. I grabbed my purse off the seat that was empty beside me. I thumbed through it just to make sure I brought enough cash with me. I sat my purse on the desk in front of me. We locked eyes with each other. Veno always stacked his currency by $10,000.00 after that he'll rubber band it. I had to make sure I brought more than enough cash with me. I had over $100,000.00 in $10,000.00 increments. Haus eyed me intently as I placed the bills on the desk. He grabbed the bills and checked to make sure nothing was counterfeit. I sat back in my chair and folded my arms across my chest. Haus took a seat in front of me.

"Who is he and what did he do?" He asked. A small laugh escaped my lips. I'm sure he thought I hired him to take my husband out but that's not the case at all. I hired him to take a bitch he can't let go out.

"It's not a he, it's a she. She needs to stay the fuck away from my husband," I argued and sassed. I meant what the fuck I said. I made that shit clear and I shouldn't have had to. Riley knows that he chose me so I don't understand why she would still be trying to pursue a married man.

"Oh, okay. What did she do to you for you to want her head on a platter?" He asked. His eyes were trained on me. Riley never done anything to me. I can honestly say that she bowed out gracefully. Yeah, we had one fight and she got the best of me only because I was a little tipsy. She came back to Georgia for a reason, so I know it's because of my husband. I caught them.

"Too much to discuss. She doesn't know her fuckin' place but she needs to understand mine. My husband is off limits. I don't give a fuck about what they shared prior to me," I argued and explained. She killed your child move on and let that be the reason but that's too much like right. He's neglecting my needs because of her and I'm sick of it. I'm pregnant with your current child.

"Do you have a picture of the subject?" He asked. Of course, I had a picture for $100,000.00 I got it all. I got several pictures of the bitch. If she would've never step foot to Veno she wouldn't be in this situation. He's married bitch and you know that's more of the reason why you need to steer clear of him.

"Say less," I beamed and smiled. I slid the pictures I had of Riley in an envelope to him. I couldn't wait for this bitch to be a distant memory of the past. Haus looked at them and sat them down. I hope he wasn't judging me, but I don't care. I'm married to Veno.

"How soon do you want it done?" He asked. If I'm paying you today. I want that shit done immediately Riley had to fuckin' go.

"Soon," I beamed proudly. I wanted this bitch gone immediately. I don't know if Veno was still fuckin' with her while we're in a place we shouldn't be in. I'm not trying to find out. I rather dead that bitch and be done.

"I'll be in touch," he explained. I stood up and shook Haus hand. I exited the door. Haus was very easy on the eyes, but I only have feelings for Veno. There's nothing wrong with looking. I could feel his eyes on me. I put a little pep in my step. I'm pregnant and there's nothing that he could do for me. I don't know if that's a good thing or bad one. Eric and Sam grilled me, and we exited out the building. I was ready to get away from here immediately. It's creepy but I guess I couldn't be too picky because I'm here to hire a hitman to kill a bitch I fuckin' despise.

"I hope you made the right decision and I pray this shit never comes back to bite you in the ass," he argued. Sam was always going hard on me. I knew what I was doing. I've been thinking about this for a few weeks now. Riley had to go. Ain't no way around it. If she won't leave him voluntarily, I'll make her leave him the fuck alone.

"I won't," I sassed and sucked my teeth. I just got to figure out a way to tell him what I used his money for if he asks what I did with the money. I need an excuse for that. He keeps tabs on everything, and I'm sure when he decides to come back home, his safe is the first thing he's going to check. Hopefully he won't ask but that's too much like right. He'll find any excuse not to come back home. $100,000.00 missing from his safe will seal the deal.

Boss

God damn, shit got to be a real than motherfucka out here. I was that nigga to see for the right price and we could do business. If you wanted a hit orchestrated in the south, you called me. She should be glad that Sam and Eric are some loyal associates of mine or else I would've popped her ass for ordering a hit on my woman. I done seen it all. Normally women come in here all the times to have their husbands killed. Riley, though. That bitch couldn't have known who the fuck I was, because she wouldn't have even put that shit in my fuckin' face. Veno's wife. I chuckled with just the thought of her timid ass. I'm her worst fuckin' nightmare. It's crazy she wanted Riley out the way. Riley isn't her problem, her husband is. Veno wasn't a threat to me because I already knew where Riley and I stood.

I know everything about her past with that nigga. She told me about the abortion, and I didn't agree with that shit but, it was before my time. I'm ready for Riley to have a few kids of mine. We've been practicing for a minute. I tried to keep my composure for as long as I could, but I couldn't. I've been a Hitman for years and I've never turned a job down before. But ain't no way in hell I'm taking out the love of my life behind a bitch ass nigga that can't get a clue.

What I will do is take that bitches bread and hit up her nigga a few times and let her know it's nice doing business with her. I got to get up with Riley to see what the fuck is up with her and Veno because his wife wants her head. I would never let her know that Vanessa ordered a hit to be put on her. I grabbed my phone to call Riley to see what she was up to. I needed to ask her a few questions. She answered on the first ring. Riley and I are very honest with each other.

There were no secrets between us. I knew the last time she saw Veno because I pulled down on the two of them and I didn't like what the fuck I saw. That nigga doesn't want any problems with me, and his wife paid me $100,000.00 for my girl's head and it should be his.

"Hey baby, what are you up to?" She cooed through the phone. I love Riley with all my heart. I can't think of one female that I've said that about. I hope she isn't entertaining that nigga. I want to give her the fuckin' world.

"Nothing baby, I just finished handling some business. I'm on my way home. Let me ask you a question and I want you to be honest with me Riley," I explained.

"What's wrong, Boss?" She asked. I could hear the concern in her voice. I knew I had her attention. I always had that.

I need her to keep it real with me. Our relationship was built on honesty.

"Nothing is wrong. When was the last time you saw Veno and I want you to be honest with me?" I asked. I had eyes on her just in case shit popped off, but I wasn't watching her every move. Riley gave me the rundown of the last time they saw each other. I didn't like what I was hearing but she was honest. She started crying and I hated that her past always brought her to that place.

"Riley, when the fuck was you going to tell me that shit. Stay the fuck away from him. He wants you. You and I both know that, but you're not up for grabs. I got a problem with that. He looks at you the same way I do. If you need a shoulder to cry on about what the fuck you did, you can always have mine. Do I make myself clear?" I asked. Veno's making problems that he's not even ready for. I told the nigga to his face to stay the fuck away from her. I see now that he has a hard time listening. I put it on his life he'll wish he had because now he has a target on his back.

"Yes, you're very clear, Boss. I already told Tianna I wouldn't be coming around anymore," she cried. I don't like motherfuckas like him. Why are you trying to guilt trip her because she aborted your fuckin' child? I'm glad she did because this nigga is nothing but a fuckin' problem. He doesn't want a fuckin' problem with me. He needs to tend to his jealous pregnant wife. Who just paid for a hit on his ass?

"Stop crying baby, I'm on my way." I knew Riley was in her feelings and I hate that I'm not there to console her. The last thing I wanted her to do was cry because of him and what he was doing to her. It wasn't going down like that. He needs to love the one he's with instead of the one he let go.

"Okay Boss, I love you and only you," she explained. I knew Riley loved me because if she had something to hide, she would've never told me about what the fuck happened between the two of them. Vanessa is mad at the wrong person. Be mad at your husband.

"I love you too, baby." I'm about two hours away from home because of traffic. Riley is sensitive as fuck and I love that shit. I had to stop and get her some flowers. I wanted to cook her a nice hot meal. It was still early, and I had time to do that and more.

Chapter-14

Kaniya

I haven't been to Jamaica in a few years and this would be my first time here in Ocho Rios, Jamaica. I've been to Kingston, of course, but never Ocho Rios. I wanted to see the Dunn's River Falls. I've heard so much about it. It was so hot and humid when we stepped off the jet. My first week here was crazy and amazing. Tariq had a condo on a private island. It was so beautiful and spacious. It sat right on the ocean and we had access to a private beach. You know I'm a freak, so I insisted that we have sex on the beach; it doesn't get any better than white sand and ocean blue water. I'm a promiscuous gal.

We went horseback riding, scuba diving, and we rode jet skis. Tariq was romantic, so we had a candlelight dinner every night on the beach while the sun set. We had some of the best Jamaican dishes that Ocho Rios had to offer. We had nice wine and White Hennessy on demand. I could get used to this. I love the Islands. We woke up every morning to watch the sunrise and we did the same when the sun set. I loved the view.

I fell asleep one night out here while I was reading this book called **Journee & Juelz by Nikki Nicole.** Man, this was a great book. The authoress has amazing talent. I couldn't put the book down. Tariq had to grab my iPad from me because I was reading so much. I have a nice tan now and I love it. I'll be mad when my skin starts to peel. We've been in Jamaica for two weeks now. I wanted some jerk chicken from a taste of Ocho Rios.

I didn't feel good today. I had the shivers. I was cold and it's always hot in Jamaica. I jumped up out the bed because it felt like I had to throw up. My stomach was hurting and before I made it to the bathroom good, I threw up in the middle of the floor in our bedroom. Tariq must have heard me because he jumped out the bed and ran up behind me.

"Kaniya, baby, are you okay? What's wrong? Your body is hot; you're running a fever. I need to get you to the hospital asap," he explained. This was not like me to be throwing up and running a fever. Something was wrong and I needed to find out what was up. Tariq carried me to the bathroom and washed my face and brushed my teeth. I couldn't walk I was so weak.

Tariq was taking me to the hospital. We were headed to Saint Ann Parish Hospital because it's the best on the island. I pray they can find out what's wrong with me and make me feel better.

"Baby, how are you feeling? We're almost there. Hold on, okay? You'll be good. Do you think it was something you ate?" He asked. I know he was concerned and we prayed it was nothing serious. The last thing I needed was to be sick miles away from home.

"I don't think so. I was fine last night, remember?" I asked. I ate light yesterday. I had a mango fruit salad and some salmon and spinach. It was good and I didn't drink anything.

"We finally made it to the hospital. I'll let you out up front so I can park. Let me get us some help first," he explained. He was so nervous. I know he wanted everything to be all right. I hoped it was just a stomach virus or something so they could give me an antibiotic to treat it. He was so attentive to my needs and I really appreciate it. I made my way into the hospital with the transporter.

She gave me the admission form and I filled it out and listed all my symptoms and I handed it back to the nurse. She advised that I would be seen quickly. Tariq came through the door looking for me. I waved my hand so he could see me, and he headed over quickly. I laid my head on his chest. It was a Wednesday morning, so the hospital wasn't that full, thank God. The nurse called me back, finally.

"Hi, Ms. Miller. Can you explain to me what's going on?" She asked. "You look pale, but you have a glow." I'm sure I looked like shit, but I didn't need her reminding me.

"My stomach hurts, I threw up, I'm cold, and I've been shivering," I stated. I knew I was sick because it's the middle of the summer and I'm freezing. I just want to lay down and snuggle under the covers.

"When was your last menstrual cycle?" She asked. I knew I wasn't pregnant because my period just left. Thank God. I wanted kids, but I wasn't trying to have any right now.

"Two weeks ago," I stated. "It was abnormal, and it didn't last very long, maybe three days or so."

"We'll give you a pregnancy test. It seems like you might have a virus with your symptoms," she explained. I hope so. I hate being sick. I was sitting on Tariq's lap. I laid my head on his chest and he stroked the side of my face.

"What if you are pregnant with my baby?" He asked. I looked at him with wide eyes. He wanted a baby by me. I wasn't ready for a baby and we haven't been using protection at all. I'm nervous as fuck. Being pregnant is the last fuckin' thing I need right now.

"I'm not ready for any kids. It's a virus, you heard the nurse," I explained and told him. I knew Lucky would kill me if I were pregnant by another man. I started to break out in sweats suddenly and I passed out just from the thought of how Lucky would react.

"Nurse! Nurse! Come, my girlfriend just passed out," he yelled. Tariq sounded as if he was shaking at this point. We were just having a conversation and suddenly, I passed out. Something serious is going on. The nurse finally came with some cool towels and patted my face and I woke up.

"Are you okay, Ms. Miller? You don't look so good. Let me go ahead and check your vitals," she said. She checked my blood. My iron was low and my temperature was 103.3. I went ahead and gave my urine sample for the pregnancy test. I knew that it was negative. I went back to join Tariq and I could barely keep my eyes open.

"Ms. Miller come with me. Is it okay if your boyfriend comes, also? We need to do an ultrasound," she asked. The nurse sounded irritated. I'm irritated too. What the fuck do I need an ultrasound for?

"An ultrasound for what?" I asked. I wanted to know what was going on. "You said I had a virus and my iron was low."

"Do you care if I discuss your personal business in front of your boyfriend?" She asked. I knew it was due to HIPPA reasons and the Privacy Act.

"Sure, I don't mind at all," I stated.

"You're about to be a father, congratulations! I need to do the ultrasound to confirm how far along you are," she explained. The nurse confirmed I was pregnant. I wish she wouldn't have told Tariq that. He was excited until he noticed my face.

"This can't be right. There must be some mistake. I just had my period two weeks ago," I argued and explained. I was annoyed; I didn't want this happening.

"Well, let's take the ultrasound to see if I hear a heartbeat for confirmation," the nurse stated. I knew I wasn't pregnant, and I'm sure my face told it all.

"Kaniya, stop fucking playing around and do what the nurse tells you to do," he argued. Tariq was heated. He hated how I was acting this way when stuff didn't go my way. I was being a total bitch and this nurse had been nothing but nice to me. At the same time, I was curious to know if I was pregnant. I knew Tariq wanted a child with me.

"I'm ready. How do you think I feel? I'm sorry if I came at you the wrong way," I explained and told the nurse.

"Undress Ms. Miller and lay back on the bed so I can do your ultrasound. The gel will be very cold. I need to hook up this equipment so it can be accurate," the nurse stated and sucked her teeth. I knew for a fact that I wasn't pregnant. I don't know why she was so eager to show me. I know most women are happy about being pregnant by their boyfriends, but that wasn't my case. I'm prepared for the worst, but I'll pray for the best. I really didn't want any kids. I was nervous and scared. My father would go crazy and I didn't believe in abortions. The nurse got the equipment hooked up and was ready to get this show on the road.

"Ms. Miller, do you hear that sound? I told you. That's your babies' heartbeats. You're about twelve weeks along. You're pregnant with twins and your date of conception is May 1st or May 2nd. Your due date is Feb 1st or Feb 2nd, 2017. It makes sense why your iron was low; your babies are consuming all your iron. You're also having morning sickness, so I'll prescribe you some prenatal vitamins. When you head back home, see an OBGYN. Take it easy, Ms. Miller. I'll have your discharge papers in a few." She explained. Fuck my life. I can't believe this shit. I'm pregnant with twins. Why me? Damn. Who fathered these kids; Lucky or Tariq?

"What's wrong, Kaniya? You don't look happy that you're about to have my kids?" He asked.

"That's the problem, they might not be yours. There's a possibility they're Lucky's," I argued and explained. I told Tariq, admitting that I fucked up good. It would be easy to avoid Lucky when I came back to the states if no kids were involved, but if he found out I was pregnant and there was a small possibility my kids might not be his, all hell would break loose.

"What the fuck you mean they might not be mine? She said May 1st or May 2nd; we were together on May 2nd. You fucked Lucky the same day or some shit, Kaniya? Make me understand this shit," he argued and explained. Tariq was fuming hot at this point. I'm sure he wanted to choke me right about now for the words that came out of my mouth.

"Tariq, please back the fuck up and calm down. Lucky and I broke up on the first and we also fucked the same day. I fucked him and left him. It's that simple. I ran into you at Mozely Park the next day and we hooked up, so that's why the shit is complicated," I explained.

"I forgot that you were with that fuck nigga. I'm sorry for snapping. I didn't even think about that shit. You keeping them, right? I saw the look on your face when she told you you were pregnant; it looked like you were having doubts. I got you 100%. I believe they are mine, though. You were with that nigga for a long time and never got pregnant.

As soon as I came along, you're knocked up. That's a sign. We're meant to be. We'll stay out here for another week or two. I still want to take you to the Cayman Islands. Don't eat any more seafood while you are pregnant with my seeds," he explained. Tariq was gloating at this point; he knew he was the father. I'm sure he couldn't wait to call and tell Mac and John the news. I was the only woman he wanted to bare his kids.

ONE WEEK LATER

Chapter-15

Chelle

I promise you I dreaded coming back to Atlanta. Something told me to stay and I should've listened to that something, but I had to come and check on my girl Sonja. She just got out the hospital from dealing with Kanan's crazy ass. I wish they would get it together before they end up killing each other. On top of that, we got to bury Deuce this week. I could've killed Sonja when she told Kanan she set him up. I don't know why she fuckin' did that. I wish she hadn't. I don't know if it was the drinks or she was just feeling herself. Either way she fucked up.

She was supposed to take that shit to the fuckin' grave with her. When she realized she said that shit, she started sweating like she had popped a molly! Yeah, she fucked up good with that one. Her fiancé got killed and her ex is trying to kill her!

She has a dilemma. I left Atlanta years ago. I hated to come back here because it brought back to many memories. Sonja and Kanan, Me and Black, Kaisha and Killian.

We were the real get money crew. I had to leave Black's crazy ass alone. He was to possessive, but I loved his sexy ass. I just got fed up and tired of the street shit, late nights and early mornings. I left his ass without a trace. I've been living in Miami for the last seven years. I've been dating this Jamaican named Couture for the past three years. We do business together and we're dating. There's nothing wrong with mixing business with pleasure. I love to get money with my man in the daytime and at the end of the night, pop some pussy for a real nigga. I'm going to miss Couture for a couple of months. I hope and pray I don't run into Black's crazy ass after all these years.

Me and Black's situation was toxic and crazy. It's something I can't forget but I don't like to talk about it. We loved each other but he couldn't do right. He had too much to prove and I didn't owe anybody shit. Black let his ego get the best of him and he thought I would wait on him while he was getting his shit together, but he was wrong. I was tired, and I didn't have anything else to give.

Black

"These bitches ain't shit! I thought Chelle was different. I thought she would always be there for a nigga. She promised me she would, and she broke that shit. I can't believe she was out to get a nigga. She wanted to be the one to bring pain and misery to a nigga. I guess I was wrong about her. She switched up on a nigga quick and left me all alone. I've been looking for Mechelle for the last eight years straight. I searched for her high and low. I even hired a private investigator and they came up with nothing. Imagine to my surprise when she was at Deuce's birthday party in Miami with some nigga. It took everything in me to not send a warning signal to Chelle. It must be a God because a nigga put his pride aside to spare a motherfucka that night because the Angel of death was taunting a nigga flesh.

I wanted to shoot her and her nigga. I knew we would run into each other soon. I had a feeling. I guess my feelings were on point that day. I wasn't even supposed to go to Miami but Kanan Jr. and Yashir have everything in control. I trained them young niggas right. Kanan told me to ride the fuck out. I thought me and Sonja was better than that. I guess I was wrong because I used to ask Sonja all the fuckin' time to give me a number and location on Chelle. That bitch would always play me to the left. I should've probed a little more.

Chelle knew I saw her because our souls were connected. I couldn't keep my eyes off her. Chelle danced the night away. She looked good and happy. I know she was fronting because she knew I was near. I wanted her happy but if it wasn't me, I wasn't comfortable with it. I was selfish when it came to Chelle. She was everything to me no matter what. I wasn't a bad nigga when it came to us. I slipped up a few times, but it wasn't nothing permanent. I fucked up and took her for granted. She was the only one I had in my corner besides my niggas. I fucked up.

I wanted to drop that dread head motherfucka she was with right where he stood. I didn't like Florida because of the Stand Your Ground law. I wanted to rush that nigga. Kanan had to stop me. It was all good though because that nigga would lead me to Chelle. I needed some answers. No excuses, but solutions. What did I do that was so bad for her to up and leave me? No letter, no nothing. If I find out that she left me to be with that nigga, Lord have mercy on her soul. We were engaged. The only thing she left was her engagement ring that she begged me to get.

I still have the ring. If she's back running with Sonja, it won't be long before we cross paths. I have a feeling it will be soon. You can run, but you can't hide forever. I gave her everything she wanted and needed financially. I didn't get to spend as much time as I would've liked, but she knew I couldn't because Kanan had just got locked up.

She fucked my life up with that shit she pulled. I can't wait to catch Chelle because she won't even see me coming. I need to get this woman off my mind before I run in Sonja's and demand her shit. My eye is twitching and shit. She got my nerves bad. I need to go box or find somebody to shoot. Kanan punched me in my shoulder. I shoved his ass back. I didn't have time for his bullshit. I had to much shit on my mind to be boxing it out with that old ass motherfucka. He was fresh out the FEDS, so he was used to working out and shit and having a lot of energy.

"Aye Black, you need to loosen the fuck up and get your mind off Chelle. She'll show her face soon. Trust me. She knows you were in the room that night. She'll come out of hiding sooner or later," he argued and explained. Fuck that I've been waiting long enough.

"Sonja is foul as fuck for that shit. I don't have shit to do with what you did," I argued and explained.

"Black chill out. You've always covered for me. Some women won't drop the dime on their girls no matter what and that's Sonja. Chelle and Sonja are close and have been for years.

Sonja knew I was getting out. She knew I was coming. If Chelle showed her face, she wanted you to see her with that nigga. She baited you and you fail for the bait. You should've killed that nigga to let her know don't fuck with you. She would've gotten the message loud and clear. We make fuckin' statements. I guess you done got soft on a nigga since I been gone. You've been hanging with Killian for too long," he chuckled. I wasn't beat for Kanan's shit. I had too much to lose so I couldn't live careless anymore.

"Never that, I got too much to lose. I'm cautious when I'm catching bodies and Florida is a no. You barely pulled that shit off. It was reckless but clean. I'm a little more calculated now," I explained. I value my freedom to much. I got shooters and assassins on payroll to handle those situations.

Chapter-16

Niema

I've been watching Don's new chick Ketta for a minute. JR was having a kickback at Gresham Park. You know I was coming through. I dated Don on and off for about two years. I'm from the Brooklyn metro area. This nigga cut my water off like it wasn't shit. I had been asking him was he dating anyone because his behavior had changed. I should've known because he stopped paying my car note then it gets repossessed. He stopped paying the mortgage on my townhouse and now it's in foreclosure.

I called that nigga and asked him who she was and what was up. This nigga hits me with 'oh she's wifey and she got her own so need you to back the fuck off. I told you a long time ago when I find her you were cut off so don't count my money and depend on me. I had to see about this chick that came and captured my meal ticket. I had an issue with that and was ready to solve it. To make matters worse, one of my friends said they were at Gresham Park at JR's kickback and Don was tonguing the fuck out of her. They sent me the picture, so I had to pull up.

My friends didn't know that Don and I were no longer together. I wouldn't dare tell them that for them to judge and talk down on me. Don and Ketta were about to hear from me today. I had my friend Sade riding with me in case shit went left, she would have my back. Don made me plenty of promises that he never kept. I always hinted around that I wanted more than what he was offering. He was always saying that he wasn't ready to settle down. I know that's the farthest from the truth.

I knew we were friends and I wanted more than that. I thought I had a chance because he did a lot of nice things for me. I guess that was wishful thinking. I don't know where we went wrong. The moment he met Ketta everything changed for us. He cut me off and I wasn't with that. He changed his number a few times, so I knew whoever she was to him had to be serious.

Ketta

Things have been going great for me and Don for a while now! We've been living together for the past two months. It's been amazing. Still no word on Kaniya and she's been missing for over two weeks now. Barbie told me Mrs. Kaisha told her that Tariq kidnapped my girl. This shit is crazy. This nigga kidnapped my girl and had us catching bodies and shit in front of Magic City. I'm a registered nurse and I can't be doing shit like that.

We're still in Atlanta. Barbie and I were headed to this kickback that one of Don's friends was having in Gresham Park. Don and Julius were tying up some loose ends which was, why we're still out here. I didn't mind it one bit. I thought about renting out my townhouse, but I opted out. Barbie and I made it to the park. It was a cool day, not to hot. Don and Julius were playing basketball.

"Ketta, do you see that Lexus that keeps riding past us?" Barbie asked. She keeps mentioning a Lexus, but I didn't see anything. My mind is in the gutter and if it ain't directed it ain't respected.

"No, I'm not paying attention. What's up?" I asked. If Barbie mentioned something out the ordinary, I'm sure I needed to pay attention to see what's going on.

"Look, there it goes again," she stated. I tried to turn around as fast I could, but I was too late. Barbie roughly touched my shoulder so I could see what the car looked like. The car slowed down, and two girls jumped out. It piqued my interest because I didn't have any beef with anybody, so I was confused. I stay in my lane and the moment a bitch has the balls to swerve it's going down.

"Which one of y'all hoes fuck with Don?" She asked. I looked at this bitch like she crazy. She knew who was fuckin' with Don because it ain't no fuckin' secret. The worst thing a bitch can do is send for me and I haven't sent for her. She had so much bass in her voice and she had a fuckin attitude. All I can say is choose your words wisely because I'm not the one and she doesn't want me to make her the one.

"Which one of y'all hoes wants to know?" I asked. I had so much bass in my voice too. I was giving her what she gave me. I had to let that bitch know I wasn't Don's hoe. I was his woman and I'm sure those hoes know that.

"Me," she beamed and said cheerfully. I can't stand a stupid ass bitch because clearly, she knows what I am to him. I don't even know why I was entertaining this bitch. I had nothing to prove because I know where I stand with him.

"I'm not just a fuck, we're in a relationship and you know that. Don checked your duck ass plenty of times. What's your issue?" I asked. I knew exactly who this bitch was. She's a part of his past. Don told me all about his past relationships so there are no secrets between us.

"Niema, I know you're not about to let this bitch check you like that?" Her friend asked. Who was this bitch because clearly her friend hasn't told her the truth? I don't mind letting a bitch know what the fuck it is between Don and me. I'm playing for keeps behind that one.

"Don is Ketta's man, bitch. Why are you running your dick suckers?" Barbie argued and asked. Barbie wasn't fuckin' playing with these bitches and neither am I. I don't bother any fuckin' body, but see these bitches are swerving and I don't mind fuckin' serving them with these hands.

"Fuck all that talking, Niema. Do something because I didn't come to do any talking," she argued. Did these bitches come to fight because I'm confused? I ain't never fought a bitch over a nigga that wasn't hers. I never knew she had any beef with me.

Before she could finish her last sentence, I punched Niema in her fucking head so hard that bitch fell to the ground. I rocked that hoe to sleep and I kept punching her in the forehead. I promise you I have never had to fight where a bitch doesn't get one lick in the fight. What she thought this shit was? Don and Julius came running down the hill, trying to get me off Niema, but it didn't work. I heard sirens and I dropped that dusty bitch quick. Don was shaking his head because he didn't want me going to jail behind Niema's duck ass. I didn't want to go to jail either behind some trash.

I jumped in the car with Don, slammed the door, and he pulled off driving all crazy. I don't know why he was mad at me because I didn't do anything. She started with me, so I finished it. I could feel him grilling me. He pulled over and I knew he was about to go in. He threw the car in park and hopped out. He opened my door and pulled me out the car.

I stood in front of him and folded my arms across my chest. He closed the gap between us and was now all in my personal space. He cupped my chin forcing me to look at him. Our lips were touching each other.

"Babe, are you okay? I love you Ketta and I don't want you out here laying hands on bitches that aren't irrelevant. You got too much to lose. I don't want you to lose anything, you feel me?" He asked then placed a kiss on my lips.

"I'm okay, Don. I know I got a lot to lose. You know I don't start drama and you know that I don't know her. I never seen a picture of her. She came here to fight me because of you. She had a problem and I solved it. I didn't want to, but you know how I feel about disrespect. Babe, she was reaching so I had to touch her," I explained.

"I know babe, I promise you that shit will never happen again. I don't know what her problem is but I'm sure she got the message loud and clear," he explained. We exchanged a few kisses before getting back in the car and heading to dinner. I'm sure she got the message loud and clear. I wasn't playing behind him.

Chapter-17

Sonja

The time has come for me to finally lay Deuce to rest. I was still in my feelings about what happened in Florida. I didn't want to let Deuce go because he didn't deserve to die. I should've kept my mouth shut and we wouldn't be here. I can't believe Kanan done that shit. I knew the moment I saw him walk into the club with Yasmine some shit was about to go down, but I wasn't prepared for it. A small scowl instantly appeared on my face because he knew I despised that bitch. You run back to the same bitch that I despised but you here ruining something that's special to me because you're jealous.

Kanan and I can always agree to disagree. I love Kanan but Deuce held a special place in my heart also. I can't deny I was attracted and addicted to him. I loved him. He taught me how to love again. He mended my heart that was broken. I didn't even recognize the lone tear that started to slide down my cheek. I fanned my eyes to stop the tears from falling. I heard a knock at my door, and it was Lucky. We had an appointment at the funeral home to talk to the director.

The whole ride was awkward. His phone kept ringing and judging by the conversations he had, a lot of shit was going on. I wish I didn't hear half of it. We gave the funeral director Deuces suit that he would be laid to rest in. I chose a double-breasted white Armani suit, a white Armani shirt, and a white Armani tie to match. I had purchased him some nice ass gold cufflinks to bring it out. He had on his gold Audemars Piquet watch to match. On his left ring finger was the nice engagement ring I gave him because we had a matching set. I left his black socks and all-white Air Force Ones at the funeral home to be put on. We made small talk. Eddie, the funeral home director, came in and discussed our plans.

We decided on a beautiful white casket with gold trim. We discussed the arrangements and the obituary. I let him know that I had the perfect song that I would like to hear. I wanted this to be a home going celebration, and not just another sad funeral. Damn, I can't believe we're doing this. I finally told Lucky and Quan the truth about everything, and I do mean everything.

I told him I knew once Kanan got out of prison, he was going to come looking for me. I knew he would try to stake claim to me. I told them I loved their father and that would never change. I loved him and I had fallen in love with him. I never wanted to see that happen to him.

Kanan still held a piece of my heart. He hurt me with the shit he did behind my back. Everybody got secrets and scandals and I still got a few that I'm holding on to.

THE FUNERAL THE NEXT DAY

I swear I dreaded this day. I had a bad feeling about this funeral, but I don't know why. We were all lined up and ready to walk into the church. My hands were sweaty, and I kept wiping them on my skirt. Lucky, Quan, Chelle, and I headed inside of the church. It was packed already. A lot of people came out to show their respects for Deuce. I was glad to have my girl here with me since Kaniya couldn't be here. We were all sitting here listening to the same preacher who was supposed to be marrying us.

"Good afternoon ladies and gentlemen! We're gathered here to celebrate the life of Calvin Rogan. Can I get a standing ovation and a round of applause for him?" Everybody stood to their feet clapping their hands. I was listening to everything he was saying. I felt like somebody was watching me. I looked over my shoulders to see if I saw anything. I didn't see anything. Something was about to happen. I could feel it in the pit of my stomach.

I became nervous and started sweating! I felt some shit was about to go down and I was hoping and praying that nothing happened. I guess that's just wishful thinking because before I knew it, Kanan came into the church. He walked up to the front row, grabbed my ass right up. I looked at him as if he were crazy. Lucky and Quan both had scowls on their faces.

"Not now, Kanan." I sighed and sassed. I didn't want to raise my voice because all eyes were already on me and I didn't need the extra attention. Kanan was doing too much and I'm sick of his ass. Why would he come here and do this? I swear Kaitlyn should've swallowed him.

"Sonja, bring your motherfuckin ass on before I walk you up out this church my damn self. If you want to continue breathing, you better not say one fuckin' word or look back. Your good deed has been done," he argued and explained. He was embarrassing me. I can't stand him. He turned around and looked at Chelle. He had an evil smirk on his face. Chelle turned her head instantly and acted as if she didn't know him. I knew Kanan wasn't going to give her a pass.

"Chelle, if you know what's good for you too, you would walk your short ass in front of me. Black is outside of the church, front and center, waiting on your ass right fuckin' now. Judging by that nigga's appearance he's mad as fuck at you and you know why." The moment we stepped outside of the church. I went in on his ass. I don't give a fuck who heard me. I wanted him to hear me.

"Kanan, why are you here doing this? You've done enough, let me lay him to rest. I'm sick of you and your shit," I argued. I was trying to talk some sense into Kanan's thick skull, but he wasn't trying to hear me. If it wasn't his way it wasn't no way.

"Sonja, I don't give a fuck. You knew I was coming here. You heard what the fuck I said. You don't have to do any of this shit. You did what you had to do, and you don't need to do anything else. You're disrespecting me by even being here doing this shit," he argued and explained. It was pointless to even have this conversation with him.

"Kanan, I'm not trying to do this with you. He was my fiancé rather you like it or not. I'm not asking you; I'm telling you. The funeral is almost over in the next couple of hours, you'll never have to hear Deuce's name again. If I meant to you what you're constantly trying to act like I do, then you would let me bury my fiancé," I argued and explained. My free hand was rested on my hip and my finger was pointed in his face.

What the hell possessed me to say that? Kanan was sexy and built nice. This crazy motherfucker slapped the hell out of me. "I know you didn't do that shit?" I smacked the fuck out of him back. He cupped my face and shoved his tongue down my throat. He was so fuckin' disrespectful.

"You heard what the fuck I said. This better be the last time that dead nigga's name rolled off your tongue," he argued. I hated my body still responded to him. My pussy was wet as fuck. I don't know if I pissed on myself or had one of those out of this world orgasms, but that shit felt good as hell. He let me go. I straightened my clothes and looked at him. I turned around quick. I didn't want him to catch me staring. He nodded his head at me. I bit my bottom lip the moment I turned around. I didn't want him to see me doing that. The funeral was almost over. I rode with Lucky, Quan, and Tianna. I think I'll catch me an Uber back. I couldn't ride with them after Kanan just showed his ass. Black stopped me at the door, and I looked at him.

"Sonja, let Chelle motherfuckin ass' know the moment this shit is over, her ass is coming with me. I got an issue with her. I thought you didn't know where the fuck she was. If she tries that shit she did seven years ago, there won't be a funeral for her ass because I'll bury her alive or cremate her," he argued and explained. If Chelle was smart she would've left and cleared this motherfucka already. Anytime you saw Kanan you knew Black was somewhere close and the last thing I wanted was for her to get caught up in my shit.

I swear I can't stand those two motherfuckas. Black and Kanan do the fuckin' most. The two of them need to let everything in the past go. I wish they stop holding onto shit. Black and Chelle haven't been together in years. The moment Kanan got locked up and went to the FEDS Black was handling everything in Kanan's absence.

He was running the streets and stopped coming home like he should. Chelle got tired of that shit and left. I knew where she was, but I wasn't about to give the drop on her. I made it back inside of the church. I eased back to my seat and Chelle was nowhere in sight. I knew she cleared it. I'll shoot her a text when

I leave the service. Lucky and Quan were up next to speak about their father. Lucky spoke first.

"I never thought I would be the one giving reflections on my father. I always hoped that I would go before him. The day those pussy ass motherfuckas took my father away from me, woke me up. On the outside looking in, one would think that I'm fine but I'm not. He didn't deserve to go out like that. He was a provider and businessman. He helped his community. My father was a good man and he would give you his last. My brother and I will forever carry on his legacy," he explained. Lucky was taking Deuce's death hard. I felt so bad. I knew he was talking to me.

Chelle ☆

If looks could kill, I would be a dead bitch and shitting fuckin' bricks right now. Oh my God I had an outer body experience. Being in the same room with black almost killed me. Woo child-sweet-baby-Jesus Hallelujah. My heart dropped instantly when Kanan jacked up Sonja in the fuckin' funeral. Black was staring a hole in the side of my face. I felt his glare and it was icy as fuck. You know how when someone is staring at you and you can feel it. Well, that's how Black's glare felt. I turned around and locked eyes with him. He looked like he wanted to body me. I pulled the brim of my hat down and turned around quickly. I swallowed hard. I'm sure everybody could hear it.

I hated Black's ass. I used to love everything about him, but he ruined us. He promised he wouldn't switch up but the moment he stepped up in Kanan's position his situation changed and he became Kanan. I knew all about what Sonja went through and I vowed I would never put myself through that. I warned Black that I would leave, and he waived me off saying I was tripping but I wasn't. I left him to prove a point, but I was tired mentally way before that.

I can't believe Kanan and Black walked in this funeral like they were running shit. I wanted to be here for Sonja, but damn I couldn't. I didn't want to run into Black at all and here he is in the flesh. Why would Kanan come here? I'll have to figure out a way to get out of here. I'm sure they have this place swarmed. I don't want to talk about shit that happened seven years ago. I left his ass in the past for a reason. I hate to be on my phone during this funeral, but I needed a ride out of here. I was about to Uber my ass up out this funeral.

I refuse to go anywhere with Black and talk. For what, so I can end up missing or in the hospital like Sonja's ass? I don't date crazy niggas or thugs anymore. I left that lifestyle in Atlanta. I like corporate thugs. Kanan and Black are still on that hot boy shit from years ago. Old ass niggas still with the shits, disrespecting this man's funeral and shit.

I wish Deuce would come back from the dead and put a bullet in Kanan's crazy ass. You already killed the man, what more can you do? If I was Sonja, I wouldn't even fuck with him at all. He's crazier now than he was before he got locked up. Lord, please forgive me for cussing in this funeral.

Chapter-18

Kanan

Let the games begin. Sonja thought I was playing with her motherfuckin' ass, but I wasn't. The twins called me yesterday and told me what Sonja was up to. The shit was only pissing me off. I intercepted that shit. They sent me a picture of Chelle because they wanted to know who she was. I showed Black that shit and he was furious. He knew she would show her fuckin' face, and guess what, she did. I told Sonja not to go to that fucking funeral or have him one at all. We brought havoc to that funeral. Black wanted to snatch Chelle up and get some fuckin' answers, but her slick ass slipped out undetected. I knew she wasn't too far.

I've been kicking it with this little chick named Amber that's thirty-nine. Things are serious for her, but I'm not serious about anybody, to be honest. I wasn't in the business to commit to anyone. I wanted that old thing back. I was entertaining her and getting familiar with her pussy. She wanted to meet Sonja. I don't know why she wanted to do that. I kept trying to spare this chick, but she was very persistent. I wanted to fuck with Sonja because I know she was feeling me.

Amber claimed the only reason why she wanted to meet Sonja was because that was my longtime girlfriend. More of the reason why she needed to mind her business and not fuckin' mine. Everybody in the streets knew about me and Sonja. If she met her, that would clarify that we had something serious going on. I looked at this bitch and laughed. She was crazy as fuck and she wanted those problems I'll gladly give them to her. I called Sonja up. It took her a few rings to answer. She finally picked up on the third ring.

"What, Kanan? Why are you calling my phone? Don't call me unless you're coming to get your kids," she sassed and sucked her teeth. She knew I wasn't coming to do that shit. Kanan and Yashir are old enough to watch themselves. I was getting Sonja acquainted with them before I moved in.

"Watch your fuckin' mouth. I want you to meet me for dinner tonight because I want you to meet my fiancé," I chuckled. I knew that shit would get to Sonja. I had to rub it in and fuck with her.

"Kanan, so you want me to meet your fiancé, seriously?" She asked. Sonja knew I was fuckin' with her. I was playing a dangerous fuckin' game, but Amber wanted it, so she needs to be prepared for what's coming. She was persistent about meeting her.

"Kanan, I wish you would stop fuckin' playing with me and cut your bullshit out. You ain't even my nigga so why would she want to meet me. If you got a fiancé that's cool, I'm happy for you. I wish I could've lived happily ever after with my fiancé, but you ruined that. You're getting to be a bit bold," she argued.

"Yes, she wants to meet my baby mother," I chuckled and laughed. I knew I was getting up under her skin. She had the nerve to let some slick shit roll off her tongue.

"Last I checked, that bitch was dead, right? You watched me pop her ass. Wherever you buried her, you and your fiancé can meet her there," she argued. "Kanan, stop playing these childish ass games. I know you miss me, but damn, you're doing too much. I'm not with it."

"Stop playing and meet me at Spondivits at 9:00 p.m. Be on your best behavior. Leave that hood shit at the door; you know how you can act," I chuckled. I knew Sonja was getting pissed, and I also knew that she would show her face. She loves a challenge. She's never been one to back down.

"Whatever games you and your little bitch are playing Kanan, I'm warning you now, you don't want to fuck with me. I'm sick of you and your bullshit. You need to grow the fuck up," she argued and yelled. "I'm tired of you and all the extra shit you've been doing. Just yesterday, you walked in Deuce's funeral being very disrespectful. Here you go today with some more bullshit. I feel like shooting your motherfuckin' ass. Leave me the fuck alone. My life was so much better when you were in jail."

"You started this shit, so I'm going to finish this shit. Don't be late," I stated. I'm very intrigued by Sonja's last statement. I knew she was tired of me. I also knew that she wasn't going anywhere. Any man that attempted to date her had a price on their head, just like Deuce. One shot, one motherfuckin kill. Not too many men were willing to die for being with a female that's off limits. If they did, they were looking for a reason to die anyway. If they wanted me to take them out of their misery, then I had no problem doing that.

Sonja   ☆

I can't believe Kanan called me with this bullshit. He had my blood pumping. I wanted to smack the shit out of his ass so fuckin' bad. We're grown as fuck, but he still wanted to play games. I looked at the phone and had an evil scowl on my face. I wish he would've saw my facial expression. A part of me wanted to stay at home but the devil was on my back telling me to pull this nigga and this bitches hoe card. She couldn't have known who the fuck I was and what I meant to him. It's cool because she was about to get introduced. I got rolled up and I put on my Sunday's best. I had to put on for this nigga and this bitch since they sent for me. Spondivits was the spot and it's no telling who I might run into and hurt Kanan's feelings in the process.

I made it to Spondivits a little after 9:00 p.m. I wasn't arriving on time just because he said so. I don't know who Kanan thought I was but I'm still the baddest bitch. Ain't a damn thing changed. I gave the host my name and she escorted me back to where he was seated. I stood there for a minute and looked at this crazy ass nigga. I can't believe him. I knew he was reaching. I'm wondering what the hell could be going through his damn mind.

Kanan has gone batshit fuckin' crazy approaching me with this ditzy ass bitch named Amber.

She looks familiar. I can't remember where I know her from, but I know that bitch. He's talking about he wanted me to meet his new fiancé. Oh really, motherfucka. Last I checked, you killed mine, but you got a fiancé suddenly. I swear he's too old for this shit. I'm not even going to knock her young ass out, because she's a beautiful lady and now she's mixed up in his bullshit with a target on her back. I'm just saying though, why are your kids at my house?

What I am going to do is fault her young dumb ass for not taking the time out to do her damn research. She couldn't have gotten the full background check on me. She should've really taken the time out to inquire about me because a motherfucka would've told her I'm not the one. I looked at Kanan and just smiled. I knew he was up to no good. He looked at me, begging me with his eyes for me not to cut up. He already knew what was up.

Amber reached her hand out to me, attempting to be cordial. She wanted to shake my hand so bad. I didn't trust this bitch she had the biggest smile on her face.

Something was up with this bitch. The worst thing a bitch can do is write a check that she can't cash. My name holds weight out in these streets when it comes to fuckin' with this nigga. I just looked at her hand. I wasn't shaking it.

"I'm not trying to be rude, but you can take it how you motherfuckin' want too. I don't know what HE fuckin' told you about me, but there's no need for introductions. If you valued your life, YOU would think twice about this situation and stepping in the room with me on some slick shit. Tell Kanan it was nice fuckin' knowing him.

Baby girl let me tell you something and trust me on this one. It's a fact and not an opinion. You really don't want or need the extra drama that's comes with fuckin' with a nigga like him," I argued and sassed. She just stood there looking stupid, so I politely opened my purse. I pulled out my Glock 45. It was purple and so fuckin' cute. I stepped in her personal, showing her how real shit was about to get. I pressed my gun to her temple. "Listen you got about five minutes to clear this motherfucka or else your smile, along with all thirty-two of your teeth will be plastered all over this fuckin' restaurant." Kanan just stood there looking at me with a big ass grin on his face.

"Sonja, you need to chill out with all this bullshit you're doing," he argued and yelled. Kanan wasn't talking about shit. He wanted me to do this, that's why he called me here.

"Whatever. You sent for me, so I came. I'm not fuckin' with you. You're the one that keeps fuckin' with me. You and your bitches. I don't mind offing these bitches and stacking up my body count. Long as you feel like it's cool to constantly bring these broads to my face, then I'm cool with rocking their ass to fuckin' sleep. One thing for sure and two things for certain, Sonja Harris ain't never been scared to pop the fuck off," I argued and explained. I left out the same way I came in.

Amber

I couldn't stand that bitch Sonja for nothing. I'm not for sure if she knew who I was but I felt like she was trying to piece together a puzzle. She got everything she motherfuckin' wanted, when she wanted it. It was cool though because I had some shit on her that would shake up her and Kanan's world. I'm sure after I drop this information her and Kanan will be a thing of the fuckin' past. If he knew what I knew he wouldn't want her anymore. I was coming for Sonja extra hard for this reason alone. I wanted her to look me in the face because I was that bitch that was about to set her fuckin' soul on fire. She gave me nothing but her ass to kiss.

I wanted to be patient and approach her by herself with this situation, but no, she wanted to fuck with me when she saw me with Kanan. She was putting on and showing out for what. He brought you here to let you know that we were together. It was all good because in the end, I would have the last laugh and Kanan. Nobody fucks with Amber Bum Biyae and lives to laugh about it. Let the games begin. I'm bringing it bitch. Let me call my brother, but I need to muster up my crocodile tears first. I started crying in the phone instantly so he would know that something was wrong. He answered on the second ring.

"Amber, what's wrong? Did he put his hands on you?" He asked. Ali Bum Biyae is my oldest brother. I knew he was curious as to why I was crying. "I want to know why my sister is fuckin' upset. If Kanan put his hands on you, it's going down. It's fucking over for him and I mean that shit. Amber, do you hear me?"

"Yes, Ali. Sonja and I just had a little scuffle, that's all. She messed my face up," I cried and lied. Fuck Sonja. That bitch had something I wanted, Kanan. I knew my brother was still in love with Sonja, but I didn't give a fuck. That bitch had some secrets that I needed light to be shed on and I needed him to help me air them out.

"What happened Amber, and don't leave shit out?" He argued and yelled. Ali knew how overdramatic I could be. I didn't want him to know that I was lying about this shit. I gave Ali the run-down of what happened between us. Ali knew I was dangerous and couldn't be trusted sometimes. He was my brother and he would ride with me regardless.

"She's mad because Kanan chose me over her. He introduced us at dinner tonight. She was so upset that she put her hands on me," I cried and lied. The lie just rolled off my tongue perfectly. Damn, being messy I just slipped up. My brother didn't even know shit between Kanan and I was that serious.

"I thought you said you and Kanan were friends. When did shit get serious? Why would Sonja be mad? Last I checked, she was mourning the loss of her fiancé. Are you telling me that her and Kanan are messing around again," He asked and argued?

"I'm not for sure if they're messing around Ali but I think they are. Kanan and I are serious. He wants to marry me. I think he told Sonja that and she requested to meet me, and we had a fight," I cried.

"I'm livid. I can't believe this shit. Sonja must be ready for Kanan to die. I know she didn't forget about our agreement. Stay away from Kanan because I don't want you to get caught up in their shit. It's dangerous," he argued and explained. Ali and I finished talking. He gave me the rundown of the agreement Sonja had with him years ago. I couldn't believe the shit he was telling me.

Ali said he was coming to the states and he had some valuable information that would be at my fingertips in a few days. Sonja's going to regret the day she ever crossed paths with me because the secret that she's been hiding is liable to land her with a bullet in her mouth soon. I wanted to be there and capture the moment.

A MONTH LATER

Chapter-19

Kaniya

Ugh, today was our last day in Jamaica. I didn't want to leave at all. I begged Tariq to stay another week. He gladly declined. You see how men do. I didn't want to come here in the first place, but now I don't want to leave. He's been spoiling me like crazy since he found out I was pregnant. I'm fourteen weeks now. I'll know what I'm having in four to six weeks. I want two boys. We went to the Cayman Islands last week and it was so beautiful. I mean the water was so beautiful. If you were swimming, you could see tons of fish, sea urchins, and jellyfish. It was a sight to see.

I wanted to eat some conch, but Tariq refuses to let me eat any fish that he hasn't heard of, so oysters and snails were out of the equation. I have accumulated so much shit these past four weeks, you wouldn't believe it. Even though I couldn't drink, I was bringing back three cases of Hennessy White. Oh lord, it was almost time to face the music. That's the real reason I wasn't ready to go home. I didn't want to run into Lucky and explain this shit.

I'm a big girl and I can own up to my mistakes. Ever since I found out I was expecting; my stomach has started to grow. My mom is going to trip. I hate to have this conversation with my dad. I'm looking forward to speaking with Killany, Barbie, Ketta, Riley, and Tianna. I know Killany will tell my dad as soon as she finds out.

"Kaniya, let's go. It's time to board the jet," he yelled. I took my time because I didn't want to leave this. He looked at me and smiled. My face was turnt up and my lips were pouty. "I'm ready to leave Jamaica. I feel like we've been gone long enough. It's time for me to resurface. I'm ready to go home and I need you to see some doctors in the USA to make sure my seeds are good."

"Okay," I pouted and whined. Tariq and I took our seats on the jet. I wasn't ready to go home yet. It is what it is. Why did I have to get pregnant with twins? I knew that shit would happen. It'll be just my luck the babies were Tariq's and Lucky would kill me.

Kaisha

I'm so glad my baby is back. Kaniya's ass is fuckin' pregnant. She's been gone for four weeks and the only thing she's been popping is pussy. She said she was fourteen weeks pregnant, and she's not sure who the father is. It's between Lucky and Tariq. Only my child would be able to pull some shit like this off. She knows I'm too fly to be a grandma. Hot ass doesn't even know who fathered her children. Yes, she's having twins! Tariq don't even care, he wants to be with her regardless.

Lucky, on the other hand, is going to flip the fuck out. Tyra is haunting me from her grave. I hope and pray Kaniya's babies aren't Tariq's. I will dig Tyra's ass up and spit on that bitch. I like Tariq for my daughter to be honest. For that reason, I won't tell Kaniya about my past. I still need to have a conversation with Sonja. Let me call her ass. It's been killing me not to reach out to her. It's been long overdue. Kanan gave me her number, so I'll called her.

"Hello, can I speak with Sonja," I asked and sucked my teeth. I knew that was her. She still sounded the same, but you could never be too sure.

"This is she, who is this?" She asked. She had an attitude. She knew it was me, Kaisha with the motherfuckin' K.

"Your worst fucking nightmare," I sassed and sucked my teeth. I could hear the attitude and irritation in Sonja's voice.

"Kaisha, I know this is your messy ass. Don't to many people call my phone talking shit besides your daughter," she laughed. "I can't believe you Kaisha. You're still messy and with the shit like you used to be. I see where Kaniya gets that shit from."

"What's up, Sonja? How are you? I heard you were on the run from Kanan. I'm sorry for your loss," I explained. Deuce was a good guy, but he didn't have a chance fuckin' with Kanan. Sonja knew Kanan told me everything about the two of them, but I didn't want to go into too many details.

"Girl, I'm not paying Kanan any attention! I heard you were in town stalking Killian. I was wondering if you were going to call me for drinks and lunch," she laughed. Sonja wanted me to know that she had been talking to Killian. I'm sure he told her about me bodying one of his hoes.

"You heard fuckin' wrong. Don't play with me! Kanan will find Killian dead if I was really stalking him. Yes, we need to meet up. I can't believe you let Tariq's grown ass get ahold of my daughter. You know I have to see you about that shit," I sassed and sucked my teeth.

"Wait a damn minute, Kaisha! I told Kaniya's hardheaded ass to stay away from him. Did she listen? Hell fuckin', no. She's hardheaded just like her momma's hot ass. I told Tariq too!"

"Sure, you did! When are we meeting up?" I asked. I was ready to see my old friend at this point. It's been to long since we had seen each other and had fun.

"We can meet up Friday! I'll shoot you the time and place. Is that cool with you?" She asked. Hell yeah, we could link up. I was ready to see Sonja's crazy ass.

"You have my number, text me the spot." It felt like old times talking with Sonja again. I can't wait to see her. It's been too long. I knew we were about to have some fun. We had lots of catching up to do. Sonja was a good friend of mine when I lived in Atlanta. I should've stayed here and raised my girls. Sonja is going to get more than drinks and food when we link up. It's to many secrets and it's time to air a few of them out.

I spoke with Kaniya and she agreed to come out with us. I pray every night that Kaniya's babies aren't Tariq's. I know that's bad and the only thing I should pray for is my daughter to have a smooth delivery and healthy kids. I don't want anything related to me to have the same blood line as Tyra Harris. That bitch was a pain in my ass. I had to give it to her, though. She had some balls when she knocked on my door, but that bitch should've asked about Kaisha Miller in these motherfuckin' streets. I invited Killian to come through so Kaniya can tell him that she's pregnant. I hope that nigga doesn't ask who the daddy is because he will nut the fuck up.

He'll have enough drama, so he won't be able to dig in to Kaniya's ass just yet. She's so scared to tell him that she's pregnant. She can tell Killany herself. I hope she's ready because I'm ready to get this show on the road. Her fat ass takes all day to get dressed. I was ready to go back home anyway. I don't think she'll be able to have the birthday party she wanted since she's pregnant. She needs to focus on Work Now Atlanta. Tariq refuses to let her come back to her house. He keeps security on her ass like she's Michelle Obama. He loves her though. I love how he loves her.

Sonja

Kaisha's crazy ass made my fuckin' day. I haven't heard from her in years! Killian told me she was in town. I was wondering when she was going to reach out to me so we could kick it. I wish Kaisha and Killian would've worked out. I never knew what happened between them, but I know Kaisha left his ass and took the girls. Speaking of girls, I forgot Kaisha had twins. Where the hell is the other daughter? I'll ask her when I see her.

"Auntie, can I go with you to meet Kaniya's mom? I want to meet her," Raven asked. She wanted to meet Kaniya's mom since she's heard so much about her. I think Raven would like Kaisha because she's crazy about Kaniya.

"Sure, you can come. I'll call Chelle to see if she wants to come also. I'm sure she'd love to see Kaisha too. It'll be so much fun. Kaniya is Kaisha all over again, but worse. I'll call Kaniya so she can come too!" I noticed her car was gone from my house. Since when does she come to my house and not come in? She knows I'm going to cuss her ass out. She must have something she's trying to hide. Tariq hasn't called me either. I called Chelle and she answered on the first ring.

"Hey, Chelle, I'm having dinner and drinks with Kaisha Friday. I want you to come," I stated. I invited Chelle because I knew she was crazy about Kaisha too. Back in the day we used to cut the fuck up. I knew we would have some serious fun.

"Oh, hell no, my girl Kaisha is in town? Hell yeah, I'm coming. It's about to be some shit." Chelle couldn't wait to see Kaisha. I knew the fun and fuckery was about to begin because Kaisha was a fool.

"Girl, her crazy ass just called me talking shit. I can't wait to see her," I beamed proudly. I was so excited too. I knew how Kaisha could be and we always cut up together.

"Me either. I'll be ready. Whenever you come, just pick me up. I'm getting drunk Friday," she explained and laughed. Chelle was ready and it's just what she needed to feel a little better about being in Atlanta.

"Okay, I'll talk to you later."

Barbie

My sister called me on FaceTime as soon as she got back. I was so happy to see her. She said Tariq had her ducked off in Ocho Rios, Jamaica. I knew she had a good time because it was written all over her face. She was glowing. That nigga was laid up behind her while we were on Facetime. I can't lie because I've never seen the two of them together, but they did look good together. She was happy and that's all I wanted for her. Why would he kidnap her like that, though? He apologized for the casualties. We had so much catching up to do. I need to book a flight because some shit needs to be discussed in person.

I can't believe she's pregnant and doesn't know who fathered my nieces or nephews. I need to hurry up and get my ass back to Atlanta. I told her Lucky was going to kill her ass when he caught her, and she didn't find shit funny about that. She needed to be prepared for that shit because it was coming. Atlanta is not that big and trust me that nigga can smell her a mile away. I also told her that the two of them need to schedule a sit down.

Don't get me wrong, I don't care much for Lucky, but I know for a fact they love each other. I know before she left, they were working on them. He took her kidnapping hard. She said she did call him, and he was talking shit. What did she think the man was going to do? Now she's popping back on the scene with Tariq, and that shit don't sit right with me. Lucky isn't about to let that shit go down.

I'm all for trying new shit, but I just don't see this working out well. I just want my sister to be happy no matter who she's with. I'm happy she's back and in good health. I hope Tariq's ready because Lucky will be bringing it. Tariq didn't appear to be a pussy ass nigga. I'm sure he could hold his own. I need some popcorn for the shit that's about to pop off. I hope the twins are Lucky's because if they ain't, Kaniya won't live long enough to have them.

Ketta

I'm so happy my best friend was back, alive and in good health. I was worried sick about her. I can't wait to see Tariq because I'm going to punch his ass. I'm Team Tariq, though. I like him for Kaniya. I know Lucky will be pissed once he finds out Kaniya's pregnant and it might not be his. I don't even want to be a fuckin' fly on the wall when he hears this or even see it.

Kaniya told us her and Tariq were having sex. If she had sex with him, baby his dick had to be extra good because she's pregnant suddenly. I remember when she told us all he was doing was eating her pussy. Nah, that nigga was laying some pipe too. You see sneaky pussy always get caught up. It's cool, though. I can't judge her because I'm ready to give Don a baby now.

Don said he had a bone to pick with Kaniya. He couldn't wait to come back to Atlanta to see her ass. She sounded good and I was glad to hear from her ass. I told her we had to stay in Atlanta for an extra three weeks because we were under investigation for the murders she helped commit. She fell out laughing. We stayed on the phone for a few hours reliving that night.

That's what we were supposed to do after we left the club. She said she wanted to see us. I wanted to see her too because I missed her. I can't lie our summer has been lit as fuck. I told her about the fight I had with Niema and she was pissed that she didn't get to beat any ass. She had the nerve to ask me if Barbie recorded it. She is too much, man. I felt Don walk up behind me and slid my panties and leggings down. I already knew what time it was. I arched my back giving him access to fit in my tight and wet walls. Don placed his hands on my ass cheeks. He started plunging away. It was hard for me to keep my perfect arch. He bit my ear. I could never get used to Don and his back shots. I swear I could feel him in my stomach. The only sounds you could hear was ass slapping against his balls.

"Ketta, I want you to have my child," he grunted in my ear.

"I want to have your child too. I'm ready," I moaned. I thought I would've been pregnant by now. I can't think of the last time Don has pulled out.

"Make an appointment with an OBGYN so we can see what's up. I know we should have something cooking by now," he explained. I guess he was reading my mind. I had plans to do that.

TWO DAYS LATER

Chapter - 20

Yirah

So, I've still been chilling and kicking it with Lucky for about two months now. Lately, well since Kaniya is out the picture, we've been kicking it heavy, real fuckin' heavy. He has the keys to my crib, and I've been using a few of his whips as my daily driver. We're not in a committed relationship, but I like him. Shit, I love him. He does real boss shit, and he's been catering to all my needs. I think the reason that he didn't want to commit to me is because of Kaniya.

He thought I was stupid, but I know he's waiting for her to come back. If Lucky only knew what I knew about his ex, he would've committed to me a lot sooner. I've seen the pictures of Kaniya and Tariq in Jamaica. They looked happy and good together. I also noticed a pudge. I know all of this because Tariq and my brother, Mac and John, are best friends. Tariq has been in love with Kaniya for a very long time. I met her at his coming home party in May where I exposed her ass. Let me tell you this, that nigga was so into her, he didn't even recognize the other pussy in the room. Their chemistry lit up the room. I wanted Lucky to see what I saw.

I hate to rain on Lucky's parade, but Kaniya isn't coming back. My loyalty is with Mac and Tariq! If Lucky was my man, then yes, I would put him up on game but he's not yet. He's about to be and I got this nigga in the bag. It is what it is. He's doing him and I'm doing me. Tariq deserves a good girl. Shaela dogged him out when he did his bid. From what I've heard and seen, Kaniya is a rider. I'm rooting for them.

Mac told me that Tariq and Kaniya were back in town and that shit was like music to my fuckin' ears. I'm going to invite Lucky to Mac's party. I wanted him to see Kaniya and Tariq together, pregnant. If I could get her out the picture for good and secure my position in Lucky's life, I was willing to do that. I don't give a fuck whose feelings would be hurt. My feelings wouldn't be hurt. I'll be there waiting with my arms, mouth and legs wide open.

Tariq

Kaniya and I have been back in the states for about four days now. It's the first of the month and I had to get back to this fuckin' money. I had to re-up and do a lot of shit. I got three mouths to feed so it's time to grind because I didn't want Kaniya to lift a finger. Since Kaniya was carrying my kids I had to buy us a house. She picked out something that she liked a few days ago. So, we've been busy picking out furniture and shit and whatever else she wanted. Today was my niggas Mac birthday! He was having a kickback barbecue at his house. It wasn't anything to big or small, just a few people that we kicked it with from time to time. I couldn't wait to get up with my niggas.

Yirah was throwing the kickback for him. John and I gave her the money a few weeks ago. I know Mac was waiting on me to show my face real soon. I said I would be there, but he didn't believe me. He'll see me in the flesh in a few hours. I've been busy handling business since I've been back. I haven't had the time to pull down on them yet. John sent me a text and he wanted to know if I was going to make it or not. I told him I was in the city handling business. We have some major work to do. I wouldn't miss this shit for the world. I missed to many birthday's and I wasn't missing this one.

Kaniya acted like she didn't want to go, but that wasn't an option. We were together so I wanted everybody to know. When they see her in the streets, they need to know that's me. I have a lot of stuff to do for this barbecue since it starts at 7:00 p.m. I had to get super fresh. Louie this, Louie that, Louie everything! My nigga made it to see twenty-nine with no kids or felonies. Mac was a straight bachelor.

He has a couple special females in his life. I hope he wasn't inviting any of them to my barbecue because his game wasn't too tight. The last thing I wanted was for my nigga to get caught up in some bullshit on his birthday. My first stop was the barbershop. I need a fresh line, my goatee trimmed, and my dreads re-twisted.

Kaniya

Tariq and I finally came back to the States after being in Jamaica for a month. I loved Jamaica, but it's just too damn hot. I couldn't eat the Jerk chicken like I wanted to because of heartburn. Tariq didn't want me eating anything spicy. Baby, when I say Tariq plays for motherfuckin' keeps out here. I knew I would love him way too much. First, I feared that shit, but now I'm open and ready to accept what he's offering. This man had me so fuckin' gone already and he didn't even know it. I swear he's swept me off my feet.

We've been home for a few days now. Yes, I said home because I agreed to move in with him. So, he brought us a house. The only person that knows I'm home is my mother. Yes, it's official. Tariq and I are together, and I don't care who knows. I'm fourteen weeks pregnant with twins. The babies are kicking my ass and I'm sick all the time. They could either be Lucky's or Tariq's. I told Tariq and he was livid at first, but now he's cool and he knows the chances. He's so easy to talk to and that's another plus. I can lay my feelings on the line with Tariq because our relationship is different. I'm not scared to tell him what I'm thinking.

Ugh, I don't even know how to tell Lucky. Let me correct that, I don't want to tell Lucky because I already know how he's going to take this. He is going to trip, I know him. I'll cross that bridge when I get there. I really don't care because I can raise my kids by myself. I don't need a nigga to front me shit. I'm always buying my own. Tariq refuses to let me go to my house. He made me move in with him. He thinks I'm going to run back to Lucky but I'm not. He hasn't given me a reason to do that so I'm good. We are going to Mac's birthday party tonight. I really didn't feel like going anywhere, but he insisted. I'm still having my birthday party, pregnant or not.

I had to find something cute to wear. I was showing. My stomach was already sticking out a little. I found a cute little white maxi dress. I took a bath earlier. I washed my hair and styled it into a Mohawk. I wanted to be comfortable. I slid my feet into a pair of white Chuck Taylors. It's too hot for make-up. I just coated my lips with a nude pink lip. Tariq walked up behind me and placed his hands on my stomach. He rested his face in the crook of my neck.

"I love you," he stated. I rested my head on his chest. Our eyes connected.

"I love you too."

Lucky

I've missed Kaniya something serious. She's been gone for over a month. We've never been apart this long. I know our last conversation wasn't the best, but she knew where the fuck I was coming from. I don't know if she's okay or not... I take that back; I know she's okay, probably more than I would like her to be. I must move on, I got to. I know she gave my pussy away to that nigga. I have needs also. If it's meant to be, we'll find our way back to each other.

I've been kicking it with Yirah for a few months. I really liked Yirah. Unlike Melanie, she knew how to play her position, her lips weren't loose. I liked Yirah way more than I should. She knows all about Kaniya and our situation. We both agreed we should just be friends and I was cool with that until my heart comes back. Honestly, I don't think I could take Kaniya back after this. She up and disappeared with a nigga and not just any nigga, but Tariq. That shit doesn't sit well with me at all. In due time he and I will see each other. I'm not going to do too much talking. I can't take Kaniya back after this, but Tariq will feel me, though.

Yirah invited me to her brother's barbecue. This would be the first time I would meet some of her family. Something was telling me not to go, but something was telling me to go. The only reason I considered going was because she damn near begged me to. I would do it just for her. She's been a good girl and very patient with me. I wasn't planning on staying that long. I had to meet up with Quan later anyway.

I never met her brothers and I don't think I know him. I pulled up to his spot. He stayed in Cobb County. I didn't fuck with Cobb County to tough and that's another reason I wouldn't be staying too long. I called Yirah to let her know that I was outside, and she said she was coming out front. She made her way to me. Yirah was beautiful and very bad. I needed to cuff her. I loved her lips and her body was sick. She could do a little something in the kitchen also.

I had feelings for her, and that shit was foreign to me. I wouldn't give her my heart though because that was taken. We made our way to the backyard and the setup was nice. I met her brother and I feel like I knew that nigga from somewhere. I couldn't remember from where, though. How about my DJ was on the ones and twos tonight!

I chopped it up with her brother and some of her people. Yirah fixed me a plate and we sat on one of the benches that were outside, and she fed me bite for bite. She knew how to cater to a nigga. I appreciated her for that. We chopped it up and talked for a while. I was enjoying myself. No drama, this barbecue was cool.

"Bae, I need to go use the bathroom. You cool out here by yourself or do you need to come to the bathroom with me?" She asked. Yirah wanted me to escort her to the bathroom. I knew she wanted to fuck. She can't stay off this dick. She poked her lips out and started pouting. She ran her tongue across her teeth. I knew she wanted to suck on me. "You look edible and I want to taste you."

"I'm good. You just want me to go to the bathroom with you. I'll break you off later," I explained. Yirah went to the bathroom. She was gone for a minute, so I was sitting back, checking shit out paying attention to my surroundings. I looked up and I saw Tariq and Kaniya. I had to do a double-take to make sure my eyes weren't playing tricks on me.

My blood started pumping instantly. What were the chances I would run into these two motherfuckas? I sat back and peeped shit out. I know this is Yirah's brothers shit and I'm out numbered but that's still my bitch. Tariq already knew we were about to have some motherfuckin' problems. Ain't shit pussy about me. He knew it was on right motherfuckin' here. I don't give a fuck.

Ain't this some shit! Mac, John, and Tariq chopped it up for a long time. That's where I knew that nigga from. He runs with Tariq's weak ass. That nigga knew who I was the whole fuckin' time. Yirah invited me to this shit, she insisted that I come. I wonder if she knew these motherfuckas would be here. She had to know they were going to be here. I'm glad I came though because this nigga was about to feel me. I owed him one. I can't believe Kaniya and Tariq are here. I was just thinking about her fuckin' ass before I pulled up. Kaniya has gotten thick as fuck and that confirmed my suspicions that she was fuckin' this nigga. The DJ played **Future's Astronaut Chick**

> **You amaze me on a whole another level**

> **Me and you we light up the room when we're together**

> **Every time we have sex, we gotta break a sweat**

It's a wrap. The devil was on my back telling me to air this motherfucka out. A motherfucka can't disrespect me without any repercussions.

They danced liked no one else was in the room. He kept rubbing her stomach and he kissed her on the mouth. That shit set me off and made me sick. I had to call Quan and let him know this shit. She was really booed up with this nigga. I must let her, and this fuckin' nigga know. I'm up in this bitch and I see them.

It's taking everything in me not to walk up and smack her ass and leave this nigga leaking. I got a good look at her stomach. Oh hell no and she's fucking pregnant.

That's why he was feeling on her stomach. I need some answers. Tariq is about to feel me today. Ain't no hoe shit over here. I don't give a fuck where I'm at or whose crib I'm at. I told this nigga when I see him it was on, and today was the day. Don't believe me, just motherfuckin' watch. I ran down on Kaniya and Tariq. I tapped her on her shoulder like I was the motherfuckin' police. I damn near took the skin off her shoulder.

"Hey Kaniya, baby I missed you," I argued and yelled. I wanted her to feel me. I pushed up on her the same way she did me when she caught me and Melanie together. I bet she wasn't expecting this shit. I heard her mumble under her breath, she wasn't too loud but enough for me to hear what the fuck she said.

"Oh shit, what the fuck is Lucky doing here?" She asked. I knew her heart dropped. I could see the blonde hairs appear on her neck. She knew shit was about to go left quick with me and Tariq in the same fuckin' room after the kidnapping happened. Tariq looked at me. He already knew what fuckin' time it was.

"What's up kidnapper, you finally brought my heart back? I told you when I see you it was on. I'm not going to shoot this bitch up, but it's on," I argued and yelled. I pushed Kaniya out the way and I was in this niggas face. I grabbed the gun out of my back pocket quick. I smashed that motherfucka in Tariq's face quick. I went in on Tariq's jaw and we started fighting. We were going blow for blow. I don't give a fuck. I guarantee you this nigga will tap out before me. I had one up on Tariq because I smashed my gun in his face. Tariq shook it off and bounced back quick.

I heard somebody yelling for John and Mac and they ran over. I guess they thought they were about to gang me to help this nigga. If they ganged me, I put it on Tariq they wouldn't live passed midnight. I got a fuckin' pump in my trunk that will lay everybody fuckin' down. Oh yeah, they were about to try me.

"Oh, hell motherfuckin' no, this shit is not about to go down on my watch. Don't get me wrong, I like y'all John and Mac, but y'all motherfuckas will not body HIM on my watch. Tariq knew this shit was coming. I'm strapped anywhere I fuckin' go," she yelled. I heard Kaniya cock back two fuckin' guns. I looked over my shoulders and she had two Mac 11's. I just shook my head. I knew she was about to let that motherfucka rip. John and Mac really drew down on me. Kaniya had the Mac 11's rested on their temples. I knew she had one in the chamber. She let those niggas know what fuckin' time it was.

"Y'all pussy as niggas better fuckin' kill me," I argued and yelled.

"I need y'all to raise the fuck up off Lucky before I let this shit rip. I'm counting to motherfuckin' two. Mac, I don't want you to die on your birthday and at your crib, but this isn't your mess. This is our mess. I understand Tariq is your nigga and you have his back, but Lucky was my nigga and I have his back in these types of situations, when nobody is here for him. For that reason alone, I can't let you do him and I won't let you do him." She made that shit clear to John and Mac. I raised up and kept my eyes trained on these motherfuckas. I might not kill these motherfuckas today BUT TOMORROW ain't fuckin' promised. She didn't give a fuck who was watching. If they wanted smoke, she was going to smoke these two motherfuckas out.

"Kaniya, put that shit up before you get hurt and you're pregnant with my babies," he argued and explained. I know Tariq didn't say what the fuck I think he said. He wanted to let me know that Kaniya was pregnant by him.

"Kaniya, please tell me you are not pregnant by this nigga and babies? Are you having twins?" I asked. I was fuming hot at this point to know that the love of my life was pregnant and possibly by another nigga.

"It's possible that they're yours, too," she explained. "I had plans to tell you that I was pregnant, but I didn't plan on telling you today at this fuckin' barbecue," she explained.

"How far along are you?" I asked. I wanted to know if there was a strong possibility that I fathered her children.

"Fourteen weeks," she sighed. She knew I was calculating the time in my head.

"Oh, they're mine, that's unless you were fucking him the whole time," I argued and yelled. I knew for a fact they were mine, but it makes sense now why Tariq would think they were his also. He fucked Kaniya around the same time, too. I knew she fucked that nigga, but she wouldn't stop lying about that shit. She knew I would've beat her ass for fuckin' off.

"You know what, Lucky? We can discuss this shit somewhere else and at another time," she sassed and sucked her teeth. I knew Kaniya was mad, at this point. "I don't like your choice of words, and I don't want everybody in my fuckin' business. I ain't got shit to hide since you're putting it out there. I don't care who fathered mine because I'm their mother. Regardless MINE will be straight with or without their father." I felt somebody walk up behind me and wrapped their arms around my waist. I knew it was Yirah. Kaniya's eyes were trained on me and this is the last thing I needed.

"Baby, what's going on?" She asked. I know she witnessed everything go down.

"I'm having a conversation with my baby's momma," I explained. I need Yirah to shut the fuck up. I tried to dismiss her nicely.

"Mac, I'm sorry about your party. Tariq, I'm ready to go home. Can you take me home? You can come back and chop it up with your niggas," she sassed and sucked her teeth. If she wanted to go home, I'll take her.

"I'll take you home because we need to talk anyway," I explained. I swear I'm going to fuckin' hurt her the moment we pull off. I'm on one right now. I can't believe she had been fuckin' Tariq the whole time. I wanted to put my hands on her. She deserved to be smacked since she had me out here looking like a fool.

"I got her. She doesn't live there anymore," he explained. What the fuck did he mean that she didn't live there no more. I know she wasn't living with this nigga. Kaniya wants to fuckin' die. "She ain't your business Lucky, she's mine. I refuse to let you take her anywhere." He didn't want her running back to me.

He already knew what it was between us. He knew Kaniya was mine and she was coming back home regardless of what the fuck he was saying. She just should tell him who her loyalty was with.

"You're scared I'm going to kidnap her? I just need to holla at her. I'm not trying to step on your toes even though you stepped on mine. Walk me to my car Kaniya, so I can holla at you. I'm leaving anyway," I argued. I was cool on her. I wanted to smack the shit out of her, but I opted out for now because my heart was aching and I couldn't believe this shit. She walked me to my car and no words were spoken between us. I don't even want to hear her mouth. She knew I was about to spaz out. I can feel it and I can't let this shit ride.

"So, this is what we are doing now? You're pregnant with my kids and you're letting this nigga fuck on you. You've been out of town for a month. Did you think to call me? It's a possibility that they are not mine? That means you cheated on me. Your pussy is sneaky. I want to be at every fuckin' doctor's appointment. If these kids are not mine, you won't live to know about it; that's a promise.

Did you think I wouldn't find out? I knew you were pregnant the last few times I fucked you because your sneaky pussy ass was extra wet. If they are mine, I don't want him around my kids. I want full custody. I don't want to be with you anymore. I can't wait until that nigga fucks up. Just know that you can't come back to me.

You ain't shit to me but an average ass bitch that doesn't know who fathered her children. That's some hoe shit. I appreciate you for having my back out here. That's the most you could do. You're loyal, but your pussy ain't. I want to strangle your ass so fuckin' bad. I'll let you live another day because you might be pregnant with my seeds.

When did you start fucking him? Can you answer that for me? I knew you fucked him, but you denied it every time. That's the one thing that you couldn't keep it real about. You were supposed to be my most prized possession, but you gave that nigga my pussy. Fuck you, Kaniya. Don't call me for shit but when you find out the sex of my seeds. You're free to be with that nigga. Tariq, you can have her. She ain't shit but an average ass bitch," I argued and yelled. I hopped in my car and pulled the fuck off.

Kaniya dropped that shit on me like that. I wanted to die! I wanted to kill everything fuckin' moving! She will feel my pain for every day that I don't know if her babies are fuckin' mine. I'm sending her black roses every fuckin' day. I can't explain it. It's like the air left my body. She's still my little shooter. She didn't give a fuck who was around. She was ready to empty the clip on those niggas. She said she was counting to two and she was letting that bitch rip.

Yirah was sneaky, too! That's why she was pressuring me to be there. She wanted me to see that shit. That bitch wasn't down to ride. I guess what goes around comes around. I had plenty of bitches that were screaming they were pregnant by the kid! Every test came back, you are not the father'. Kaniya never knew about any of that shit.

If I never prayed in my life, I prayed those babies were mine. I promise you I'm taking them, and she can pay fuckin' child support. She was supposed to be my wife. Karma is a bitch when she eventually comes back around. I had to talk bad to her like that since I couldn't put my hands on her. I was so harsh on her because I wanted her to feel my pain.

Tariq

I can't believe Kaniya pulled this shit at my nigga's birthday party. I don't even know if I can rock with her after this. She disrespected the fuck out of me. I wanted to kill Lucky for talking so fuckin' reckless to her. I heard their whole conversation. I was surprised she didn't say shit or feed into it. I can't wait to dig in her ass. As soon as she hits the seat and we pull off its on. She's pregnant and she shouldn't be doing all that extra shit.

"Kaniya, you know you're wrong for that shit you pulled. Did you really think I would let you and your nigga draw down on me and my niggas for Lucky? Both of you would've motherfuckas would've died tonight. You had no fuckin' business doing that," I argued and explained.

"I'm not about to argue with you, Tariq. If you were in his position, I would've done the same thing for you, no questions asked," she argued. I knew Kaniya was irritated that I questioned her, but I don't give a fuck. My niggas looked at me like I needed to fuckin' choose. She had an attitude about what she was doing.

"Kaniya, I understand that, but I don't want you fuckin' doing that. You could've been hurt. Don't ever fuckin' disrespect me like that again," I argued. I was fuming hot with her.

"Oh, it's all about you now? What about me? Niggas and bitches are looking at me sideways. All I did was have my nigga's back and that was it," she sassed and sucked her teeth. I stopped at the stop sign. I can't believe she said that shit. She slipped up and mentioned that Lucky was her nigga.

"Oh, you consider him your nigga still?" I asked. I wanted her to know that I caught that. I wasn't letting that comment slide. She still considered Lucky as her nigga.

"You know what the fuck I mean, don't act," she argued. "Tariq, I don't appreciate what you were leading to. You know at this point fuck this conversation because it will never end."

"That's the problem. He's your ex and I'm your future, Kaniya. You need to ride with me at all fuckin' times," I argued and explained. "I don't care about what you meant. I don't want you to ever refer to Lucky as your nigga."

"The nerve of you, Tariq! Are we really having this fuckin' conversation? You are the reason this shit popped off. You kidnapped me, remember? You knew this day was coming, motherfucka. That's why I didn't want to come here. I wanted to avoid shit like this," she argued and yelled. I knew Kaniya was pissed. "You don't give a fuck about my feelings because you're still in your feelings and you're the one that caused this shit. You knew the day was coming just like I did. You just didn't know it would be today."

"You brought this on yourself, remember? You were the one fucking two niggas," he argued and yelled. I wanted to piss her off more than what she already was.

"You know what, Tariq? I'm not even about to argue with you about nann nigga I was fuckin'. My pussy was so good you had to kidnap me. My kids will be A1 regardless, trust me I got them with every breath in me. I don't need a nigga for shit, not even no hard dick. Take me home to Chateau Miller, please," she argued. "Tariq just know that I'm going to my home tonight. I refused to lay beside you with the shit that just rolled off your tongue. Fuck you. You're on my shit list now."

"Oh, so you want to go home now. I'll kidnap you again, Kaniya. You think this shit is a game but it's not. You told that nigga to meet you there, huh? You're trying to give him some of my pussy again. Guess what, I'm not taking you home. Every time we have a disagreement you want to run. That's not how relationships work. If you want to be with somebody, you work that shit out.

We can go home and work it out," I argued and explained. I refused to put up or feed into her antics. I wasn't taking her home. The thought of Lucky popping up was a strong fuckin' possibility… I couldn't seem to shake the thought. Whatever issues we had we were working them out tonight. I refused to lay alone and wonder if Lucky had got a hold of her. I couldn't take that.

"We can work it out another day because it will not be today. I'll call Uber or my momma, but I'm going to my house. I don't even want to talk to you with your disrespectful ass. You've done enough talking," she argued. "I refused to hear anything else out of your fuckin' mouth. You've said way too much already.

"You want me to hurt you, huh? I've told you about your mouth numerous times. Listen to me, Kaniya. Let me keep it real with you, Can I do that? You don't like the truth. I'm sorry, I shouldn't have said any of those things. I'm sorry, I apologize. God don't make no mistakes. I don't care about the circumstances. I'm with you and my kids regardless. You're the only woman that matters to me.

I'm sorry, I didn't mean to come at you like that. Let me make it up to you. I love you, Kaniya. I want you to be my wife. Will you marry me? Tell me you love me. You're that stubborn you can't say it back," I explained. I noticed Kaniya's whole mood change and she wasn't budging. I had to pull out some stops. I knew the shit I said just put my ass in the doghouse. She was trying to get to her house and away from me. "Since you want to be quiet, I hope that you're thinking about everything I just said. I'm ready to marry you, Kaniya."

Kaniya

Tariq doesn't play fair! All I wanted to do was go to my home, be by myself, cry it out and think about this shit that just happened. I never wanted Lucky to see me, not yet anyway. Eventually, we would have to see each other and have a conversation. I just didn't think that today would be the day. What am I going to do? I really don't care who fathered the twins; it's going to be some shit regardless on Lucky's end.

He talked to me like I was an average bitch in the streets. Never again after everything we've been through. I understand that he was hurt, but he didn't have to talk to me like that. Tears started pouring down my face instantly. I wiped my face with the back of my hand. He moved on with Yirah, but I didn't even bother to shed any light on that. It makes since now, why that bitch was so fuckin' friendly at Tariq's party. She probably was fuckin' him then.

I didn't even say shit back to him. I didn't even feel like arguing. I'm past that shit and fuckin' over it. That's another reason why I chose Tariq. He's grown and not immature like Lucky's ass. We can never stay mad at each other for too long. He suffocates me with love and attention, and he caters to all my needs. Yes, I will marry that nigga if he was serious. He keeps a smile on my face. I don't think I've been this happy in a while.

I'm glad he kidnapped me and fucked some sense into me. Despite what people may think, on the outside looking in, I do love Tariq. He's a breath of fresh air. I still needed to have a conversation with Sonja about Tariq and me. I spoke with Raven over the phone and she was happy for us. She was glad that Tariq and I finally made it official. The whole ride home Tariq kept catching glances at me, but I refused to look at him. I didn't want him to see me crying.

We finally pulled up to our house. He pulled in the driveway and killed the engine. He jumped out and opened the door for me and I pushed passed him. He was right on my heels. I went upstairs to our room and started packing a few of my things up. He snatched the bag out my hand. I tried to exit out the room, but he stopped me. He cupped my chin forcing me to look at him

"What, Tariq? I'm going home, I can't do this with you right now," I sighed.

"You are at home. Kaniya, I'm sorry. I didn't mean it; please stay I'm begging you."

Chapter-21

Kaniya

These past two weeks have been crazy. I swear my life is like a fuckin' roller coaster. After our little run in with Lucky, things between Tariq and I have been shaky. We argued the whole night after we saw Lucky. We haven't had sex in over a week. I couldn't go anywhere without him. He thought I was trying to run off with Lucky, but I wasn't. I called an Uber so I could go home, but he shot at the Uber driver. My mom said she wasn't coming because she didn't have time for our bullshit. I have too much stuff going on to be worried about what he thinks I'm doing.

I've been putting my time and energy in to Work Now Atlanta. I guess Lucky knew I was up here at my office working. He sent black roses to the office every fuckin' day. My office space was filled with black roses. It was just ridiculous. I wasn't bothered by it one bit.

He's been emailing me constantly about us. I refused to respond; I'm not opening those cans of worms again. He said what he had to say so I didn't know why he was still talking. Work Now Atlanta will be open in a few weeks. I've had a few applicants coming through today for some job training and resume workshops.

I'll offer those workshops here for free. I wanted to provide additional training for the community. I wanted to help people get back to work. I wanted to provide black women and men with successful resources and dress for success tips. I've linked up with a couple of businesses that are willing to staff some of the people from my agency.

If their qualifications and skills match and they have a clean background, they were guaranteed a position. I was thankful for that because that would mean I would have tons of people registering here a lot. I wanted my staffing service to be a facility that people can vouch for that puts you to work and not sending you on tons of interviews without any results. I wanted my business to standout.

Lucky

I was finally able to get ahold of Kaniya. Tariq has her on lockdown. Everywhere she goes, he's with her. I can't believe she had the nerve to have that Range Rover that I bought her towed to my fuckin' house. She thought I was playing with her, even though I wasn't fucking with her. I meant what the fuck I said when I told her I wanted to be at every doctor's appointment. I haven't been to one yet and it's been about two weeks since I last saw her.

Look at her sexy motherfuckin' ass. She knows she's not supposed to be drinking coffee with my babies. She's too busy on her laptop and not paying any attention to her surroundings. I know she's checking her emails, because I've been emailing her for weeks and she hasn't responded to one. She was posted up at Starbucks without a care in the world. I started to run up and snatch her ass, but I didn't get down like that.

"So, this is how you're doing shit now? I know you hear me fuckin' talking to you, Kaniya," I argued and yelled. I snatched her laptop up off the table at Starbucks. I had her attention now. Whatever she was working on would have to wait. She folded her arms across her chest. I heard her suck her teeth. She should choose her words wisely because I'm not the one.

"What, Lucky? What do you want with a hoe?" She asked and argued? I knew Kaniya had an attitude with me? She was still pissed about the last conversation we had. "I'm so fuckin confused about why you're here."

"Stop fucking playing with me. You know what the fuck I want," I argued and yelled. All eyes were on us. I was starting to get pissed with her and her nonchalant ass attitude. "You know what the fuck I want and you know you've been ignoring me." She tried to grab her laptop and walk to her car. I was right on her fuckin' hells. I grabbed her shirt, she turned around and looked at me.

"Lucky, I'm not even about to argue with you and get my blood pressure high today. I gladly pack up my shit and walk off. I'm not beat for your shit Jamel Lee Williams," she sassed and sucked her teeth

"You can't hold a fuckin' a conversation with a nigga? We'll be co-parenting soon," I argued and chuckled. I wanted her to know whether she liked it or not we were going to have to talk.

"We'll talk when that time comes," she sassed and sucked her teeth.

"Don't fuckin' walk away from me Kaniya, when I'm fuckin' talking to you. Just because you with that nigga you still fuckin' belong to me. You're really pissing me off with the way you're acting," I argued.

"Don't touch me or talk to me. What do you want Lucky, because I'm fuckin' done here?" She asked. "As far as I'm concerned, there was nothing for us to talk about. I was about to leave anyway."

"I want to talk to you. I've emailed you numerous times and you haven't responded," I argued. "I wanted to know why you're avoiding me. I know I talked crazy to you the last time we saw each other, but you know me, and you knew how I would react. What did you fuckin' expect, Kaniya?"

"You've talked enough, remember? Anytime you email me regarding us, you will never get a response," she argued and sucked her teeth. "Lucky, you've been emailing me like crazy wanting to meet up and talk about us. Nigga, there isn't an us. I'm not coming back this time."

"I just want to know why? Can you give me that much?" I asked. "Kaniya, I know I shouldn't be asking you this shit, but damn. I want to know how you just up and left me on some fuck me type of shit? For real because when you left, we were fuckin' working on us?"

"Lucky, when you cheated on me, did I ask you why? The difference is, I didn't cheat on you, we were broken up. The day after we broke up, I kicked it with Tariq and one thing led to another," she argued and sassed.

"Kaniya, you want to come clean now about how you fucked another nigga. Why are you just now telling me?" I asked. "I can't fuckin' believe you. Bitch, the day after we broke up. You let another nigga fuck. I wish I could choke the life out of your ass. Why did you fuckin' lie though?"

"Lucky, you have to many questions. Telling you I had sex with someone else was the hardest thing I ever had to do. I didn't want you to know, so there you fuckin' have it. Why do I have to explain? You never explained anything to me. I must go. I have a doctor's appointment on the 23rd at Emory, you're welcome to come," she explained. "I don't feel like answering any more questions. It's getting hot and I don't feel so good."

"I'm not finished talking. You've been gone over a month and all I can get is ten fuckin' minutes?" I asked. "Clearly, you're in a rush for some reason, but I want you to slow the fuck down."

"Saved by the phone," she beamed. Kaniya was busy smiling in her phone. She didn't notice me walk up. I snatched the phone out her hand. Tariq sent her a text. Her future I swear I'm going to fuckin' hurt her.

Wifey - Baby, I was getting some work done at Starbucks and Lucky popped up.

My Future - I know I have eyes on you, are you good? Do I need to pull up?

Wifey - I'm good. What do you want for dinner?

My Future - It doesn't matter. I'll cook if you want me too.

"Fuck your phone. Can you put that shit up before I break it? You checking in with that nigga, huh? You think he's your future, Kaniya. You and I both know I'll never let you ride off in the sunset with him," I argued. I'm pissed. She had the prettiest smile on her face texting that nigga.

"We're in a relationship and we check in with each other. I did the same thing with you, but you never responded. I guess some hoes had you occupied. What do you want to talk about? I have a meeting in an hour so make it quick," she stated. I knew she was lying.

"Answer this for me and you're free to leave. When that bitch ass nigga kidnapped you, we made love the same day and we were working on us. You're back and now you're in a full-fledged relationship with another man and you're pregnant with my seeds. Explain that shit to me," I argued. "I want you to explain this shit to me because you started a fuckin' war that you can't even put out."

"Yes, we were working on us. Even though you've moved on also. We don't need to have this discussion. You can talk about some other shit, but not us. We are not up for discussion," she stated. "I know you want answers, but I don't have them to give. When I wanted answers from you Lucky, you couldn't give me any."

"You don't want to shed light on your situation. Let me make this shit clear to you. I see you happy with that nigga. If you think for a minute that I'm about to let you and that nigga walk around here on some in love type shit and there are no consequences, you're sadly fuckin' mistaken. You know I'm not letting that shit happen. Every time I see that nigga, I'm bussing.

Don't get caught up in the crossfire. You'll make Fox 5 News also a pregnant woman shot. I don't want you, but I'll be damned if I let you be with him. Learn to be happy and single without him. You got me fucked up. I'm not sparing him. He stepped on my toes, so he'll get stepped on."

"You're so miserable. What did I ever do to you? Why can't I be happy without you? You can't stand to see me with somebody. It's cool for you to cheat on me and live a double life. I moved on and found somebody that's truly for me and I'm all that matters to him. He doesn't have time to entertain other females. I'm more than enough for him. You want to take that from me because I'm not with you. Fuck you. We can play body for body," she argued. "I'm tired of you with this crazy shit. Leave me the fuck alone."

"You're feeling some type of way about that, huh? You're really feeling him. Do you love him? I think you do. You remember how I killed ole boy in Miami and made you watch? I'm coming at Tariq the same fuckin' way, but harder, so be ready. You better not be in the way or I'll shoot your ass too, pregnant or not," I argued. I cupped Kaniya's chin roughly. "I can't wait to see my babies with or without their mother." Kaniya scratched my hands begging me to remove them from her face.

"I can't stand you. Stop fucking following me, stalker," she argued. I knew Kaniya was pissed at me. I couldn't accept the fact that she moved on and she was happy.

"I love you too, baby momma, more than you'll ever know," I laughed and blew her a kiss; I knew just what to do to piss Kaniya off.

"I like you too, baby daddy, probably less than you would like me too," she sassed and sucked her teeth. She knew that would piss me off also. I had something for Kaniya's ass. I can't believe she's in love with that nigga like that. I'm not even going to kill him just yet because she's pregnant and I don't want her to be upset, but I'm about to do some other shit.

When we were in Miami at my OG's birthday party, the chick that Tariq was with in Miami, I got her number. I knew this bitch would be useful in the future. I'm a smart guy and I didn't trust Tariq. I knew that fuck boy would be on some take my bitch type shit, but not kidnap my bitch type shit one day. I hate to rain on Kaniya's parade, but it is what it is.

I understand that nigga kidnapped you, but you do what you must do to survive and come back to me. I forgive you for whatever y'all did, but when you touched Georgia soil and you knew you were pregnant with my seeds, you should've ran off on that nigga the first chance you got, but nah, you wanted to continue to play house with him.

It's unfortunate Kaniya must deal with the consequences that's coming her way. I'm about to create some karma for her and Tariq. She thinks he's perfect. Let's find out and see if he can handle this pussy, I'm about to throw his way.

Chapter-22

Kaisha

I couldn't wait to meet up with Sonja tonight. Our schedules were a bit tight, so we couldn't see each other but today we're going to link up. It's been too long, and this link up was long overdue. Kaniya agreed that she's would come with me. I wanted to kill Lucky's black ass and Tariq after the text Kaniya sent me a few weeks ago. She sent me a text and told me they were at a cookout and Lucky was there with another bitch, but he got mad when he noticed Tariq and her together. Kaniya said Lucky talked so bad to her like she was an average bitch out here in these streets in front of everybody.

To make matters worse, her and Tariq got into it. He had the nerve to say she shouldn't have been fuckin' two niggas. You weren't worried about who she was fuckin' when you kidnapped her, though. I see he has a lot of mouth like his fuckin' mammy. I was going to Lucky's house to shoot his motherfuckin' shit up. Kaniya begged me not too. I called his ass up and gave him the business.

I let his motherfuckin' ass know off top. Don't you ever in your life fix your fuckin' mouth to talk bad about my daughter in front of people. When you know for a fact that you're a dog ass nigga too. You mad at her because she's with somebody else, but you already moved on with somebody else. Kaniya should've smacked the fuck out that bitch. To make matters worse, these niggas were about to kill you, but my daughter saved your fuckin' life. Now her and her nigga are beefing about you. Get the fuck out of here.

I gave his Keith Sweat begging ass the motherfuckin' business. I told him don't ever call my fuckin' phone again crying and begging me to get Kaniya to talk to him. I'll get Killian to beat his ass again. Please don't threaten my daughter about shit or you'll come up fuckin' missing. I don't make promises that I can't keep. I come through. There's a lot of females that talk about what they'll do. I do it. I don't talk too much. My theme is show and tell motherfucka.

Murder for hire is my hobby. You see, hanging with Kaniya and being back in Atlanta is taking me there. You better ask about Kaisha Miller in these motherfuckin' streets. From East Lake to Kirkwood to Edgewood all up through Lil Vietnam, niggas and bitches know about me. I don't play about my kid's, period. I'll body anybody about mine without even blinking twice.

Sonja

Tonight, was the night me and Chelle were meeting Kaisha and Kaniya at Cozumel Mexican Restaurant on Old National Parkway. Raven was also coming with us. It felt so good. It was nice out today, not to humid with a nice breeze. I was ready for this lady's night out. We arrived early and got a table. Kaisha sent me a text and said they were ten minutes away and to go ahead and order. She wanted two tacos and an enchilada. Kaniya wanted fajita nachos. We made idle chat until Kaniya and Kaisha pulled up. They finally walked through the door looking like twins. Before Kaniya could sit down good, I was ready to dig in her ass.

"Hey, Kaniya. I see you've been acting funny with your auntie. I told your hot ass to leave Tariq alone. I noticed you came by and got your car, but you didn't come in. You must be hiding some shit with your sneaky ass." I argued.

"I'm pregnant, Auntie Sonja," she beamed proudly. "I really dreaded telling you this or anybody for that matter. It's my business and nobody else's."

"Pregnant by who? Kaniya, please tell me it's not Tariq's. Lucky is going to kill both of you," I asked. I had a motherfuckin' flashback of when Lucky kicked my door in and threatened to kill Tariq and me.

"I'm having twins and it's possible they're Lucky's or Tariq's. I'm not afraid of Lucky and Tariq isn't either. It is what it is," she sassed and sucked her teeth. "Sonja, Lucky already knows and it was already a mess with the threats and black roses every day."

"I can't get a 'hey, how you doing' or nothing? You went straight for my daughter. What's up with that, old heifer? Well, since we're putting shit out on the table, I got some tea. Who is this girl with y'all? Can we talk in front of her or not? I don't want to tell my business or air shit out to just anybody. I don't trust bitches. It's to many snitches out here," she explained. Kaisha was already on her level. What type of fuckin' tea does she have to spill? I have a bad feeling about this. I could always tell when Kaisha was on her good bull shit and tonight, she was.

"You remember my sister Tyra? This is her daughter, Raven; she's good," I explained. Kaisha gave me a devilish smile.

"Oh REALLY? Hi, Raven. I'm Kaisha, Kaniya's mom. You look just like your dad and sisters. I have some stuff I need to say to your auntie. Please don't take offense to what I'm saying. Damn this is perfect timing. She looks just like Killian and Killany. How does Kaniya not know this girl is her fuckin' sister?" She asked. I knew she didn't say what the fuck I thought she said. How did she know that? She couldn't know that.

"Wait, who is my dad and sisters? What the hell is your mom talking about Kaniya? I don't have anybody but Tariq and Sonja," she explained. I don't want Raven looking at me sideways. She was looking at me for an explanation. Damn, it's about to go down. Tyra told me on her deathbed that Killian might be Raven's father, but she wasn't 100% sure. I didn't know that Kaisha knew that, fuck. The cat is out the bag and it's about to be some shit. Everybody was looking at me for a fuckin' explanation.

"Sonja, do you have something you want to tell me and Raven before I air this shit out? You can hold water. I understand that Tyra was your sister, but you were smiling in my face knowing damn well she was fuckin' my husband. Raven, Kaniya here is your sister and her father, Killian, is your dad," she argued and explained. Kaisha was so fuckin' messy. She didn't have to do this shit here. "Real bitches do real shit, no matter what." Kaisha was on one and I was the fuel to her fuckin' fire.

"Hold up Kaisha, let me make some shit clear to you. I never knew Tyra was fuckin' your husband. I found out on her deathbed that Killian might be her daughter's father, but she said she wasn't 100% sure," I argued and explained.

"Good. Sonja, it has been confirmed he is the father and he signed her birth certificate. I know your loyalty is with your sister but on some real shit, you could've told me. I was cool with Yasmine and I told you about her, and Kanan's every fuckin' move because I fucked with you. I never wanted you to be in the dark or looking like a fool about anything," she argued. "I've always been the realest bitch on my team. If don't nobody got Kaisha, I got my mother fuckin' self. That's why I left. I wasn't with the fake shit."

"I'm whose father," he argued. Killian, Kanan, and Black walked in the motherfuckin' building. Kaisha set this shit up. I asked Killian and he swore on his momma Raven wasn't his. He hoped and prayed Kaisha never found this shit out; but that's too much like right when she knew everything.

He swore he would take this shit to the grave with him. Looking at Raven, she looked just like him. She was his and he fuckin' knew it.

"You sold me out, Kaisha. You got me fuckin' caught up," Kanan argued. He needs to sit the fuck down. "I can't believe you Kaisha, you sold me fuckin out. You were the one who told Sonja what the fuck I was into. Killian you better get your fuckin' wife." Black walked up behind Chelle and placed his hands on her shoulders.

"What's up, Chelle? Bring your ass on right fucking now. You know I got a few fuckin' bones to pick with you, I can't fuckin' believe you. Look at me when I'm fuckin' talking to you, Chelle," he argued. Black was upset. Poor Chelle was scared to turn around to look at him. Kaisha sucked her teeth and rolled her eyes at me.

"Yeah, Kanan, I sold your dirty dick ass out. The fuck you gone do about it. Raven meet your father, Killian. Killian meet your daughter, Raven, Tyra's daughter," she argued and sassed. Who in the fuck called these niggas up here? I was ready to go before Killian shoots Kaisha's ass. I noticed Kaniya tried to ease out, but Killian's eyes were trained on her. I heard Kaniya mumble something under her breath.

"Oh, shit. I didn't want my dad to see me pregnant. I'm texting, Killany. That bitch done set me up and sent my dad up here," she mumbled. I noticed Kaniya tried to make her way out to the car. She didn't want him to see her. Killian stood right in front of her blocking her from leaving.

"Kaniya, you ain't slick. Sit your pregnant ass down. Yeah, Killany told me. I swear this child of mine likes fuckin' with me and making me gray. I don't want to be nobody's grandpa. I'm sorry, Raven. I never knew you were my daughter until today. I always knew it was a possibility, but it was never confirmed. I did sign your birth certificate; you do have my last name.

We were unable to get the DNA test done due to your mother's circumstances. I'm curious to know how my wife knows for sure, but I'm sorry for not being in your life. I'll spend the rest of my life making it up to you. I promise you I hate to tell you these words because you're my baby girl. I've never been a deadbeat. If Kaisha knew this the whole fuckin' time, why didn't she tell me? She loves to throw everything else up in my face," he argued. Killian had his eyes trained on Kaisha.

"I got my ways. I know people. I had her mouth swabbed. Here you go, Mr. Miller. Therefore, I left your dirty dick ass years ago for a reason. I'm sorry, Raven, no offense to you but your mom and your dad ruined my marriage. I hate you had to witness this, but it is what it is.

Let's go, Kaniya. I'm ready to go, I'm hungry and my food is fuckin' cold. This shit right here has got my blood pressure high and opened some old wounds, but I got this shit up off my chest," she argued. Kaisha grabbed her food and stormed out. Kaniya was right behind her but she stopped and talked to Raven before leaving out.

"I love you, Raven. Call me later or tomorrow so we can talk, or come over, sister," she stated and smiled. Kaniya and Raven were already close and acted like sisters. I was glad that Raven had a relationship with Kaniya. That explains their connection and their bond.

"I love you too, sis. I'll be over tomorrow. I can't believe this shit," she stated and beamed proudly. Raven's eyes were focused on me. She shook her head and looked at me with wide eyes looking for an explanation. I hope she didn't think I knew the whole time because I didn't. I'm going by what her mother told me.

Kaisha

Kaniya and I walked to the car. I couldn't leave the Cozumel fast enough. Sonja fuckin' knew. She's not fooling me. She never revealed who the other possibility could've been. Bitch get the fuck out of here with that fake ass shit. I just want Killian to grant me my fuckin' divorce, that's it. I was walking so fast Kaniya couldn't even keep up with me. I opened the door for her. I couldn't wait until she slid her ass in these leather seats so I could pull off. She hopped in, slammed the door, and I pulled off.

"Ma, what the fuck was that about back there?" She asked. I knew Kaniya had questions and I didn't mind plugging her in. "Momma, you know I'm curious and know you can hold some damn water. How long have you been knowing about this? I can't believe Sonja. What was up with Uncle Black and Auntie Chelle."

"I told you I had some tea on your daddy. I see you sipped it very well. I don't know what's going on with Chelle and Black. Ask Sonja and see if she'll tell you," I laughed. I hope Kaniya doesn't start questioning me about this shit. I don't want to explain anything to her nosey ass.

"Ma, why you didn't tell me my dad cheated on you with Tariq's momma? It makes sense now why you don't want me with him. Is that your fuckin' reason? I know you can hold grudges but damn," she argued and explained. I love Kaniya but she should pick the right fuckin' side.

"I didn't want you to hate your daddy like I knew you would. Who called him up to Cozumel?" I asked. "I wanted to know who sent him because he wasn't needed." Killian tried to play like he didn't know. Motherfucka you knew because you gave her your last name. Niggas wasn't just doing that.

"Killany, of course. I was texting her when you were popping off. She told him I was pregnant. She talks to damn much. I wish I wasn't pregnant so I could catch a flight to her house now and check her ass," she argued. Kaniya is going to get enough of telling Killany her fuckin' business because when it comes to her father, Killany loyalty lies with Killian

"Remind me when I see Killany to pop her in her fucking mouth. She talks to fucking much," I sassed and sucked my teeth. Killany needs a life and some dick to slide on. I must do something about her loose ass lips, just watch.

"So, Ma, how long did you know that Tyra was fuckin' my dad? Who killed her and did they ever find her killer? Why

are you just now telling me this? Who swabbed Raven's mouth?"
She asked. Damn Kaniya wanted to know it all. I guess I had a lot
of explaining to do.

"Cut your phone off and give it to me. I don't talk about
none of my personal business with phones on. You like texting
Killany and telling her all your business when shit pops off. You
won't tell any of mine and get me caught up on some murder
cases," I sassed and sucked my teeth. I motioned with my hand
for Kaniya to pass me her phone. I'm serious. I didn't play that
shit. Technology was too much for me. I didn't want to get caught
up at all.

"Really, Ma?" She asked. Kaniya didn't believe me, but
this was serious for me. I got too much to fuckin' loose. She cut
her phone off and gave it to me. I sat it in the arm rest.

"Kaniya Nicole, now we can fuckin' talk. Don't ever
repeat this shit. Take this to the fuckin' grave with you and I
mean that shit. If I find out, you told Killany you'll be the only
fuckin' child and I'm not fuckin' playing. Yes, that bitch came to
my house talking shit about your father. I killed that bitch. I
swabbed Raven's mouth when she was born. I have connections
everywhere.

A friend of mine told me she delivered, and Killian's ass was out there with her. I made my way up to Emory hospital, dressed as a nurse and got that shit done. The results came back the same day. I thought you knew since you, Raven, and Sonja were so cool," I explained. "I thought you just didn't want me to know."

"Ma, you're really are the realest chick I know. Kaisha plays for keeps. You were serious about your husband Killian Miller back in the day. Bodying bitches and bagging coke," she laughed. "Ma I can't believe all this shit went down back in the day. Y'all was lit. Tell me some more about Kaisha with motherfuckin' K." I cut my eyes at Kaniya. She so fuckin' silly.

"Kaniya, don't you start. Last, I recall, you bodied two bitches behind Lucky and Tariq. Yasmine was a good friend of mine. Her daughters should've never crossed you, though. You killed both of her daughters with your petty ass. Don't look at me like that. I haven't bodied as many women as you have behind some dick. Pick up your face and don't tell Killany about none of this shit and I mean it.

You can tell her all your business, but don't tell her none of mine. She'll fuck around and get me caught up on a cold case," I laughed. Killany was hell with her diarrhea of the mouth. She gets it's from Kaitlyn, Killian's mom.

"Ma, she isn't that bad," she laughed.

"Sure, Kaniya, just keep me out of your conversation. I won't forget, trust me. When I see Killany Denise, I'm popping her in her fuckin' mouth. I can't wait to see Killany, I owed her one.

Raven

I can't believe none of this shit. I've always thought I didn't have any family besides Sonja and Tariq. I ain't never looked at my birth certificate before, but my last name is Miller. Kaitlyn Raven Miller. I wanted to look at that shit. I can't wait to get back to California to pack my stuff up and check out my birth certificate. I always wondered who my father was and now I know. My daddy is crazy. I'll never forget how he pulled up at Deuce's party.

Kaniya's mom revealed that shit tonight and it was a mess. I didn't even get to eat my food. I'm speechless. I can't believe I met my father tonight. He knew about me. Where the hell have you been all my life? He's been in plain sight. I'm glad that Kaniya is my real sister. I can't believe she's pregnant and Tariq might be the father. I know my mom is smiling down on us… maybe not. She might think this shit is funny. Kaniya's mom was livid. My sister and brother might be having a baby together. Sonja was caught up in the middle.

I guess my prayers worked because I prayed for them. I'm moving back to Atlanta. I'm going to enroll in Georgia State. I want to be with my sister more than anything. Kaniya has always been there for me. I'll get to know Killian or whatever his name is later, but I want to be wherever my sister is, regardless because she's my real protector. I noticed Kaisha said sisters.

Did I have another sister that I didn't know about? I'll have to call Kaniya in the morning so we can sit down and talk. Uncle Kanan was my real fuckin' uncle. I swear it's a small world. I couldn't wait to tell Tariq this. I guess that's why me and Kaniya always were close because we share the same blood line.

Kaniya

I can't believe this shit, my daddy has another child. Raven, Tariq's sister, is my real sister. Isn't this some shit? Boy, when Kaisha comes to play, baby, she's coming for the jugular. I never saw my mom pop off before. I always heard about her, but I've never been there to witness it. My dad acted as if he didn't know about Raven. I'm not buying that shit. He fuckin' knew.

I'm petty as fuck. I couldn't hold this water. I couldn't wait to smack this shit up in Killany's face. Daddy couldn't do no wrong in her eyes. Guess what, Killany? Daddy has a new little princess that he must make up for lost time with and she's the spitting image of you! I'm a mommy's girl—no competition there. Killany was livid. She was catching a red-eye flight in the morning. I bet she had a heart attack when I told her that our dad had another daughter?

That really pissed her off. I was glad he had another daughter because he'll be up in Raven's business now and less in mine. He needs to get to know Raven, anyway. Kaitlyn Raven Miller. Hell nah, it makes perfect sense now. Raven's real name is Kaitlyn, but she hates that name, so she goes by Raven. She was named after our grandmother. My daddy thinks he is slick.

He's a lying motherfucka. He knew she was his daughter and Sonja did also. You wouldn't give anybody your mother's name if you had doubts. He knew for a fact she was his.

"Ma, peep this shit out: Raven's real name is Kaitlyn Raven Miller." Nothing about her name is coincidental. My daddy ain't shit.

"Kaniya, stop fucking lying. You are fuckin' kidding me. I know you motherfuckin' lying," she argued.

"I'm serious, Mom. She hates the name Kaitlyn, so she goes by Raven," I explained. I figured that shit out. You gave her your mother's name.

"Oh, Sonja definitely knew. She hates that bitch, Kaitlyn, just as much as I do. Killian knew too. That's a lying piece of shit. I'm good, though. Everything you do in the dark comes to the light," she explained. I can't believe all these lies were unfolding by the minute.

Chapter-23

Killany

I can't believe my dad has another daughter that's younger than me. I tell my dad everything and he tells me everything, or so I thought. To say I was livid was a fuckin' understatement. I've always been daddy's little girl. I wanted it to remain that way. I called my dad to find out if it was true or not. He answered his phone and said, 'not now, Killany' and hung up. Yep, that confirmed it. She could've been anybody. Why did she have to be Raven, Tariq's sister? Raven and Kaniya already had a bond that couldn't be broken.

This chick stole my daddy and now Kaniya? Oh, hell no. I'm taking a trip to Atlanta to see what's up with all this shit. The only person that could cheer me up and make me feel better would be my mom. Let me call her up. She answered on the third ring.

"Hey, Ma," I sighed. I couldn't muster up a smile if I wanted too.

"What, Killany Denise?" She asked and sassed. My mother answered her phone with an attitude. She must have known I was only calling because I heard about my dad's news. I can't lie I feel some type of way. I've always had my dad in the bag so to know that I'll have to share him with someone else fucks with me.

"Ma, is that how you answer your phone when your favorite daughter calls you?" I asked. I had to lay it on thick. I knew she would love to hear that.

"Favorite, huh? Killany, cut the bullshit. You know that's how I answer my phone. I don't care if the president is fuckin' calling. You miss your mom? Come see me, you know where I'm at. Your sister's pregnant ass is getting on my last nerves," she sassed and sucked her teeth. "Killany, you think you're slick. Your father must have pissed you off for you to be on my line."

"I don't know, Ma," I laughed. I wanted her to beg me to come see her.

"Stop fuckin' playing games, Killany Denise Miller. You know you want to come and see your dad's new little princess. Get your ass here. You haven't seen Kaniya since she's been kidnapped.

You're running around telling everybody's business. I'll expect to see you tomorrow," she explained. "Killany, I hope you bring your ass out here. I can't wait to pop you in your damn mouth." My mother and I ended the conversation. I had to call my grandmother. I dialed her number and she answered on the first ring. She's going to go ballistic.

Mrs. Kaitlyn Miller

I'm fuckin' livid. I can't believe Killany called me upset. She told me that Killian had another daughter. I swear since Kanan has been out I haven't seen much of them two motherfuckas. I don't appreciate that shit one fuckin' bit. Killany is my favorite grandchild. I don't give a fuck who knows it... well, my only grandchild. Kaniya is just like her damn mother. Kanan Jr. and Yashir—they're the fucking devil just like their damn father. They're not welcomed back to my house anymore. I was so glad the day they released Kanan from the FEDS because I didn't have to be bothered with those two motherfuckas tearing up my damn house and eating every fuckin' thing.

Killany is the daughter I never had. When she hurts, I hurt. I'm going to cuss Killian's yellow behind out. He's a big fuckin' liar. To make matters worse, you had a baby by Tootsie Pop Harris' daughter, Tyra Harris? Yuck. She was a well-known hoe just like her momma and Sonja too. Killany even told me the child's name was Kaitlyn Raven Miller. He crossed the motherfuckin' line with that one. I really lost it then because that was supposed to be Killany's fuckin' name. It shouldn't have been handed down to Tyra's daughter.

Why would Killian name a child after me without my fuckin' approval? I can't believe this mess. Killany woke me up out of my damn sleep with this bull shit. I just left from a dice game over at OG Lou's. Killian hasn't called and told me a motherfuckin' thang. I remember when he brought that bitch Tyra to my house years ago, and she was pregnant. I asked that lying motherfucka was it his and he said he didn't think so. I took his word for it. I'm not the least bit surprised Kaisha was still running around keeping up mess, her and Sonja both.

Kanan and Killian didn't choose women well at all. It was just something about Kaisha and Sonja that I didn't like. I didn't like them two bitches. They made me fuckin' sick. For one, Sonja was an offspring of Tootsie Pop Harris. She and I grew up together; she was always jealous of me. She wanted Killian Sr. so bad she drugged him and had sex with him. I beat the fuck out that bitch too. Fuck she thought this was.

When my sons started to make a name for themselves in the dope game, it was Tootsie Pop who made Sonja pursue Kanan. A mutual friend of ours, Willie Belle, told me how Tootsie Pop was raising her girls. I didn't like Sonja or Kaisha. Ugh, the thought of those two.

I knew they only wanted my sons for their money. The love they had for my sons wasn't genuine. Kaisha walked around like she was fuckin' Princess Diana and that bitch wasn't shit but dirt under my fuckin' shoe. I really stopped liking Kaisha when she gave birth to her twins. She fuckin' lied to me and said she was going to name Killany, Kaitlyn.

I wanted Killany named after me so bad it hurt my soul that she did the opposite. She had the nerve to name them Killany and Kaniya. She thought the shit was funny, her and Sonja. I'll never forget when they laughed at me in my face about it. It took everything in me not to choke Kaisha's ass out when she was in the hospital.

Killany told me all about Kaniya being pregnant and not knowing who fathered her kids. Sounds just like her momma all over again. I know Killian wasn't the only nigga Kaisha was fuckin' while she was pregnant. Chelle was the only one I liked out of Kaisha and Sonja. My nephew Black sure picked him a good one. I hate she left Black.

Chelle

I knew I should've taken my ass back to Miami yesterday. I had a feeling that I should've done that. I should've listened to that fuckin' something. I wanted to see Kaisha and have some damn fun. Fuckin' with Sonja and Kaisha and all these God damn secrets. I was looking like Kermit the fuckin' frog sipping my damn Margarita after everything started coming out. The moment Killian and Kanan walked in. I knew Black's old bitter motherfuckin' ass wasn't too far behind. I was right too. That crazy motherfucka walked up on me like we had some shit fuckin' going on and we didn't.

I damn near chocked on my fuckin' drink when he gripped my fuckin' shoulders and applied pressure. Black kidnapped my ass. I dodged his ass at the funeral and got away. I wish I could smack myself right now. Black pushed me out of Cozumel Mexican Restaurant off Old National Parkway on the South side so quick he had his gun pressed to my back.

Damn, I'm fucked. He threw me in the front seat of his Porsche. I kept trying to jump out the car. He looked over at me and let out an evil laugh. I knew the child lock was on. I couldn't jump out this bitch. He started driving like a bat out of hell when he jumped on I-285N. He knew I hated that shit. Just fuckin' kill me because that's what you're trying to do. It felt like all the Margaritas I drank were about to come up at any minute. I wish they would because I would lean over and throw up on his ass. He knew I hated when he drove fast like a Nascar driver. Why is he doing this stupid shit?

Just let this shit go and let us go. It doesn't even have to be this way. I'm going to kill Sonja and Kaisha my damn self. I swear I am if I ever make it out of this shit. I'm listening to their damn drama from some shit that happened twenty years ago, not paying attention, and Black's psychotic ass done snatched me up. I love my friends, but damn, I'm going to love y'all hoes from a distance. Black is the last motherfucka that I wanted to be alone with. He's not playing with a full deck.

Black

Damn, Chelle thought she was slick. She really didn't want to fuck with a nigga. She got away good at the funeral. I don't know how, though, but she did. I just wanted some answers. Trust me, I'm not chasing behind no chick or trying to keep a chick that doesn't want to be kept. I made sure I drove extra fast on I-285 doing 200mph. I wanted to scare the shit out of her. I knew she hated that shit.

"Slow this fuckin' car down," she argued and yelled. I knew Chelle was scared, nervous and about to throw up. Ask me do, I give a fuck? I don't give a fuck. She should've thought about that shit before she started running and hiding. Chelle knew it was going to be consequences. She should've taken her ass back to Miami or wherever the fuck she was staying at.

"Oh, so this is what the fuck I got to do to get you to fuckin' talk?" I asked. We've been riding for thirty minutes and this is the first time she's said one word. She must come better than that.

"You know I hate this shit, Black. You know what the fuck your, inconsiderate ass doing," she argued, sassed and sucked her teeth. "What the fuck do you want from me?"

"I hate you left seven years ago. Why in the fuck did you do that shit Chelle? You see now you don't have shit to say now. I'm driving extra fast just because I don't like being ignored," I argued and explained.

"I'm sorry, Black. Please slow down before you kill us. I should've just walked away instead of running away and let you know what was up. Please Black, I'm damn near pleading with you at this point to slow the car down. I don't want to fuckin die," she begged and pleaded.

"You sorry, now? You got a lot of should've, could've, would've to say now. I don't care about dying. I died a long time ago. I don't care about you dying tonight, either. I thought you were dead already until I saw you in Miami at Deuce's party with that nigga. You had me looking like a fool, but you are living a whole new life with some new nigga.

You know you got me fucked up right. I play for keeps, in case you forgot. Murder is always my case. I knew you were going to show your face sooner or later fucking with Sonja. Call that nigga up now and tell him you ain't coming back," I argued.

Chelle really had me pissed the fuck off right now. It's like I couldn't forgive her and move on, fuck ass no.

"I'm not doing that shit, fuck you. I refused to tell Couture a lie;" she argued and explained. I could've sworn I heard her mumble under her breath she loved him too much. It took everything in me not to reach over and choke her motherfuckin' ass.

"Oh, it's fucks me, Chelle? We can fuck. Give me your phone before I shoot you in your mouth, spitting that hot ass shit you talking. You think this shit is a game? Do you know what the fuck I want to do to you? Get that fuck nigga on the motherfuckin' phone and tell him you'll see his ass in seven years," I argued and explained. I'm pissed and I can't believe her. I'm ready to put my hands on her because she was to fuckin' disrespectful.

"Why does it have to be this way, Black? I'm not telling him shit. Just kill me if that's what the fuck you want to do. Just make sure you can live with it. Take me out of my fuckin' misery," she argued. What the fuck does she mean take her out of her misery.

"You ain't afraid to motherfuckin' die? Chelle, you forgot how real this motherfuckin' shit gets. Let me pull over so I can show you. You think this shit is a game; get your ass out of the fuckin' car right now. Move, quick. You are moving to fucking slow. Talk that hot ass shit you were just spitting. I'm in your face now, what's up?" I asked. I'm ready to get this shit popping. My blood was fuckin' boiling. I heard her mumble under her breath.

"Oh lord, this nigga done lost his damn mind," she mumbled. I heard her phone ring. I snatched the phone out her hand. I pressed the gun to her mouth. I'm tired of fuckin' playing with Chelle. It was that nigga calling.

"Unlock your motherfuckin' phone and call that pussy ass nigga up," I argued and explained. Chelle did as she was told. The nigga answered the phone on the first ring. "Daddy. Oh, you are calling this motherfuckin' nigga daddy?" I smacked Chelle in her motherfuckin' face. She got me fucked up.

"Chelle, baby, are you at the airport? I'm on my way," he asked in his Jamaican accent.

"Nah, pussy ass nigga, Chelle isn't on her way no damn where. She'll see you in seven years. Black is back on the fucking track, bitch," I argued and yelled through the phone.

"Who the fuck is this calling me from my girl's phone? You want to go to war, pussy, behind my pussy? Couture will bring the pain, pussy. Vest up, I'll see you soon, bitch," he argued and yelled. I laughed at that motherfucka. I ain't never feared nann nigga.

A WEEK LATER

Chapter-24

Jassity

Men, what would the world do without them? So, Lucky hit me up a few days ago. I smiled just thinking about his fine ass. We exchanged numbers in Miami. He had a business proposition for me. He was going to pay me $10,000.00 if I could seduce and fuck Tariq raw and record it and send it to Kaniya. I told him it was going to be hard just because I haven't heard from Tariq in over a month. He wanted me to keep hitting him up to see if he would bite. I needed the money. The last time me and Tariq talked he mentioned something about he was going to Jamaica. Lucky told me he was back so try to hit him up.

I was really feeling Tariq and he was feeling me too. The time we spent in Miami was amazing. He thought I was crazy, but I knew he was feeling ole girl that took a picture of us at the party. He couldn't keep his eyes off her. Everywhere she went, he all sudden wanted to go and do shit to piss her off. I know he was using me to piss her off, but she never reacted. I noticed how the bitch kept calling me Jasper and shit. I wanted to check her, but I always wanted to remain a lady.

Lucky told me that old girl was Kaniya, his ex, and her and Tariq are in a relationship together. She must have some liquid gold between her legs. Lucky is paying me to break her and Tariq up. I shot Tariq a text and told him I was in Atlanta for a few days and I wanted to see him. Guess what? The nigga texted me back finally and told me he wanted to see me also and we could hang out tonight. That shit was music to my ears. I wanted to make my last impression my best impression.

I sent Lucky a text to let him know I got him. I wanted Tariq and I was going to make sure I got his ass, too. I feel sorry for Kaniya, but money was the motive tonight. I was paid to get Tariq out of the picture. This was the end of their story and Lucky was paying top dollar. I was playing for keeps tonight. No man has ever shown me the attention that Tariq showed me when we were in Miami, but I wanted him only for tonight, though.

I was going to do whatever to get that $10,000. I got some tricks up my sleeve and I'm pulling all of them out tonight. I'm not sure where we are going, but he said he would text me the location in an hour or so.

Tariq

I don't know what the fuck is up with me lately, but I haven't really been feeling Kaniya to much. She's been on my bad side for a few weeks now. I know for a fact that she's not keeping company with Lucky. I have security on her daily. I got John and Mac in my ear all the time talking about how I shouldn't be with her. I know they were still tripping after the shit she pulled at Mac's house with Lucky. I'm stuck because I know my niggas riding with me right or wrong and I'll never have to question their loyalty. I must question Kaniya's loyalty because she switched up on me quick at Mac's house. My niggas were looking at me sideways because I was sleeping with the fuckin' opps. If they would've shot Lucky, I know she would've popped them.

If she had to choose between me or him; clearly, she was going to ride with him. I didn't even know she had any guns on her. What the fuck is she doing walking around with two Mac 11s in her big ass purse? I love her, or do I lust her? Kaniya got my heart I can't even lie but that's the question, do I got hers. I know I fucked up her situation with Lucky, but so fuckin' what? There's a possibility that her kids might be mine. I really don't know what to do at this point.

I can't talk to Sonja about this shit because she told me plenty of times to leave Kaniya's alone. Did I listen? Hell no. I just made a fuckin' mistake. Jassity hit me up and told me she was in town and she wanted to see me. I hit her ass back and told her we would hook up. There's nothing wrong with casual drinks and dinner with an old friend, right? I'll go home and play it off with Kaniya that some shit popped off so I can leave the house later. She's cool, she doesn't trip that much. She's tired most of the time anyway.

I made it to the house a little after 6:00 p.m. As soon as I hit the kitchen, I smelled the aroma of food. I knew Kaniya cooked. She always made sure she kept a nigga fed. I looked in the microwave and my plate was in there. Barbecue ribs and baked beans. I'll eat my plate after I finish getting dressed. I walked upstairs to our room. Kaniya was laid on her back reading her Kindle. I snatched her Kindle out of her hand because I needed her attention.

"What you do that for?" She asked and pouted.

"Some shit popped off, I got to make a few runs later is that cool?" I asked. She nodded her head yes. My plans were in motion.

Kaniya

I've been relaxing in our bed for a while now. I fell asleep a little after 9:00 p.m. I just didn't want to get up and use the bathroom. Tariq had to leave earlier. Something came up with some of his businesses. He's been gone already for about four hours. I wanted to wait up for him, but I couldn't because I was tired. These babies are kicking my ass. I dozed off and when I woke up, I noticed that Tariq still wasn't in bed with me. I looked up at the clock and it read 4:00 a.m.

Where the fuck was, he at this time of the morning? I was about to grab my phone to call his ass, but my phone alerted me that I had a text message. It was a Miami number. This was a new phone number, so I was curious. I opened the message; the number was an iPhone user also. The text read:

305-688-2691: Do you know where your man is?

That's the first red flag. It was a video with the message. Tariq was fucking Jasper raw. My heart dropped. I couldn't believe this nigga. How could he? I'm not about to be anybody's fool. I forwarded him the video message so he would know why I was gone. I packed my shit up and emptied out all his safes. I'm tired of niggas playing with me. You can never play me, but you can motherfuckin' pay me.

I'm taxing his ass the same way I taxed Lucky, but more. I wasn't about to shed anymore fuckin' tears, though. Jasper barked up the wrong tree. Bitch, I don't play with mutt-faced hoes. I'll get you in the worst way. You think that video was cute? Wait until I slaughter your silly ass. The bitch had the nerve to add a laughing emoji. Game on, bitch. I'm savage and the best to ever do it. You'll regret fuckin' with me about my nigga. To think I was falling in love with him. Tariq was no different than Lucky.

Kaisha

Kaniya called me and told me that Tariq cheated on her and she was leaving. The chick sent her a video of her fuckin' Tariq. That motherfucka was a hoe just like his momma. My baby was upset because she trusted this nigga. He kidnapped her and took her from Lucky to cheat on her. I told my baby to do what she had to do. I also told her to quit running from every relationship. That's the problem with this generation today, they're so quick to give up and not work shit out. I had to stop for a minute and practice what I preached.

I know I haven't made the best decisions in my relationships, but I wanted the best for my daughters. I had to choose my words wisely. History has a way of repeating itself and karma was a bitch when she finally came back around. Kaniya was just like me in so many ways. She was truly me all over again. When I look at her, I see me. I had to guide her and not entertain her.

I had to let Kaniya know it's okay to love and it's okay to leave his ass also. I also wanted to school her and make her understand what I was saying. What goes around comes around. It's just karma from the way Tariq and her did Lucky. Kaniya just got caught in the middle of it. If she loves Tariq like she claimed to me that she did, she will fight for their love. I wanted Kaniya to be strong and independent.

I wanted her to stop running all the time. I understand she's pissed, but don't let no bitch run you up out of a house you and your man share or get your man that easy. She gave up to quick with Lucky and she's throwing in the towel with Tariq. She gives up to quick. I should've fought for Killian, but I didn't. I let my pride and street cred get the best of me. I've spent twenty years looking for Mr. Right when I had Mr. Right. If she wants to body a chick, Momma will do it, but don't give up on your relationships so quick.

Tariq

I can't believe this motherfuckin' shit, man. I went to kick it with Jassity for about an hour or two. She kept throwing the pussy at me, but I wouldn't take it. I knew what the fuck I had at home, but I fucked up. I think she drugged me. I know that bitch drugged me because I didn't smoke or drink shit. I woke up drowsy in her hotel room with my dick hanging out. I grabbed my phone to see what time it was. It was 9:00 a.m. and I knew Kaniya was going to dig in my ass. I had a message from her.

Wifey- You dirty dick bitch! I'm gone, please don't come looking for me.

There was a video attached to it. I looked at the video from her and it was forwarded from Jassity's phone number. It was me and Jassity fucking raw. Damn, I fucked up, but I felt like I was set up. I know that bitch set me up, but where the fuck is, she? I know Kaniya's going to leave me. This bitch set me up. I've lost my family behind this shit. I'll murk Jassity's sneaky ass my damn self.

Damn, I got to hurry up and get home. I hope and pray she's still there. Lord, please save her for me. How could I be so fuckin' stupid? Kaniya will not forgive me for this. I thought Jassity just wanted to talk and chill. That bitch wanted to fuck me and let my bitch know about it. I got something for her ass. Bitch, I will fuckin' kill you if Kaniya leaves me behind you and this shit you just pulled. I called Jassity's phone and her number was disconnected. I can't believe that bitch set me up. I had $5000.00 in my back pocket and the hoe didn't take that.

I made it home in about thirty minutes. Kaniya's truck wasn't in the garage. I ran upstairs to take a shower. I know she's at her home and soon as I get myself cleaned up; I'll go over there to see about her. I went in my closet to find something to wear and my safe was wide the fuck open. I looked in my safe and everything was gone. Kaniya emptied out my shit and she attached a cute little note.

Tariq

Fuck you! I fuckin' hate you. I took everything and it doesn't even make me feel better. I thought you, were different? I guess the joke was on me. If you wanted to fuck a bitch; you didn't have to lie.

Kaniya

Kaniya

Damn you got to be careful who you give your heart to. This shit hurts so fuckin' bad. I wouldn't wish this feeling on my worst enemy. I really love Tariq and I could see myself being with him forever. For him to go and cheat on me and lie to leave our bed to go fuck another bitch. I'm not accepting that at all. To make matters worse, the bitch wanted me to know that she fucked my man. *How did she get my number?* My momma is talking about don't run and don't give up on your relationship. Don't leave him because of one mistake. I'm done giving out fuckin' passes. Shit, that nigga left. Ain't no coming back.

I swear a motherfucka should thank God I'm pregnant because if I wasn't, I would've been gone. I'm nobody's fool. He was so anxious to leave the house last night he just didn't know that he was going to get caught up. I emptied out all his safes. I took all his cash, and shit. That still didn't take away the pain. He had the nerve to come to my house afterward with the same shit he had on smelling just like that bitch with that cheap ass perfume, begging me to hear him out.

I don't want to hear shit you have to say. Lucky has been emailing me like crazy, do you see me leaving my bed to go meet with him? Hell no. Out of all the niggas, Tariq swore he would never hurt me or make me regret being with him. This is the main reason why I didn't want to take it there with him because of shit like this.

Now he wants to beg a bitch like Luther. Bitch take your ass on and forget about me because I've forgotten about you. I told him to let Jassity know when I drop my babies, I'm coming to Miami to put my foot on that bitch's neck. I'm not leaving until I find her. Whatever you and her got going on, leave me the fuck up out of it. The worse thing a bitch can do is send for me because trust me it's motherfuckin' repercussions.

A WEEK LATER

Chapter-25

Chelle

Black has made my life a living fuckin' hell these past few weeks. He had the nerve to bring me back to our old house that we used to share. To make matters worse, he's sharing it with his new bitch. I was a little jealous at first, but I had to think about it for a minute. I left his ass for a better man, and I didn't lose anything. I've gained a lot. Couture has exposed me to so many opportunities that I've never thought about doing or pursuing.

I just didn't understand him. If you have somebody, what the fuck did you want with me? I didn't have a phone or anything. I wanted to call and cuss Kaisha and Sonja ass out so fuckin' bad but I couldn't. Kanan came by here last week. You know this nigga took me with him to pick out Sonja's engagement ring? I told him to make Black let me go.

His lying ass said I'm working on it. I know Couture was hot and he was going to come and look for me. I heard the venom in his voice. Black has started a war and he didn't even know it. Couture isn't your average businessman. He's a real street nigga but many people wouldn't realize it because he doesn't do typical street nigga shit.

The whole time I was here, I made sure to piss Black's chick off. I would walk around nude all day just for the hell of it. I knew she didn't like it but what the fuck were you going to say to me? I mean literally, this nigga would sleep with me every night and yes, we were having sexual encounters.

I was extra loud on purpose. This chick wouldn't budge. She would still have his breakfast ready before 9:00 a.m. I've been blind to some shit but never dumb. Black is still on that bullshit. I know he still wants me, but I was good on him. He still has hoes by the pound. I was planning on escaping today. Black was going to Savannah and I was going to act like I was sick so this dummy would take me to the hospital, and I would be long gone.

"Chelle, are you okay? You don't look so good, is something wrong today? Chelle you aren't walking around nude, you're covered up," she asked. The moment at bitch think you're slipping she got all the questions in the fuckin' world.

"Madison, I don't feel good. Could you take me to the hospital?" I asked. She fell for the bait. It's on.

"Sure, are you ready?" She asked. I heard her mumble underneath her breath "Oh, this bitch doesn't feel good today. I sure will take her to the hospital. I hope she runs and doesn't bring her ass back." I didn't even respond because I just wanted to get the fuck out of here.

"Yes, I'm ready," I coughed. My voice was low. I was really laying it on thick like I was sick.

"Oh, let me lock my house up… I meant your house up," she sassed and sucked her teeth. Madison was trying to be slick with me. I guess since she thought I was sick, she didn't think I would give her much pushback. I will put a knot on her fuckin' head. Yes, this bitch is dumber than I thought. I'll be out of here so quick. I caught that little slick shit she was just spitting. I'll let it ride today because I'm on my way back to Miami.

"What's wrong with you?" She asked. Wouldn't she like to know? I heard her mumble under her breath. "I hope she's not pregnant by Black. I hear her fucking my man every night." I'm just saying, your issue should be with Black and not me.

"I don't know, I feel really cold," I sighed. Listen at this bitch acting like she's concerned and shit. She could give two fucks whether I lived or died.

"Oh okay. Oh, Lord, here's Black calling me," she beamed proudly. "I love when Black calls to check up on me in the middle of the day." She had her eyes trained on me. Bitch, please. She answered on the first ring. She put Black on speaker phone. I swear I don't want to hear his fuckin' voice. His voice boomed through the speakers.

"Where in the fuck are you going in my car?" He asked and yelled. Damn he's hostile as fuck about Madison taking his car without asking. A small laugh escaped my lips. Black knew he could never talk to me like this. Jokes on Madison.

"Chelle is sick. I'm taking her to the hospital," she stated in an aggravated tone. She was upset Black had yelled at her in front of me. She wanted to rub it in my face about him calling her bitch, please.

"Madison, are you fucking stupid? Call my nurse to come to the house. You are one dumb ass bitch. You wonder why I treat you like shit. Chelle ain't fucking sick. She eats garlic every other day. She's trying to fucking run. Put me on speakerphone. Chelle, you think this shit is a game? I know you are trying to run and if you do, I'll kill your old ass momma and daddy. I know where you have them tucked and hidden," he argued and explained. "Madison I can't believe you're so naïve and dumb. If Chelle gets away, I'll kill you within thirty minutes." Black hung up the phone in her face.

"You set me up, Chelle. Why would you do that? The nerve of you, bitch. And to think I was being considerate and trying to help you," she argued and sucked her teeth.

"Bitch, who in the fuck do you think you're talking too? When Black just talked bad to your stupid ass, did you say anything," I argued. "I can't believe this duck ass bitch just came at me sideways behind Black. Bitch, you better keep driving me to the hospital, that's what I do know."

"That's not the point. You already ruined our relationship. To make matters worse, you set me up with this shit," she argued.

"Madison, I can't believe you're pissed at me because I asked you a question?"

"I can't believe you're trying to leave all the good dick that Black is serving. He hasn't touched me since you've been here. I threatened to leave him. I just couldn't do it," she sighed.

"You know what, Madison, take me to the fucking hospital. I don't argue with simple bitches. I lay hands on them," I refused to go back and forth with her stupid ass.

"What's that supposed to mean? You heard Black; I'm taking you back to the house. Did you really think I was going to listen to you and not Black? I'm not getting killed behind you," she argued.

"Give me a minute; I'll show you exactly what I'm talking about." I was already pissed the fuck off. Black threw a wrench in my plans and to make matters worse, this dumb bitch is in her feelings. I punched her ass dead in her fucking jaw so fucking hard this bitch started swerving on I-285S. I started beating her ass senseless. I had so much anger and frustration built up. She was the perfect target. She finally pulled over. Damn, Madison is dumb; she didn't even fight me back.

"What was that all about, Chelle? Why would you fight me while I was driving? I can't believe you got this angry and put your hands on me like this. My jaw is swollen and my head is hurting bad," she argued and cried.

"Let me tell you something, bitch. You're a little too dumb and naïve for my liking. Black needs to watch you. I believe you have some other motives as to why you are with him. Get your stupid ass up out of your nigga's shit and give me the fuckin' keys. I'm escaping with or without you, dummy. Don't show your fuckin' face no fucking more around here before I slice you up like taco meat, bitch," I argued and explained. I think Madison is crazy or something is wrong with her ass. Ain't no way a bitch gone beat my ass while I'm driving and I'm asking why. I will toe tag a bitch quick.

Black

Chelle thought she was slick. She knew Madison was naïve and green to this street shit. She used that to her advantage. I knew she wanted to leave. I knew she would run if given a chance. I just didn't know that she was going to try and leave today. I noticed on my phone that somebody was driving my Lexus coupe. I called Madison to see if she was driving my shit. I knew I didn't tell her she could drive my car. Guess what shit she hit me with? 'I'm taking Chelle to the hospital, she's sick.'

I talked so bad to her. Madison had to be crazy; she didn't pay attention to anything I've told her. Chelle was trying to run off on a nigga again. I had a GPS on that car and a kill switch. Madison just called me upset and told me that Chelle laid hands on her and put her out the car on I-285s Jonesboro Rd exit.

She was really trying to run off on a nigga and go on about her business. I wasn't even in Savannah. I was over at my wife's house, Savannah. It would take me about twenty to thirty minutes to pull up on Chelle. I checked the GPS. Damn she was pushing it down I-285 and she just merged on I-75s she really thought she was about to ride my shit back to Miami.

I was going to kill the engine. I can't believe this chick was really trying to run after I told her I would kill her momma and daddy. She knew I was crazy and would do it with no remorse. I made it to her crazy ass as she jumped out the Lexus and started walking alongside the highway. I couldn't do anything but shake my head. She was serious about this shit.

"Get your crazy ass in the fucking car," I yelled. I swear she likes testing me and she's still hardheaded as fuck.

"For what? I'm tired of you. Let me live my life. I gave you some pussy since you begged for it. What are you trying to prove? You're still the same old Black with bitches by the pound. What do you want with me? I know all about your wife, Savannah. Yeah, nigga, I went through your phone. You can't face the fact that I was the one that got away and left your dog ass? You can kill my momma and daddy; I don't give a fuck; they knew you would come one day."

"I had to beg for the pussy. You wanted this dick just as bad, please don't get this shit confused. Don't speak on shit you don't know anything about. I can't face the fact that you got away. Correction, you ran away. Did I ever dog you out, Chelle? You don't care if I kill your momma and daddy? One call and that's all. You're that selfish that you would have your parents killed so you don't have to spend another day with me?

You're here because I want you here and I refuse to lose you again. Savannah doesn't mean shit to me. She was something to do when I couldn't find you," I argued and explained. Damn, she just put that shit out there. I didn't know that she knew about Savannah. Madison's dumb ass didn't even know that. Chelle got me fucked up. We're really on the side of the interstate doing this shit.

"You said all of that to say what? You're a married man and nothing can change that. Go home to your wife or kick it with your mistress. Let me fuckin' be. You have two women that want you and I'm not one of them. You and I could never be. I'm not the same Chelle that I used to be. I'm smarter than that. If I would've known your dog ass was married before I put this pussy on you, I would've killed you in your fucking sleep.

For you to kidnap me and have a wife and mistress on the side too. You fucked up my relationship with my fiancé is some straight bullshit and for that reason alone, I will continue to beat my two feet on I-75S. I refuse to get in the car with you. You can get the fuck out of here with this bullshit," she argued and explained.

Chelle was really spitting some hot shit out of her mouth. I was going to call my partners to pick her ass up. I see she needed to be roughed up. I jumped out of my car and ran after her. I caught her ass, picked her up, and threw her in the back seat.

"Got these white folks looking at me like I'm crazy and shit. I'll come back and pick up my car later," I argued and yelled. She got me tired and shit playing these thot games.

A FEW DAYS LATER

Chapter-26

Sonja

So much shit has happened these past few months. I can't even keep up. I hated that Kaisha and I fell out for a minute. She was a good friend of mine. I'm glad we moved on and got past this. I haven't seen much of Chelle since the blow up at Cozumel when Black ushered her ass out of there. Couture called me asking me info about Black. He said that he started a war.

I told Couture whatever war there was, I didn't want any parts of it and keep that shit away from me and my front door. I had these bad ass twins Kanan Jr. and Yashir. These little motherfuckers were getting on my last damn nerves. Kaniya had them for a week, then called me to come and get them. They were ready to come home because she was shooting at their bad asses. They stole her Corvette. Kaisha told me Kaniya and Tariq broke up because he cheated on her. No wonder her ass was back at her house.

I was having a barbecue and inviting everyone over. If they came, good and if they didn't, oh well. I knew Kaisha was coming. She was dating this boss nigga named Joshen that had some major bread. He was from New Jersey and she introduced me to his brother, Nassir. This nigga was fine and paid—just my type. We had been talking on the phone and sneaking around to see each other. He flew me out to New York for a few days.

We slipped up and he was ten feet deep in my guts. Good lawd, he was blessed down there. He hit me up and said he was in town and wanted to come through. I couldn't let this man come over here. There's no telling where Kanan is and the twins run and tell him everything. I called Kaisha to tell her my dilemma. She said she invited them over and fuck Kanan and laughed.

I cussed that bitch out just because Killian don't be acting crazy over her. I didn't want Kanan to kill anybody else. I invited Lucky and Quan also. I hope and pray Kaisha was just playing. I had my food cooking already. I smoked my ribs and chicken last night. I ordered some fruit trays too.

Kaniya

Sonja was having a barbecue. Raven, Killany, and I were going to fall through. I went to my doctor's appointment and found out what I was having today—a girl and a boy, fraternal twins. How about neither one of them niggas showed up to the appointment. That was so refreshing. I started to do a praise dance. I hoped my kids looked exactly like me. I still wasn't fucking with Tariq at all. I was cool on Lucky also.

I've been focused on Work Now Atlanta. The grand opening is September 6th and I can't wait. Since Raven found out that we're real sisters, she's moving back to Atlanta and moving in with me. Killany was envious, so she brought her ass up here too. I was ready to head over to Sonja's house because my babies were ready to eat. My skin was glowing, my breasts were fuller, and my ass was sticking out. You could sit a glass on this motherfucka. I was keeping it simple today, but I was dressed to the nines.

"Kaniya, come on, I'm ready," she pouted and whined. Raven was doing the most. She was ready to go because she was hungry.

"I'm ready too, let's go. I've heard about her gatherings," Killany beamed. Suddenly, she was ready to go to Sonja's house too. I looked at Killany and rolled my fuckin' eyes. She was competing with Raven bad. I was pulling up in my new 2016 Range Rover. I traded in the one that Lucky bought me. I got me some new new. You won't track my every move in this Rover. The Q-45 Infiniti that Tariq bought me, I traded that bitch in also for the new 2016 M56 Infiniti.

All my tags were custom made; they read SLF MDE (SELF MADE). I was always a boss before those niggas. I had to remind myself of that every time. I only needed a nigga for some hard dick and some fire ass head.

"Kaniya, do you think you and Tariq will ever get back together?" Raven asked. She wanted to know. "How do you truly feel because you never discussed the matter with me, and Tariq wanted to know." Ever since my mother told me don't talk in front of her because they could be recording me. I stopped but I didn't mind giving Raven an earful to run back and tell Tariq.

"Why, Raven? What makes you want to know? I would never take Tariq back. He did too much to get me to fuck up with no remorse. Hell no, it's a wrap. That's the reason I didn't want to cross that line because of this shit happening," I argued and explained. I let Raven know exactly how I felt. I knew she was recording me because she kept fuckin' with her phone.

"Lil sis, you have to pick a side, it's either Kaniya or Tariq," Killany stated. I looked at Killany and our eyes had their own conversation. Raven thinks she's slick. She knew her brother did some foul shit to me and to think I loved his ass.

"Do you still love him," she asked.

"I do. I will always love him, but I refuse to be with him. He did me wrong in the worst way possible. If I ever see Jassity again, it's on. That bitch will feel me. I understand that you fucked him but what made you want to send me that video to my fucking phone," I argued. I started to get pissed off just thinking about the day Tariq cheated on me and lied about where he was going just so he could go fuck another bitch.

"Sis, I'm not letting you fight with my niece and nephews. You can forget about that shit," Killany argued. I'm glad she's here. I missed her something serious. "I'm glad I'm here Kaniya, because I know how you can be." I watched Raven out the corner of my eye fuckin' with her phone. She was doing something. My phone alerted me that I had a text from Tariq

Him - Damn, my heart hurt just listening to that shit. I fucked up good. I can hear the hurt in your voice. I really love

you, Kaniya. I just made a bad decision and you're refusing to work through our little issue.

I wasn't even about to text him back. This breakup was really fucking with him. He needed more than an 'I'm sorry.'

We finally made it to Sonja's house and it was lit. There were so many cars wrapped around the block. It was crazy. I parked my Range Rover. I had to give myself the once over in the mirror to make sure I was perfect. I knew there was a chance that I would run into Tariq or Lucky.

I had to make sure I was giving those niggas something to miss. There were a lot of people here, some I knew and some I didn't. I saw my mom and she waved and motioned for us to come over. We made our way in her direction.

"Kaniya, Killany, and Raven, how are you? I wanted you three to meet some people. Follow me please, so I can introduce you guys to some young bosses," she explained. I wish my momma would sit her ass down. She would introduce us to some young bosses when I'm pregnant. Where the fuck was these niggas a few months ago. "I want Killany, or Raven to meet their futures. Joshen's nephews, Yung and Cartier. I hope y'all don't blow it. These niggas were caked the fuck up."

"Ma, you know I can't date anybody, I'm pregnant. Who are these guys, anyway? How do you know them? Raven and Killany are available," I explained. I wasn't really feeling my mom hooking me up with anyone. I don't need any extra drama in my life right now. She needs to hook Killany's ass up, shit.

"Kaniya, did you notice I didn't say your fuckin' name," she sassed and sucked her teeth.

"Mrs. Kaisha, I don't know about this," Raven stated. I don't know why she was nervous. I guess she wasn't ready to date anyone yet, especially a boss. School was her main priority. She was really scared that she'd be like me with Tariq and Lucky.

"Ma, who do you think you are now? I don't need you hooking me up with anybody," Killany sassed and sucked her teeth. Oh, lawd here she goes with this shit.

"Call me Kaisha, Raven. Last I checked, both of you were single, so let me hook y'all up. Kaniya, so what if you pregnant? Let me tell you about me when I was pregnant. I had all kinds of niggas buying me all kinds of shit that your dad never knew about. Damn, I forgot Killany's big mouth ass was here, run and tell that. Go with the flow, okay," she beamed proudly. My mother whispered in my ear. "They're acting old; they need to loosen up. I'm surprised at Raven; her mother was a hoe. She must be a good girl like the Millers?" I swear my momma don't give a fuck. I had to put my hand over my mouth so they wouldn't hear me laugh.

"Kaisha, damn, are these your daughters," they asked. My mother nodded her head in agreement. I guess they were intrigued with us.

"Yes, these are my girls. Killany, Raven, and Kaniya. Meet Yung and Cartier," she beamed proudly. Ma introduced them so they could get acquainted on their own. "Listen I put you guys in each other's presence for a reason. It's up to y'all to make it happen on your own." I swear I can't stand my momma; she does the most. Killany whispered in my ear.

"Damn, Yung and Cartier are sexy as fuck. I don't know which one I want. I want one of them, though. Momma has good taste; maybe coming to Atlanta wasn't a bad idea after all. I wonder if Raven will be my wingman. Damn, I hate you're pregnant; I know you would be down.

I'm feeling Yung, though. His swag is through the roof. I love his persona and let's not forget his looks. He can't keep his eyes off me. I can just imagine his caramel skin against mine. His beard between my honey pot and his gold grill in the crook of my neck.

Last, but not least, his big arms wrapped around my waist. Yeah, I'm having freaky thoughts to early. Lucky and Tariq are so fucking crazy. They'll ruin my shit just to fuck with you." I looked at Killany and smiled. I feel like a proud big sister. Raven tapped me on my shoulder, and she was smiling from ear to ear. She spoke low only loud enough for me to hear.

"Cartier is sexy as shit. He's been eye fucking me the whole time. What's a girl to do? I needed to see what's up with Killany, to see which one she's feeling because dammit, I want Cartier. Mrs. Kaisha's not bad after all, she's a cool ass mom.

Cartier is the finest man I've seen in a long time. His green eyes, caramel complexion and curly hair have me mesmerized. I'm intrigued with his physique. He's so tall and handsome. I hate looking into his eyes, it's like he's reading my soul. I hope your pregnant ass isn't checking for any of these niggas, she stated. I looked at Raven with wide eyes. I can't believe her.

"I'm good," I beamed proudly. Raven and Killany were talking about Yung and Cartier. I hope they make it happen. Men were the last thing on my mind.

Lucky

I spotted Kaniya a mile away. It's like I could feel her presence. I decided to fall through Sonja's cookout to see what's up. Who is this knock off Kaniya that's with her? I guess it's over between her and Tariq. That's the best ten thousand dollars I've ever spent. I need to call and thank Jassity for a job well done. She looks so much better without him.

Who is that nigga's face she's all up in? Let me go stop this shit right now. She has me all the way fucked up and she's pregnant with my seeds. I was grilling the shit out of that nigga. He saw me looking at his ass. She was off limits. I'll have her back no matter what. She will always and forever be my rider. I had to walk up on her and approach her now. I grabbed her from the back. She didn't even see me coming.

"Hey, baby. My babies miss me, don't they," I asked. I still had her heart five years later.

"Get your ass off me, Lucky. They wouldn't miss you if you came to the doctor's appointment. The nerve of this nigga to walk up on me from behind like we're cool like that," she sassed and sucked her teeth.

"I didn't come because I didn't want to look at your mutt-faced ass nigga. Who is this knock off that's with you?" I asked. I noticed this girl looks exactly like Kaniya. Who the fuck is she and where did she come from?

"Oh Lucky, this is Killany, my twin sister," she beamed proudly. Kaniya introduced us.

"I already know you Lucky, though. I saw you in some pictures and stuff," she explained. Kaniya sister knew me but I didn't know her.

"Why am I just now finding out that you have a twin sister and shit? You sure can keep a secret," I argued. I don't know what to believe about Kaniya any more. Shit, do I even know her?

"It's nice to finally meet your dog ass, too. Ain't shit knock off about me," she sassed and sucked her teeth. Kaniya must have been telling Killany our fuckin' business.

"I take it your sister has already dogged me out to you, huh? Don't believe everything you hear," I explained. Kaniya should've hooked her sister up with Tariq's bitch ass. I looked at Kaniya and her eyes were focused on something else. I heard her mumble under her breath.

"I know this nigga didn't come here with a bitch and we just broke up two weeks ago. He's so fuckin' disrespectful." I smiled and kissed her on her cheek. I noticed Kaniya checking out Tariq and his chick. I wanted her attention on me and not on him.

"Baby, what are we having," I asked. I needed to know what the doctor saw. I was ready to start buying shit and my mom was excited. I wish my dad was here.

"I'm having a boy and a girl, fraternal twins. The twins are kicking my ass. It's probably the girl more than the boy," she beamed.

"Baby momma, I see it's trouble in paradise. The grass isn't always greener on the other side. I'll let you come back since that nigga fucked you and left you. I know all three of my babies miss me," I chuckled. I had to put that out there. "I see Tariq and his new chick, that's a good look for him."

"I'm cool, Lucky. Thanks for the gesture, but I'm good as you can see. I like being single. I guess you saw Tariq and his chick that he brought through here?" She asked. I nodded my head in agreement.

"Let me feed you and my babies," I stated. I wanted Kaniya in the worst way. I couldn't seem to shake her for nothing. She still held the key to my heart.

Chapter-27

KC

I was invited to this little barbecue by my partners in crime, Yung and Cartier, invited me to. I like Atlanta, but I could never live here. Atlantic City was my home. That's where I run the streets and ball. I need to call my Auntie Amber and let her know that I'm here for a few days and I want to see her. She'd go nuts if she knew I stepped in her city and didn't reach out. I made my way to the barbecue; it wasn't far from where I was staying.

It was a nice house and it had a nice crowd. Yung's silly ass sent me a text talking about we got some sisters and they bad, too. This nigga here is a fool. He knew damn well he couldn't settle down for shit. I couldn't wait until the day came when a chick was able to tie him down. I couldn't care less about whatever females were here because Armony had my full attention.

No female could compare to her, not even my mother who ran off on me when I was a jitterbug. For some reason, lately, I've been thinking about my mom more than ever. Every time I would ask my dad or auntie about her, they would brush me off. I wanted to meet her so I could spit in the bitch's face for abandoning me twenty-eight years ago.

I was going to fall through this spot for a minute to see what these fools were up to. My aunt texted me back and said she would fall through in a minute. My flight leaves tomorrow at 10:45 p.m. I wasn't missing it for anything. I was missing Armony something serious. I was ready to take my ass back home. I'm pissed she didn't want to come with me.

She knows that she's the air that I breathe. She gives me life. I'm ready to marry her and she keeps hinting if I don't soon, she's leaving me. I wish she would, I'll kill her mom and grandma, now play. I texted Yung and Cartier to let them know I was pulling up so they could be looking out for me. I didn't want to be pulling up at this spot by myself. I didn't know these folks.

Tariq

Damn, I fucked up. I didn't know that Kaniya would be here. I fucked around and brought Gabrielle with me to this little barbecue at Sonja's house. Raven failed to mention that they were falling through. I've been kicking it with her for about two weeks. I wasn't feeling Gabrielle. She was just something to do. Who was that niggas face Kaniya was smiling in like she was single and shit? Kaniya got me fucked up. I started flexing and shit. It was about to go down.

"What's wrong, baby?" She asked. I guessed Gabrielle noticed my whole mood had changed. Something had my attention and it's not her.

"I'm good shawty, I just have some shit on my mind," I explained and brushed her off. Why is she questioning me? Stay in your place.

"Oh, I see what has your attention, lying ass nigga. You're still checking for your baby momma and it looks like she's checking for somebody else," she argued and sucked her teeth. I waived Gabrielle off. I wasn't trying to go there with her. I don't owe her an explanation. I had enough of watching her and Lucky and this other fuck nigga. I had to remove her and myself from this situation. I left Gabrielle and started approaching Kaniya. I could tell she had an attitude. Ask me did I care. I didn't want to make a scene, though. I motioned with my hand for her to come over to me. She started walking my way. She stood in front of me and folded her arms across her chest.

"What's up, Tariq? What you want? Where's your bitch at that you brought with you?" She argued and asked. "I had to let you know I saw you, and you're caught."

"Give me a hug, Kaniya. Damn, I miss you something serious," I explained and smiled. Kaniya wasn't budging. I had to force her to give me a hug. I heard her whisper.

"I missed being in your arms."

"I miss you too." I picked Kaniya's ass up and carried her up out of here. I walked to my car quick. She was slapping me and punching me in my face. I threw her ass in the car and put the child lock on.

"I don't want to ride with you. I don't want to be kidnapped by you again. The nerve of you Tariq, to pull a damn stunt like that," she argued. She smacked and punched the fuck out of my face.

"I'm sorry, damn, what more do I have to do?" I asked. I was pleading my case at this point; I wanted to get past this shit. All niggas fuck up.

"You don't have to do shit. Do you see me sweating you and running up behind you, begging you to be here with me? I'm good. You fucked up, not me," she argued.

"You don't want this anymore, Kaniya?" I asked. I pointed between her and I. "Is it really over between us?" I wanted to know what's in store for our future. I wanted to marry her.

"It's over, Tariq. It was over before it started. Let me out of your car. I'm glad to get that off my chest. You're free to move on and so am I," she stated.

"It's not over until I say it's over. I'm not leaving and we're not breaking up. You can forget about that shit," I argued and explained. I was about to pull off.

"Oh, so you want to pull off now. You can't force me to be with you. Did I force you to fuck Jassity?" She asked. Kaniya was livid. I couldn't believe she was acting like this.

"I was drugged and fuckin' set up. I knew Jassity set me up, but I can't prove it, though," I argued. Somebody started shooting suddenly and the air left my tires. I pushed Kaniya down on the ground.

"First, you're drugged, now someone is shooting at us. What the fuck, Tariq?" She argued. She tried to open the car door to fire some shots back thank God I had the child lock on. "I don't know what the fuck you got going on."

"Didn't I tell you about toting that shit while you're pregnant with my seeds?" I argued and asked. She's hardheaded and you can't tell her shit.

"Open the fucking door Kaniya, and get your ass out of this car now," he yelled. "I don't know what the fuck you and Tariq got going on." I know that wasn't Lucky at my fuckin' car.

"I can't, he has the child lock on," she explained. "Tariq, you know you're a childish, crazy ass, motherfucker for pulling this bullshit."

"Oh, you back fucking him now?" I asked. "You got me fucked up. You're already back with this nigga. I can't believe you, especially after the way he talked to you a couple of weeks ago at Mac's birthday party."

"Unlock the door so I can get out," she argued. "I don't have time for your bullshit today or any other day."

"So, you're adamant about getting out of this car to go fuck with him?" I asked. She has me curious now. She's very persistent about getting out of here.

"I'm killing this nigga today, watch me." I argued. I'm sick of Lucky. She thinks I'm fuckin' playing, but I'm dead serious. I'm sick of him and her.

"Do what you got to do. Let me up out of this bitch. I don't care about your threats today," she argued. I had to step out of the car to see what this nigga wanted and why he shot my tires out.

"What the fuck you want?" I asked. Today was the fucking day. I'm tired of him coming at me sideways.

"Let my baby momma up out your motherfuckin' shit. You can't be holding her against her fuckin' will. You can miss me with that kidnapping shit, partner," he argued and yelled. Who in the fuck did this nigga think he was? It was on today.

"Oh, you mad about our baby momma. Remember I fucked, too, did you forget? We're still together, don't worry about how I handle her." I had to remind that nigga there was a possibility that they were not his.

"I'm not with your dirty dick ass. I'm a free agent," she argued. "Don't be claiming me."

"Watch your fucking mouth," I argued and yelled. She couldn't wait to let this nigga know we're not together. That's why he's doing this shit. They're back kicking it.

"Whatever. That skunk you came through here with, she needs to be riding with you. It's just like, a man to be in their feelings when they came with a chick. You're stalking me for what, though," she sassed and sucked her teeth.

"Get your ass back in the fucking car, Kaniya. I'm not going to tell you any more." She's really trying me and being extra slick at the mouth.

"Aye watch how the fuck you talk to her," he argued. "You're really trying to handle her out here like that shit was going to fly with me."

"Let me guess you're back fuckin' her so that's why you got an issue, but Lucky, this ain't what you want today. Move around partner and mind your fuckin' business and not mine," I argued. The way I'm feeling, this nigga doesn't want it; he can get these slugs.

"Kaniya, get your ass in my fucking car right now. This shit is about to get real really quick," he argued and threatened. I'm killing this man today and I don't need her ass in the way.

Kaniya

Oh my God. It was about to go down in front of Sonja's house. Lucky and Tariq were about to shoot it out. Tariq was doing to fuckin' much. I wasn't trying to be the obedient chick. I was on my messy shit. I did what I was told and got in Lucky's coupe. I knew that would piss Tariq off, but so what. What did I do that shit for? Tariq is grilling the fuck out of me now. I know he wants to lay hands on my ass. He must have forgotten I do what the fuck I want to do.

"I'm about to kill his ass now," he yelled. Lucky was on one. "I made that shit clear to you Kaniya. I already told you I was going to make you fuckin' watch."

"No, you're not, Lucky. Let this shit go, man. He ain't worth it. I'm not letting you do it," I pleaded. "Please don't do this."

"You love him that much that you're begging me not to kill him? I already told you don't get in my fuckin' way or I'll hit your pregnant ass up, too. One of us has to go and it damn sure ain't me," he argued and explained. "I don't even know why you're stressing because you know how this shit goes."

"Fuck that, Lucky. It's not that fucking serious. I can own up to my mistakes. I shouldn't have fucked with him, but he's not worth the hollow tips and I don't want that shit on my conscience," I explained. I made my way out of Lucky's car and back to Tariq. I was not about to let him die today. I sent Killany a text to get out here quick.

"I see your back-dick hopping," he argued and grilled me. "I should've listened to John and Mac. They said you would ride with that nigga until the wheels fell off."

"I'm stopping this nigga from doing something to you," I argued and sucked my teeth. He's coming at me sideways. This shit is deeper than Lucky and me and whatever he thinks we got going on.

"Oh, he's on some fuck shit. He wants to kill me behind you. I want to kill his ass too. I'm begging for a nigga to try me. I got some hot shit for his ass, too," he argued and yelled. Tariq was hyped. He went to his trunk and grabbed his AK-47. It was on today.

Yung

I was feeling Killany. I liked her style and her whole demeanor. We exchanged numbers and shit. We've been texting the whole time I've been at this barbecue. Her sister, Kaniya, was bad, too, but she was pregnant and had some shit with her. Each time we would talk, two different niggas would start grilling me. I didn't have time for that extra heat. I wanted to get to know Killany a little better. She had me in a trance. I couldn't keep my eyes off her. I wanted some alone time with her. This barbecue wasn't doing me any justice. I had to hit her up to see if she wanted to get away.

Yung - Run off with me.

Killany - When?

Yung - Now.

Killany - Alright. Meet me out front. My sister got shit popping out front and she needs back up.

I knew her sister had some shit going on with her. We made our way out front to see what was going on. Those same two niggas that were grilling me were out here with AK-47s and AR 15s about to set this shit off like it's the Fourth of July. Her pussy must be lethal, damn. I don't want any of that shit. I can tell she plays a lot of games, though. I feel like I need to protect Killany, though.

"This shit is crazy, what in the fuck has Kaniya gotten herself into this time? Last time I checked, she wasn't entertaining neither one of these clowns," she whispered.

"What happened?" I needed to know what type of shit was going on. Her sister had two Glock 40s out. What the fuck is she doing with that shit and pregnant? Killany pulled out a Desert Eagle?

"It's a long story," she sighed. "Fuckin' with Kaniya, she's about to get me caught up in her bullshit. The first nigga that I'll shoot would be Tariq's ass."

"If you're going to be my woman, no secrets," I stated. I kept my eyes trained on Killany. She really didn't want to tell me what the fuck was going on, but she pulled out a Desert Eagle.

"Did I just hear you correctly? What makes you think I'm going to be your woman?" She asked. "You're cute and all, but damn, it's to early to be putting a title on shit."

"I just know you want me as bad as I want you." She can front all she wants to. I know she's feeling the kid. She can cut that acting shit out. I can take her to Hollywood if she's ready.

"How do you know I want you, though?" She asked.

"I see you and your sister are one in the same. You play games too and I don't have time for that high school shit. My money is to fuckin' long and I'm a young fly rich nigga. I'm not chasing no female that don't want to be kept," I explained. I had to let Killany know that's how I'm coming because this shit Kaniya has going on, I'm not with it at all. She can chalk it.

"Oh, you're mad, huh? I'm sorry if I offended you. I'm iconic. My sister and I are night and day. You can't speak on something you don't know anything about. I'm not looking for anything. I'm running up a check, too," she sassed and sucked her teeth. Killany had an attitude. "Yung just so you know, please don't get this shit confused. I'm not looking for a come up. I have my own money, so I'm not impressed by that."

Kaniya

"Look, I'm sick of y'all two with this little boy shit. It's enough black on black crime in the community. I refuse to let you two be the next niggas on a R.I.P. tee shirt or hold a candlelight vigil for the both of you. I'm so tired of this shit. Niggas are dying every day behind some bullshit. If I could change back the hands of time, trust me, I would to avoid this shit every time we run into each other. I can't change the past, but I can mold the future. I'm sorry but I don't want you two beefing behind whatever. All three of us are in the wrong. I can own up to my shit but y'all can't. Please let this shit go," I argued. I'm sick of Lucky and Tariq. This shit must stop every time we see each other.

"This ain't about you, Kaniya. It's deeper than that," Lucky argued. I knew he was pissed but let it go please. "There're rules and levels to this shit. He crossed them, so he must pay."

"I don't give a fuck Lucky, cut the bullshit. If I never would've dated him, you wouldn't have any beef with him, so let it go, please. Don't die behind me, I promise you I won't be able to live with this shit. Let this feud go that you two have going on.

Tariq, there's no more us, you blew it. Lucky, it's been a wrap. If the issue is deeper than that and y'all still want to shoot it out, and y'all are willing to die behind this shit. Well, let me shoot both of y'all niggas for playing me like I'm an average bitch." I argued. I've had enough of this shit. It's time for them to let it go and move on. I walked Lucky to his car. Tariq was still looking at me and I don't know why. Focus on the bitch you brought and not me.

We made it to Lucky's car. I was waiting on him to get in and pull off. He just stood there and looked at me. I said what I had to say, and I don't have anything else to say. I started to walk off, but he grabbed my hand. I looked over my shoulder to see what he wanted.

"I miss you, Kaniya. You know I love you," he stated.

"I love you too Lucky, and I miss you." I tried to walk off because I wasn't trying to get caught up with him again. I've been there and done that. He grabbed my hand.

"Why are you walking away when I'm trying to talk to you? Come here." I stood in front of him. He placed his hands on my stomach. "I know I fucked up and I'm sorry for that. I promise you I'm going to get this shit right for them and you." Lucky wrapped his arms around me. I missed him.

Chapter-28

Cartier

Raven, Raven, Raven. Damn, she was a bad girl. I need to make sure I thank Ms. Kaisha every day. Raven was going to be my wife. I already knew it. She couldn't keep her eyes off me. She liked what she saw and so did I. She has a story, her eyes told it all. Every time I would catch her looking at me, she would hurry up and turn her head. I knew she was feeling me. I guess I was going to be that nigga that brought her out of her shell.

When Yung and her sister exchanged numbers, I looked her dead in her eye to see if she wanted mine and she didn't budge. I knew she was playing hard to get. She turned her head quick, but I wasn't leaving here until I got her number. I don't mind the chase or the effort. I can tell she's worth it. I'll wear her ass down. I'm irresistible.

I just need to prove to her that I'm worth it. I'm tired of watching and thinking about her from afar. I needed to make my move. Now was the perfect time. She had her back turned. I was approaching her from behind and she didn't even know it. Damn, she smells good. I wrapped my arms around her waist and put my nose in the crook of her neck. I whispered in her ear and told her "I want you." She looked over her shoulders and smiled at me. She tried to pry my arms from around her waist but that wasn't working.

I grabbed her phone and put my number in it. I told her, "Aye, you should make use of my number within twenty-four hours or I'm coming to find you." I just put myself out there. Now it's a waiting game I hope she uses it.

Raven

Damn, what is Cartier trying to do to me? I want him in the worst way. Listen at me, I don't even sound like myself. He wrapped his arms around me. Oh my gosh, it felt so right. My heart melted and my body vibrated. He smells so good. His Creed cologne invaded my nostrils. I began to get moist between my legs just thinking about our encounter.

He has me mesmerized. Mrs. Kaisha is so fucking messy, taking pictures of us. Tariq would kill me if he knew I was dating. I'm curious about Cartier, he has me intrigued. I want to know what it is that he wants from me. I'm still a virgin. Why is he interested in me? I'll need some relationship tips from Kaniya.

I can't ask Killany because she's so full of shit and secretive. This past week I've been trying to get to know her and she hasn't opened, up to me at all. I bet she could've told you everything about me and then some, though. I can tell she's envious of me and Kaniya's relationship, but I'm not going anywhere. Kaniya has been my sister before we found out that we share the same DNA. Killany can move around with that little side shit that she has going on.

Yes, I moved in with Kaniya. She was so happy because she would call me damn near every week when I was in

California. She knew I didn't have any family out there to check on me and make sure I was good. When I asked her if I could move in, she begged me to.

She's the best big sister ever and always has been. Despite Kaisha's dislike for my mom, she treated me just like her daughter. I never felt out of place or unwanted. She included me in everything.

Sonja

I can't believe this little barbecue was turning out nice and very laid back. No drama at all. I forgot all about Kaisha's ass having twins. They never mention Killany at all. She looks just like Killian's ass, it's crazy. Raven looks just like her sisters. Hell, she has moved out of my house and with her sister. Nasir had sent me a text stating that he was on his way. I'm sweating bullets. Kaisha has invited this man's whole damn family to my house.

I saw his nephew Cartier pushing up on Raven. I didn't like that shit. She was innocent and still a virgin. He was a straight dope boy. I didn't want her exposed to that shit at all. I wouldn't have to worry to much because her sister wouldn't let her go down the wrong path, not to mention her crazy ass daddy. To this day, Killian and I aren't seeing eye to eye because of this little incident, shit.

He never asked me, so hell, I assumed she wasn't his or he didn't want anything to do with her. I just hope and pray that Kanan's crazy ass doesn't show up over here. Yashir and Kanan Jr. reports to Kanan every fucking thing that goes on over here. I told them to quit telling my fuckin' business and mind their own.

I wish Kaniya would come take them back to her fuckin' house, shit. These past few months Kanan has been driving me crazy. I went to my primary care doctor and my blood pressure was sky high. I've been seeing Dr. Sims for the past sixteen years. When Kanan was away my blood pressure was never high. She knew he had to be out because my blood pressure hasn't been this high in almost seven years. I received a text from Nasir saying he was about to pull up and the that he was parking now.

I needed to be discreet with this shit. Kanan Jr. and Yashir were so damn nosey. I asked them earlier did they want to go to the mall because I knew they would report some shit. I offered to buy them the new Jordan's that came out today and some Huaraches. Guess what? They said I buy them to many shoes. They didn't feel like going to the mall today.

Since when they didn't want to go to the mall and look for thots? I love them two to death. They've really grown on me. They are really Kanan's children. Oh my gosh, when they grow up, they are going to be hell in these streets.

Chapter-29

Nasir

I finally made it to Sonja's house. I noticed Yung out front with some younger chicks that looked like Kaisha. It seems like it was some heat outside. I'll ask Yung about that later. I wanted to see Sonja. Damn, she was bad as fuck to be forty-five with no kids. Also, she had no drama and no baggage. I noticed she was a little cautious to bring me to her home. I knew all about Kanan and Deuce. She told me about that shit.

We were just kicking it for the moment. If she wanted anything more than that, I couldn't offer her that right now. I make to many moves to be tied down and committed. We were just cool and having casual relations. That's all she wanted too. Her life was complicated. I made my way inside of the barbecue. I noticed there was plenty of food and drinks and everything smelled good.

Cartier was even booed up with some little cutie. I spotted Kaisha and Sonja. My brother Joshen wanted Kaisha in the worst way. I wouldn't say that Kaisha was a gold digger, but she had a few cats in her back pocket and she let Joshen know that. That's why he's not here. Kaisha told him he could come, but she had some other niggas that were going to fall through also.

"Hey, I see you made it," she beamed. I pulled Sonja in for a hug and my hands roamed her body. She whispered in my ear. "Damn Nasir, you're so damn fine. Caramel brown just like I like them. With hazel brown eyes, nice build, long beard, and nice waves that have me seasick." I grabbed a handful of her ass and a soft moan escaped her lips.

"Nice to see you, too. You see something you like? Give me a hug, shit," I stated. I stood back and took Sonja in. She was looking at me like she wanted to eat me. I wouldn't mind sampling that pussy again today.

Sonja

This man right here knows he does something to me. My pussy got wet quick just by being in his presence. Lord, forgive me for these thoughts I'm having right now. Just the touch of him gripping on my ass I'm ready to come up out of these clothes and sit on his fuckin' face.

"Aye, man, get your fucking hands up off my momma's ass," he yelled. I looked over my shoulder to see who it was. It was Kanan Jr. yelling. "Aye nigga, I don't appreciate this shit, feeling on my momma's ass out in the open." I just shook my head. I heard the flash on his phone. I bet that little motherfucka sent that picture to his dad. I knew he would be on his way.

"Watch your damn mouth, Kanan Jr," I argued. Where was this little nigga hiding at? I know I looked around and didn't see him and Yashir. I thought maybe they were in the pool or asleep.

"What the fuck? Sonja, I thought you said you didn't have any kids," he argued. "I see how women lie. You know you're too old for this shit. As wide as your hips are, I knew you carried somebody's child."

"Mom, what the fuck is going on out here?" Yashir asked. I swear I'm going to fuck up Kanan Jr. and Yashir up.

"Damn, Sonja, you have twins? These some grown little niggas, too," he asked. "Not one, but two kids. Oh, hell no. I don't have time for this shit." Nasir was showing the real fuckin' him.

"Those are her roommates that we told you about. They're fucking with you," Kaisha explained? Kanan Jr. and Yashir had Nasir shook. They act just like their daddy and uncle. Since when did Kanan Jr. and Yashir start calling me momma? They've been here two damn months and have never called me mom or no shit like that. These are some bad motherfuckers right here, fucking up my flow and shit.

Kaisha

"Sonja's bold as fuck. Kanan Jr. sent me the picture of her and some lame ass nigga. I guess it's time for Daddy to come over there and lay down the law. I tried to call my boys back and they didn't answer the phone. So, I called you Kaisha. She got me fucked up," he argued and explained. I wish I hadn't answered the fuckin' phone.

"What the fuck do you want, Kanan? Why are you on my line?" I asked. I knew those twins had gotten some shit started. Why else would Kanan be calling my phone?

"You tell Sonja and whoever else that's at the fucking barbecue they better fucking clear it because I'm on my way. Me and my fuckin' task force. Any nigga she got and you got with your old ass, I'm laying bodies down. I'm going to fire one warning shot, and after that, I'm making a fucking mess. You better fuckin' clear it now," he argued and yelled. Kanan had so much venom in his voice. He hung up the phone on me. I didn't want to hear his smart-ass comments anyway.

Who did Kanan think he was? Bitch, you bleed just like everybody else; you can get touched too. He's not the only nigga with a fuckin' task force. He didn't scare me like he scared Sonja.

Killian knows he doesn't run shit here, married or not. I do what the fuck I want, not what I can. I couldn't believe this silly ass motherfucka was calling my phone with threats.

Sonja

I knew some shit was about to pop off. Kanan just called my phone. I needed to get Nasir out of here quick. I didn't want anybody getting killed today or at my house. I lived here. I knew how crazy Kanan was. Kaisha liked drama and shit. That was a high for her.

"Nasir let me holla at you for a minute," I said. I needed this man out of my house right now. I wanted to keep fuckin' him, but I wasn't ready to let that dick go just yet. I needed him to comply and leave as he was told.

"What's up, baby? What's wrong?" He asked. "What did you need to speak with me about?" I knew Nasir wouldn't like what I was about to say but it is what it is.

"I need you to leave right now. Kanan is on his way over here and I don't want you to get hurt or killed," I pleaded. I knew Kanan would kill him just to prove a point.

"It's that serious, Sonja? I'll leave, I'm not ready to die yet. I still want to sample that pussy again. I'm not a pussy ass nigga. We're just kicking it and I'm not dying behind no pussy that's not mine. I'm going to leave, though," he explained. Thank God Nasir wasn't a dummy. He left without a hassle or asking any questions. That's some dick that I want to sample again and soon.

"You knew what time it was, huh?" Kaisha asked. I knew Kanan was crazy.

"I wanted to see if he was about that life. I haven't seen him cut up in a long time. I don't fear him, though." As if on cue, that warning shot went off. She laughed. Kanan is a damn fool I swear. I can't have shit without him fuckin' it up.

Chapter-30

Raven

Oh Lord, some shit must have popped off. Here goes Uncle Kanan firing off warning shots and shit. Kanan Jr. and Yashir must have told him about Auntie Sonja's new little friend. I'm glad Cartier left. I didn't want anything to happen to him before I even got to know him. Let me text my sisters to see where they are so they won't get hurt in the process.

Me - Where are you and Killany? Kanan shooting.

Kaniya - I know. We're out front. I see your little boo just left. It just went down and you missed it.

Me - Oh Lord, I don't want to know. Is my brother alive and safe?

Kaniya - Yes, he is.

"You forgot how real this shit really gets when a motherfucka tests me? Kanan Jr. and Yashir, where did that fuck nigga go? Point him out so I can lay him down," he argued and yelled. "Kaisha you know I don't fuckin' play any games. Why did you want to see all these innocent people get hurt? I need to talk to Killian's ass. He needs to get a better grip on you. I wish you would take your ass back home. I don't like you and Sonja

hanging together. I didn't like it then and I don't like it now."
Uncle Kanan was crazy.

"He's gone, OG. You just missed them," Yashir laughed.
He thought that shit was funny, but it wasn't. I can't believe
Uncle Kanan was this fuckin' crazy. Well, it was kinda funny. I
wanted to see how he would act when they sent pictures of Sonja
doing her.

"Why did you come over here with that bullshit, Kanan?
Do I go over your house showing out when you have company?"
She asked.

"That's the fucking problem, you ain't coming over there.
That's why I'm acting a damn fool. I told you don't have no
niggas around my sons, and you didn't want to listen. So, there
will be consequences every time. Raven keep them niggas out
your face, too. You can dead that shit that you have going on. Go
change your fucking clothes? Why do you have those tight ass
shorts on trying to be like Kaisha?

Don't let Kaisha get y'all in trouble," he argued. Uncle
Kanan threw out demands. He laid down the law for today. "It
feels good. I lived another day to put some fear up in Sonja's ass.
The task force didn't have to use any ammo."

Cartier

"**D**on't move nephew. I want to see how this Kanan nigga is moving. Ali Bum Biyae told me about him and his crew. I'm going to watch him from afar just to see what type of shit he was on. I'm glad y'all cleared this motherfuckin' spot because some shit was about to go down, and I didn't want y'all near," he explained. My uncle Nasir must have been fuckin' with one of those old heads at the barbecue.

The little barbecue was cool. We had to leave early because my Uncle Nasir said some heat was coming through and he didn't want us to get caught in the crossfire. We sat in the cut for a minute. Sure enough, ten minutes later this guy pulled up in this Bentley GT, then six black Suburban's pulled up behind him. All the men were dressed in black with assault rifles. He reminds me of an older version of my nigga KC.

"What the fuck is going on, Nasir?"

"That's Sonja's ex, Kanan. He was coming to see about me. She gave me the heads up to leave so I wouldn't get hurt," he chuckled. This fool Kanan was doing to much behind some pussy that he hasn't put a ring on.

"Damn Nasir, that man is moving like that behind some pussy," I laughed. These old heads do extremely to much behind females. I'm not doing all that shit.

"I don't want her pussy like that if he's mobbing that hard behind it," he explained. I couldn't believe this fool was doing this much just off an assumption. "She told me he was crazy, but not this crazy."

"That's nothing, Nasir, Kaisha's daughter Kaniya had two niggas outside ready to body someone behind her," I explained. Yung said the shit was foolish. I'm glad Kaniya stopped it. She wasn't one of those females that liked shit like that. I had a text come through from a number I didn't have saved.

213-780-9366: What's up, you good?

Cartier- Who is this?

213-780-9366: Ray.

Cartier - I'm good. I could be better.

213-780-9366: I was just making sure you were good. My crazy Uncle just pulled up.

Cartier - Yeah, I saw him. You were checking on your man.

I see Raven was playing hard to get. She didn't respond to my text. I'm glad she used my number, though. Trust me I was going to come looking for her. Yung mentioned something about shooting to New Orleans for a few days. He was going to ask Killany to go with him. I wonder if Ray would be down to ride with me. I'll hit her up in a few. I hope she says yes. I can tell she's kind of shy.

Killany

My sister has the life, man. Tariq and Lucky were about to shoot it out right in front of Sonja's house behind her hot pussy ass. She doesn't make shit any better. I saw Tariq carry her outside. I watched her smack and punch him in the face. I don't know what happened. Lucky was livid and he was ready to kill this nigga today. Tariq was ready to kill him too. It always goes down at Sonja's house. I witnessed that firsthand today. Yung and I were supposed to run away, but he wanted to get fly at the mouth about my sister, speaking on some shit that he knows nothing about.

I had to stop him in his tracks. Don't judge a book by its cover because you don't know what happened for them to get to this point. He was still blowing up my phone trying to get me to run away with him. I was cool on him, though. I had to make sure my sister was straight. I was her backup. I didn't know if Tariq would try and kidnap her again. To make matters worse Kanan's crazy ass pulled up with an AK-47 and some fuckin' Military men like he was fuckin' Rambo and shit. He needs to sit his old ass down somewhere seriously. My dad and him are night and day. I noticed a two door Maserati coupe pulled up in front of me. He hopped out looking fly as fuck.

"You like ignoring me, huh? I noticed you saw my texts and didn't respond," he asked. "I see now I'm going to have to break you in. You're on that tough girl shit walking around with a Desert Eagle and shit." I had to contain my smile. I wasn't about to do this with him. Not here and not now.

"So, let me guess, you're a stalker now?" I asked. Where did this nigga come from? I know he didn't think he was my dad because that's the only man I answer too.

"You can call me what you want. Let's ride, though," he explained. "Your mouth is a little to slick for my liking. I'm going to have to work on that. You need some good dick in your motherfuckin' life. I got you, though." He let out a small chuckle. I wanted to bite my bottom lip so bad.

"I'm not riding nowhere with you," I sassed and sucked my teeth. I don't know who he thought I was. I don't ride with strangers.

"Really? You're playing hard to get?" He asked. "You want me to chase your ass and do extra shit. I'm not like those fuck niggas. I lay down the law. Your sister has those niggas pussy whipped. I'm the opposite, Killany. I'll have you dick whipped. I'm not playing. I'm dead serious."

"What the fuck did I get myself into," I mumbled. This nigga Yung is very comical and persistent.

"You like for niggas to chase you, huh? And show out and shit?" He asked. "I'm a real ass nigga I command attention and respect. I'm not with that little kid ass shit or childish ass games. I've already told you once to come on and let's ride. I'm not going to tell you anymore. I'm going to show you what type of boss I am." He walked over to me and whispered in my ear.

"It's your best bet to get in this fuckin' car right now. You showed your ass enough and you don't want me to show mine." He opened the passenger side door and ushered for me to get in. I just shook my head because I wasn't ready to give in. Yung thought he was a real boss. He moved like one, though. The only reason why I chilled out was because Kaniya whispered in my ear and told me too.

"Cut it out Killany. He might be the one so go easy on him. I like him for you," she smiled. I rolled my eyes at Kaniya. I can't believe her. I did want to see what he was about, though. I slid in Yung's passenger seat praying that I didn't regret this. He closed the door and jogged to the driver side and pulled off. No words were spoken between us.

"You're quiet for somebody who just had a lot to say," he chuckled and stated. "Killany, you're to quiet for me. I got to watch quiet people because they can't be trusted."

"I'm good, I was just thinking about some shit that's all. Where are we going?" I asked. Yung was sexy. I did want to get to know him some more but he had to work for me. I wasn't just willing to be with him. I have a lot to offer. I need somebody to match my hustle and bring something to the table.

"New Orleans! Is that cool with you, Killany?" He asked. "Talk to me, what are you thinking about over there. I'm feeling you. I want to get to know you some more." Yung was talking a good game, but we'll see.

"Swing me by my sister's house so I can pack some clothes," I stated. I knew the nigga said chill but damn New Orleans to chill.

"Baby, you're fuckin' with a boss. Whatever you want I'll buy it when we get there. You don't need a bag. You'll bring some bags back, though," he explained. "I know I fucked you up with that one. I had to let you know what it was with me. Whatever you need I got it."

"Really, Yung? I'm a boss too. I'm caked up. I like to buy my own. Whatever you have is extra, it's a motherfuckin' bonus,"

I sassed and sucked my teeth. Yung was probably used to chicks going crazy about what he could do for them. That shit didn't excite me. My whole fit I had on today was Balmain from my head to my fuckin' toes.

"I hear you, Killany. I want you to stack your money and spend my money. I'm not a trick, I don't trick off on hoes. I'm a man and I want to take care of my lady," he explained. His eyes were trained on me. I can't take it. This man was trying to snatch my soul with his fuckin' words. "I put myself out there and I want you to know how I feel about you."

Raven

I sent Cartier a text to see what was up with him. I'm curious about him. He was mysterious but mainly because I knew Kanan was crazy. My uncle didn't mind killing innocent people to make an example. I just wanted to make sure he was okay. I could still smell his Creed cologne on my clothes. He was a little to close to me. I loved how he wanted my attention. I haven't dated anyone that could keep my attention. If I decide to give Cartier a chance, he would be my first everything.

He shot me a text asking me would I get away with him for a few days. I want to say yes, but I'm scared. I've never been alone with a guy before, especially not for a couple of days. This would be new for me. Mrs. Kaisha sent me the picture that she took of us. We did look good together. I need to ask Kaniya what I should do.

"Hey, Kaniya, can I ask you a question?"

"Sure, Ray what's up?" She asked. "What you want Raven? I hope you're not asking me shit about Tariq." I pinched Kaniya. Tariq and her are the last people on my mind.

"Cartier asked me to go away with him for a few days, but I don't know. I really want to go but damn I barely even know him. I have never been alone with a guy before overnight."

"Awe Ray, Cartier, and Yung ain't playing about you and Killany. Do you want to go? Killany sent me a text and told me she was headed to New Orleans with Yung. I think you should go," she explained. "Shoot Ray, you better go head. You only live once. I wish I weren't in this condition because I would've rode with them."

"I really want to go Kaniya, but I've never been alone with a guy before especially not for three days. I'm still a virgin. That's what I was concerned about. What if he wants to have sex? I'm not ready for that just yet. Sex hasn't crossed my mind at all. School's my focus," I sighed. I wasn't ready to give up my V-Card yet.

"I don't think he'll try to pressure you for sex. I didn't get that vibe from him. If he does tell that nigga no. If he insists, shoot his ass in his nuts. Do you still have your gun? Take it with you for protection. Ray, you're finally growing up and Cartier might be the one," she beamed and smiled.

"I don't get a bad vibe from him. I think I'll go. Don't tell Tariq or daddy." I'm curious about Cartier. I want to be alone with him. I hope Tariq don't find out because he'll go crazy.

"Ray, I don't either. Why would I tell Tariq? I'm not talking to him. I think you should go, too. You need to live a little. You're to old to be acting so sheltered. It's my fault. though. You're twenty-one and a Miller. Tariq needs to mind his own damn business."

"Okay, cool. He might be the one, sis. What do you think? I'm feeling him a little. I'm not going to lie. Check out our picture mom took of us," I beamed. I wanted Kaniya's opinion about Cartier and me. I think we look good together.

"I'm jealous. I'll be home all alone and you and Killany are going on a baecation. I'm happy for you guys, though. I hope Yung and Cartier are the ones for you two. Hey, momma vouched for them. Maybe one day I'll find somebody to love me unconditionally," she smiled. "I hope you and Killany get your shot at your one true love. Ray and Cartier and Killany and Yung, that shit sounds good together."

"Stop, Kaniya. You have two men that love you to death. If anything, I'm jealous of you. I want that type of hood love without the drama. I'm still rooting for you and Tariq even though he messed up. I want y'all to be together for the sake of your kids." I was telling the truth. The love that Tariq and Lucky have for Kaniya is a hood love that many dreamed of having.

Chapter-31

Kanan

It was early as fuck and I just left my Saturday morning workout. I just came from Planet Fitness. I was tired for some reason. Normally when I work out, I'm energized. I've had a lot of shit on my mind lately. I've been chilling, laying low for no reason. I don't know about everybody else but when I feel some shit brewing my body tells me to sit still and wait. My boys were ready to come back home. School was about to start in a few weeks for them anyway.

They've been giving Sonja and Kaniya hell. They refused to go back over to Kaniya's house. I've been thinking about settling down anyways. I didn't know if Sonja was ready, but I was. I don't know what to say about Sonja. She's been running around with Kaisha's ass thinking she's young again. She had no clue that I knew about her little trips to New York to kick it with some nigga Kaisha introduced her too.

I wish Killian's bitch ass would lock her down. I don't need Sonja thinking that she can do what the fuck she wants to do. I'm not having that shit. I've been meaning to call Kaisha and tell her she needs to find her a new friend and sit her old ass down. She's about to be a grandma for god sake. I was finally ready to wife Sonja. The first thing that I was nipping in the bud is that house. That shit had to go and hanging with Kaisha every day, that shit was about to stop, too.

Kaisha tries Killian and they're still married. I already bought Sonja a ring a month ago. I had Chelle to pick it out for me. She couldn't go anywhere. Black had her ass on restrictions. She didn't even have a phone to use. I didn't have to worry about her telling Sonja shit. I was going to propose to Sonja before the week was out. I wanted to blow Sonja's mind. I wanted to do some shit that I knew she wouldn't expect coming from me.

I've taken her through so many obstacles these past couple of months. The fact remains the same and she passed them all. I wanted her proposal to be special for her because she deserves this shit. I was ready to settle down. I was tired of running the streets with Black every day. I broke it off with Amber a couple of weeks ago. She was feeling me too hard. I'm sorry the feelings weren't mutual, and I didn't want to continue to lead the girl on.

The sound of glass just broke me out of my thoughts. If somebody busted a window out of my Bentley, all hell was going to break loose. I looked out of my living room window, but I didn't see anything. Damn somebody busted my windshield. I hoped the motherfuckers were still outside when I came out. They made the wrong move bringing some shit to where I lay my head. I opened the closet and grabbed my AR-15. I took the safety off. I was on my Rambo shit.

I was ready to make a mess now. It's on and popping. I made my way toward the foyer of my house. I fired a warning shot to see if anybody was out, there were no shots were fired back. I approached the front of my house and made my way toward my Bentley truck to observe the damage to my windshield.

It was some paper in between my windshield wipers. I grabbed the fucking paper. It was a fuckin' birth certificate with Sonja Harris's name and a child named Kanan Chad Harris, date of birth January 26, 1988. Oh, hell no. I know this bitch didn't have a son by me and I never knew about this shit. When was she pregnant? Let me call up my sons asap. Yashir answered on the first ring.

"Yeah, old man what's up?" He asked. I knew he was asleep because he answered the phone in an irritated manner because he was awakened.

"Where's Sonja?" I asked. I was hostile as fuck. I needed to know if she was asleep or not because I was on my way over there.

"She's sleeping, why?" He asked. "OG I'm tired of you and Sonja's childish antics. Every other week it was something."

"Duct tape her and hog tie her; I'm on my way," I stated. I'm furious as fuck that someone came to his home and placed a birth certificate on my windshield. How did I have a son that I never knew about. A motherfucka was sending me a message and I wanted to know what for.

"What's wrong, OG? What happened?" Kanan Jr. asked. He knew it was something serious. If I wanted him to do something like this.

"Don't ask me no fucking questions. Do what the fuck I said do. I'll be there in ten minutes and unlock the front fucking door," I argued. I gave the fuckin orders. I'm furious. My blood was boiling finding out this foul shit about Sonja and to think I was just about to propose.

What the fuck is going on? When was Sonja pregnant and how did I miss this shit? Where the fuck is my son? She will fuck around and get killed today if she says the wrong shit. I got to

Sonja's house in twenty fuckin' minutes. I'm surprised I didn't get pulled over for how fast I was driving.

Sonja doesn't want to play with me. She needs to answer my questions accordingly. She better explain this shit to me. I busted in Sonja's spot like I owned it because I did. Not even the good Lord himself can keep me off her. I walked up to Sonja and snatched the duct tape off her mouth. I threw the birth certificate in her face.

"What the fuck is this? Explain this shit to me, Sonja, where is my fucking son," I argued and asked. I'm livid at this point. My blood was fuckin' boiling and my heart is fuckin' racing.

"Untie me now," she screamed. I pressed my hand over her fuckin' mouth. I was livid and she was fuckin' scared. "How in the fuck did you find out about our son? Where did this birth certificate come from? Who gave you this shit?"

"Hell fucking no, explain this shit to me. When did you have my son and where the fuck is, he?" I argued and asked. She wanted me to untie her. "Fuck ass no. Now answer my fuckin' questions. I'm calling the fucking shots."

"Ali Bum Biyae took him," she whispered. Sonja was nervous. She knew all hell was about to break loose now.

"Ali Bum Biyae took my son for what? He was my connect. What would he want with my son? This shit is not making sense at all. You need to be direct with this shit."

"We had an affair—" Before she could finish her fuckin sentence, I put my hands around her throat and choked Sonja's ass out. I blacked out…

Boss

☆

Vanessa paid me for me a hit. It's to motherfuckin' bad that Riley was never going to be the fuckin' target. My mother always told me to never write a check that you can't fuckin' cash. Riley wasn't Vanessa's issue. It's her fuckin' husband. Vanessa's going to regret the day she ever decided to do fuckin' business with me. She signed her husband's fuckin' death certificate. I wasn't going to kill Veno, but I was going to hit that motherfucka up bad, real fuckin' bad.

I've been watching Veno for about a month now. He wasn't cheating on his wife, but he was still trying to get up with Riley. I told that nigga to stand down, but he didn't want to listen. Tonight, was the night. On his wife he fuckin' should've listened. I was posted up outside the club that he owns with Lucky. He leaves around the same time every night and just like clockwork he was walking out. Quan and Lucky were right behind him.

Veno slapped hands with Lucky and Quan. They walked back in the club and it was time to make my fuckin' move. Veno walked around his car checking his surroundings. I pulled my ski-mask down and cocked my Mac 10. Fuck a silencer. I ran up on Veno and I had my pistol pressed to the back of his head. I had this pussy ass nigga right where the fuck I wanted him.

"Make a fuckin' move nigga and Clayton County will have your body outlined in motherfuckin' chalk," I argued. I searched his pants. I emptied his wallet and tossed it on the ground. He didn't have anything on him.

"Pussy ass nigga you got to get me while my fuckin' back is turned," he argued. A small chuckle escaped my mouth. I punched Veno in the back of his head two times. He fell to the ground. I had the Mac 10 still placed on his head. I turned him around so he could look me in the eyes.

"I can get you in your face nigga," I yelled. "What the fuck you want to do? I'm really about this shit."

"Who sent you?" He asked. I laughed. He didn't really want to know the fuckin' answer to that.

"You really want to know?" I asked. He nodded his head yes. "Your wife, motherfucka," I spat. I shot Veno in his chest seven times but far enough from his heart where he wouldn't die.

I put a copy of the hit in his fuckin' shoe so he would see it. I jogged back to my car. I called Vanessa and she answered on the first ring.

"It's done," I stated and hung up in her face.

CHECK
MATE

Pushing Pen Presents now accepting submissions for the following genres: Urban Fiction, Street Lit, Urban Romance, Women's Fiction, BWWM Romance Please submit your first three chapters in a Word document, synopsis, and include contact information via email Nikkinicole@nikkinicolepresents.com please allow 3-5 business days for a response after submitting.

CONTEST ALERT

Two One Year Kindle Unlimited Subscriptions. I Wanted to Announce It Here First. Read, Review on Amazon and Goodreads! Tag Me in It (Nikki Taylor) on Facebook or Instagram (WatchNikkiWrite) Twitter (WatchNikkiWrite) Email Your Entry to NikkiNicole@Nikkinicolepresents.com.

Request the Book at Your Local Library Send Proof. The First 50 Reviews I Get I'm Going to Draw A Name. The First Drawing Will Be Held Once the Book Reaches 50 Reviews It'll Be Another Drawing Once the Book Reaches 75 Reviews. I Do Things in Real Time! I'm Not Holding It Until the End of The Month.

CPSIA information can be obtained
at www.ICGtesting.com
Printed in the USA
LVHW041616130819
627493LV00002B/266/P